Praise for the Western Mysteries

'. . . a fast, funny adventure that cracks along as smartly as a cowboy's whip' – THE TIMES

'Pinky is one of the most engaging heroes I have come across.' – TELEGRAPH

'You must read this book, if only to find out how a spittoon can save your life! It is thrilling, well-written and utterly engrossing, and it cannot be recommended highly enough . . . superbly good . . . you will not want to put it down until the final shot has rung out and the murderer is revealed.' – THE BOOKBAG

'pacy and full of period detail.' – SUNDAY TIMES

'With plenty of Wild West slang and an engaging cast of colourful gunslingers, gamblers and cowboys, Caroline Lawrence brings a mid-19th century frontier town vividly to life in this intricately-plotted and very funny page-turner.' – BOOKTRUST

Also by Caroline Lawrence

THE P.K. PINKERTON MYSTERIES

The Case of the Deadly Desperados
The Case of the Good-Looking Corpse
The Case of the Pistol-Packing Widows

THE ROMAN MYSTERY SCROLLS

The Sewer Demon
The Poisoned Honey Cake
The Thunder Omen
The Two-Faced God

THE ROMAN MYSTERIES

I The Thieves of Ostia
II The Secrets of Vesuvius
III The Pirates of Pompeii
IV The Assassins of Rome
V The Dolphins of Laurentum
VI The Twelve Tasks of Flavia Gemina
VII The Enemies of Jupiter
VIII The Gladiators from Capua
IX The Colossus of Rhodes
X The Fugitive from Corinth
XI The Sirens of Surrentum
XII The Charioteer of Delphi
XIII The Slave-girl from Jerusalem
XIV The Beggar of Volubilis
XV The Scribes from Alexandria
XVI The Prophet from Ephesus
XVII The Man from Pomegranate Street

Trimalchio's Feast and Other Mini-mysteries
The Legionary from Londinium and Other Mini-mysteries

THE P.K. PINKERTON MYSTERIES

The Case of the Bogus Detective

Caroline Lawrence

Orion
Children's Books

First published in Great Britain in 2014
by Orion Children's Books
This paperback edition first published in Great Britain in 2015
by Orion Children's Books
An imprint of
Hachette Children's Group
Part of Hodder & Stoughton
Orion House
5 Upper St Martin's Lane
London WC2H 9EA
An Hachette UK company

1 3 5 7 9 10 8 6 4 2

The paper and board used in this paperback are
natural and recyclable products made from wood
grown in sustainable forests. The manufacturing
processes conform to the environmental
regulations of the country of origin.

A catalogue record for this book is
available from the British Library.

ISBN 978 1 4440 1033 6

Printed in Great Britain by Clays Ltd, St Ives plc

For Clare Pearson
agent, mentor and friend.

Stagecoach route from Virginia City to Sacramento in 1863

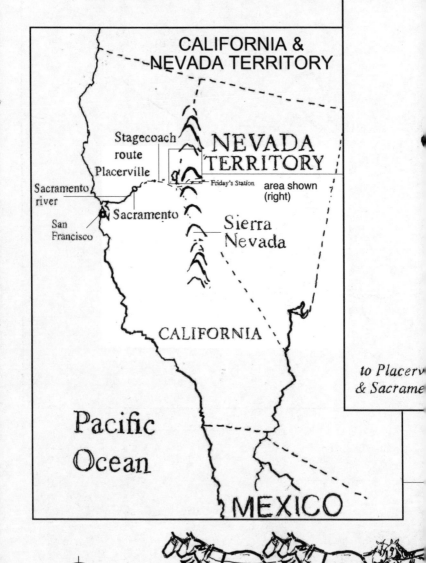

CALIFORNIA &
NEVADA TERRITORY

NEVADA
TERRITORY

Stagecoach
route
Placerville

Friday's Station

area shown
(right)

Sacramento
river

Sacramento

San
Francisco

Sierra
Nevada

CALIFORNIA

Pacific
Ocean

to Placerv
& Sacrame

MEXICO

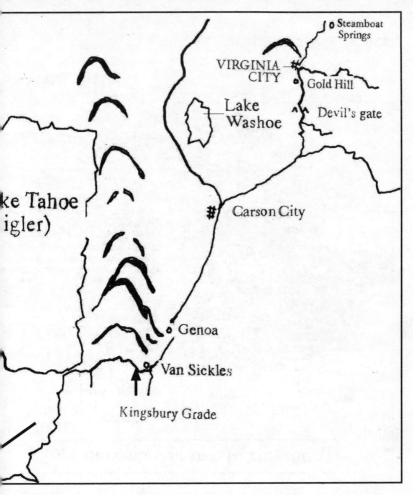

Steamboat Springs

VIRGINIA CITY

Gold Hill

Lake Washoe

Devil's gate

ke Tahoe (igler)

Carson City

Genoa

Van Sickles

Kingsbury Grade

area shown on California & Nevada map (left)

CANADA

Black Hills

CALIFORNIA

NEVADA

THE TERRITORIES

Great Plains

Chicago

United States (Union)

Confederate States

original boundaries of the Confederacy

MEXICO

NORTH AMERICA IN 1863

Panorama of San Francisco in 1863

Presidio

San Francisco
Bay

Portsmouth Square

et

Broadway
wharf

to Sacramento
by ferry

W

S   N

E

MY NAME IS P.K. PINKERTON AND I WILL SOON BE breakfast for a couple of grizzly bears.

I am trapped in a mountain cave with my dying pa. I have a small fire but not much wood left to keep it going and only 1 bullet left in my Henry Rifle.

I can hear those grizzlies a-prowling & a-growling, and I can smell them, too. I reckon I only have a few hours to record how I came to be in this sad predicament. When my fire goes out they will gobble me up. And my dying pa, too.

You may say, 'Why are you wasting the final hours of your life scribbling in a Ledger Book?'

Here is my reply:

If I write an account, people will know who done it and they can avenge me.

You may also say, 'Being half Sioux, why don't you use your Indian skills to sneak past those bears and at least save yourself?'

My answer is this:

I will not abandon my dying pa.

It all started when two strangers rode into town. I was sitting at my desk in my Detective Agency on B Street in Virginia City. I was ordering the Butterfly part of my Bug Collection. Detective business had been slow on account of a localized snowstorm, but now a strong sun was out.

The scent of melting snow swirled in as the door of my detective office opened.

It was my 14-yr-old partner Ping, with a bag of sugar & a coffee pot. He had filled the pot with pure water from the new filter in the Shamrock Saloon across the street. I could hear someone playing Camptown Races on a piano.

'Road dang muddy,' Ping said. 'Traffic should be running again soon.' He put the coffee pot on our new stove & the bag of sugar on one of the shelves.

Ping does not drink coffee, but he says the smell entices people in & encourages them to linger.

'You want game of poker?' he asked, as he turned the handle of the little wooden coffee grinder. 'While we wait for clients?'

'H-ll, yeah,' I replied.

I try to keep up my skill, because sometimes I help a gambler named Poker Face Jace play cards for money. Jace is my friend & mentor.

I put my Butterfly Tray on one of the shelves on the wall. When my office was a Tobacco Emporium those shelves held tins of tobacco. Now they hold my collections, viz: my Bug Collection, my Bullet Collection & my Big Tobacco Collection. I also have a branch with butterflies waiting to hatch out.

I opened a drawer in my desk and got out some strings of black licorice, some lemon drops & a pack of cards.

I tore off a piece of the stretchy licorice and put it between my cheek and gum, like people do with chewing tobacco.

Ping left the coffee pot on the stove to brew. He pulled up one of the chairs where clients usually sit. The door was still ajar so you could hear boots on the boardwalk & the curses of the first riders trying out the thawing thoroughfare.

I divided the licorice strings and lemon drops between us. Then I shuffled the deck and we played a few hands of 'five card draw'.

Even when I get dealt bad cards I usually win because I have learned to tell when people are bluffing. Ping's natural expression is a scowl, even when he has a good hand, but my pal Poker Face Jace says the face is the lyingest part of the body. So I ignored Ping's scowly face & scooted my chair back a little & kind of slouched down so I could see his feet. Everybody has their own 'tell' and Ping's is a common one. Whenever he has a good hand his toes point up and when he has a bad one he pulls his feet back under his chair.

If the Face is the lyingest part of the body, the Feet are the most truthful.

I spat some black licorice juice into a spittoon. I had tried proper chaw tobacco once but it made me feel queasy so I had taken to chewing licorice to make me look older & tougher.

Ping's nose wrinkled and his lip curled a little. My dead foster ma Evangeline had taught me how to identify five expressions.

No. 1 – If someone's mouth curves up & their eyes crinkle, that is a Genuine Smile.

No. 2 – If their mouth stretches sideways & their eyes are not crinkled, that is a Fake Smile.

No. 3 – If a person turns down their mouth & crinkles up their nose, they are Disgusted.

No. 4 – If their eyes open real wide, they are probably Surprised or Scared.

No. 5 – If they make their eyes narrow, they are either Mad at you or Thinking or Suspicious.

Ping's face was making Expression No. 3 – Disgust.

I felt something tickle my arm. It was my pet, Mouse, crawling on my pink flannel shirt.

Ping's expression No. 3 got stronger. 'I don't like that critter. I afraid I step on him. Make him go crunch.'

'That would be unpleasant,' I agreed. 'But he is usually in his tank when I ain't letting him perambulate on me.'

Ping shifted his gaze from Mouse to my face. His eyes were narrowed. It was no longer Expression No. 3 – Disgust. It was now Expression No. 5, which meant he

---

4

was either Mad or Thinking or Suspicious. Or all three.

'You can stare all you like,' I said to Ping. 'I am inscrutable. I can neither understand nor express emotions well. It is a Thorn in my Side. But it is useful for playing poker,' I added. 'People cannot tell if I am holding a good hand or a bad one.'

'I am not trying to tell if you have good or bad hand,' said Ping, his scowl deepening.

'Then why are you staring at me?' I asked him.

'Something bogus about you.' He tipped his head to one side. 'I can't think what.'

I pressed my lips together, wondering if he had finally guessed my secret. To throw him off the track, I wiped my nose with my finger. Then I spat some licorice-tinted spit to make me look more like a tough detective.

Ping scowled at me.

I scratched my armpit & burped.

Then I farted, just for good measure.

I was not really surprised that Ping was trying to figure out what was 'not right' about me. I knew dang well. What surprised me was that in nine months of us being pards, he had not realized that I ain't a boy.

LEDGER SHEET 2

I COULD NOT REALLY BLAME PING FOR NOT GUESSING that I am a girl.

From the day I was born my Indian ma dressed me like a boy.

She put me in little buckskin leggings, shirt and moccasins. She taught me how to ride a horse and shoot a bow & arrow and how to hunt & skin a critter. She trained me to use boy-endings for words rather than girl-endings when I spoke Lakota, and she would give me a stinging slap if I forgot.

Not that I spoke Lakota with anybody apart from my ma, for she had lit out from her tribe before I was born. She took up with a fur trader, then traded him in for a railroad detective named Pinkerton a while later, and thus was I born. But soon it was just me & her again, out in the wild frontier. I was fine with that and I was fine with dressing as a boy.

6

You might say, 'Why did your ma dress you as a boy?'

I reckon she thought if anything happened to her I would be safer as a boy, knowing how to hunt and ride and suchlike.

And sure enough, something did happen to her.

She got herself massacred on a wagon train traveling west when I was 10 yrs old.

I was out gathering buffalo chips and thus I survived. After that, a preacher & his wife adopted me. They thought I was a boy at first & were mighty surprised to discover I was a girl, you bet. But they let me keep on dressing like a boy, probably for the same reason as my Indian ma.

Unfortunately, they got massacred, too. That was on my 12th birthday, just under a year ago.

I fled to Virginia City to escape the desperados who kilt them & to avenge their deaths. I stayed on in Virginia in order to learn to be a Private Eye so I could one day join my long-lost pa, that railroad detective I mentioned earlier. That was the first time in my life I wore white girls' clothing, as a means of Disguise. I hated the thin calico dresses with their itchy lace collars & cuffs. I hated the tight, tippy-tappy, fiddly buttoned boots. Most of all, I hated the pinching corsets and puffy hoop skirts I wore while pretending to be a widow woman.

After that, I vowed not to dress like a gal unless it was a matter of life or death.

But recently my body has started changing. I have started my 'monthlies' and am beginning to develop. Not a lot, but enough so that I have to put a kind of bandage around my chest to keep myself flat. Luckily my poor dead foster ma Evangeline clearly laid out what was in store, so I was not too alarmed. The thing that worried me was this: would I wake up one morning to find I preferred dolls to Deringers? Would I get a hankering to sew samplers instead of arrange my Tobacco, Bullet and Bug Collections? Would I stop feeling like a 'Me' and start feeling like a 'She'?

I surely hope not.

I guess that is why I have taken to spitting & cussing & not stifling burps. I do not want to turn into a danged girly-girl. I may be a half-Indian Misfit, but I like me just the way I am. I do not want to change.

'I said give me two!' snapped Ping, bringing me out of my reverie.

I gave him two.

'I bet three,' said Ping. He pushed three pieces of licorice forward.

'I'll see your three pieces of licorice,' I said, 'and raise you a lemon drop.'

I showed the lemon drop to Mouse, who was perched on my shoulder, but he was disinterested. Mouse only eats live bugs, like crickets.

Once more the door opened.

It was Miss Bee Bloomfield in her tippy-tappy button-up boots. School had been closed all week on account of the Big Freeze.

Talk about girly-girls. Bee is about the girliest-girl in

Virginia City. She uses Sozodont tooth powder & lilac toilet water & is always buying new bonnets. Worst of all, she is always trying to steal a kiss from me. If she knew she had been trying to kiss another gal, she would have conniptions, you bet.

'Good morning, P.K. and Ping!' She put a waxed-paper packet on my desk. 'I brought you some oatmeal cookies baked by my own fair hand.'

Ping opened the packet & took out a cookie & ate it.

Bee frowned. 'What's that on your shelf?' She went to investigate my branch and then recoiled with a squeal. 'Oh! What are those green things hanging on it?'

I said, 'Those are butterflies in chrysalis form. I saw them last week. When it started to snow, I took pity on them & went up & broke off their branch & brought it back here so they wouldn't get froze.'

'Friz,' said a familiar voice from the doorway. *'First it blew, then it snew, then it thew and then it friz.* That is what the wags are all saying. But the thaw is here, and I believe spring is finally on the way.' The voice belonged to Mr. Sam Clemens, a local reporter. He had a skinny blond boy with him.

'Spring!' Mr. Sam Clemens cried. 'That fruitful time when young men turn their thoughts to bugs. P.K., this here is Affable Fitzsimmons.'

I nodded politely at the skinny blond boy. 'Howdy,' I said.

'How do you do?' said the boy in an English accent. I judged he was about 14. He was tall & thin with wire-rimmed spectacles & straight blond hair. He wore a palm-leaf hat & beige linen knickerbockers & canvas shoes, none of which were suitable for the snowy climes of Virginia City in April.

Bee Bloomfield stepped forward. 'Are you from England?'

'I reside in San Francisco, with my parents,' said Affable, 'but I am English by birth.'

'I'm Bee Bloomfield,' she said, showing her dimples.

'Affable is the son of the famous naturalist and jungle explorer, Sir Fitzhugh Fitzsimmons,' drawled Sam. 'Sir Fitzhugh promised to buy me a hot toddy if I could find Affable some pals his own age.'

Affable Fitzsimmons looked around the room. 'Mr. Twain said you have some interesting collections.'

I said, 'Who is Mr. Twain?'

Sam said, 'I am. It is my new *nom de plume*. I have started signing my newspaper articles "Mark Twain".'

'A rose by any other name,' said Affable, 'would smell as sweet. You can call me "Affie",' he added.

'Something in here does not smell very sweet,' said Bee, sniffing the air. She leaned towards me and wrinkled her nose. 'P.K.! When did you last bathe?'

I confess I had to ponder this question.

'December,' I said at last. 'I reckon my last bath was in December.'

'Which year?' asked Sam Clemens, AKA Mark Twain, striking a match and lighting up his notorious 'pipe of a thousand smells'.

'Last year,' I replied. '1862.'

'P.K.!' gasped Bee, clapping her hand over her mouth. 'You have not bathed in *four months*! Why, that ain't Christian!'

I pointed at Mark Twain.

'I ain't as stinky as his tobacco,' I said. 'Folk call it "The Remains" on account of it smells like a dead critter.'

Affable AKA Affie chuckled.

'At least it ain't me who stinks,' drawled Mark Twain, 'only my tobacco.' He winked at me. 'I was just being ironikle,' he said, using one of his pet words.

'Oh, I say!' Affable stepped forward to examine the pale-green chrysalises dangling from my butterfly branch. 'Don't keep them so near the stove,' he advised, 'or they will hatch too early. May I move them out of danger?'

'Sure,' I said.

As he was carefully moving the branch away from the stove, he saw my glass-fronted butterfly tray on the shelf below.

'What a bully collection!' he cried. 'And you are only missing one.' He bent closer and read the label. 'A "Buckskin Fritillary, native to Nevada & California".'

Bee said, 'What is a fritillary?'

Affie said, 'It is a kind of butterfly.'

I said, 'It was my foster pa's collection. I am trying to finish it to honor his memory. I am hoping my branch will hatch out into Buckskin Fritillaries,' I added.

Suddenly Bee Bloomfield's brown eyes went round as

quarters. 'P.K.!' she squealed. 'There is a giant spider crawling on you!'

Mark Twain's eyes bugged out, too, and his 'pipe of a thousand smells' clattered to the floor. 'That ain't no spider,' he yelped. 'That there is a deadly tarantula!'

LEDGER SHEET 3

'NOBODY MOVE!' CRIED MARK TWAIN. 'I WILL SMISH the varmint!' He grabbed an iron plate from the stove. Immediately he dropped it. It struck the plank floor with a resounding clang. 'Dam!' he cried. 'That's hot!' Then he saw the expression on Bee's face & said, 'I mean a *mill* dam, of course.'

I said, 'Do not smish him. Mouse is my pet.'

I let my tarantula crawl onto my hand. His little claws felt like tickly pinpricks.

'You dunderhead!' cried Mark Twain. 'That ain't no mouse. That is a tarantula. I encountered a passel of them in Carson City a year or so back.'

'Mr. Twain is correct,' said Affable. 'That is an arachnid of the *Theraphosidae* Family.'

'I didn't say he *was* a mouse, I said his *name* was Mouse. It is his *nom de plume*,' I added. 'If you can call yourself "Mark Twain" then I can call my tarantula "Mouse".'

Mark Twain scowled and blew on his burned fingers. 'It is no laughing matter! Those critters are poisonous. Why, an old Paiute chief died of a tarantula bite not three years back.'

I said, 'Winnemucca was old and infirm. If you treat tarantula spiders right, they will not hurt you.'

'Also,' Affie Fitzsimmons pointed out, 'they are venomous. Not poisonous.'

Ping spoke up. 'I tell P.K. he should keep it at boarding house.'

I said, 'Mrs. Matterhorn despises spiders of any description.'

'I hate spiders, too,' said Bee, who was hiding behind Affie. 'They give me the fantods. Especially that one. Why, he is as big as a saucer!'

Mark Twain picked his pipe off the floor. 'Come on, Affie! Let us hunt down your pa so I can collect my hot toddy. I need fortification badly. As soon as the roads are clear I have to flee the territory.'

'Why?' I asked him.

He puffed his pipe. 'On account of something I wrote.'

Bee said, 'Are you in "hot water" again, on account of the scurrilous & slanderous articles you often print?'

'It was neither scurrilous nor slanderous,' drawled Mr. Mark Twain. 'It was a delicate, a *very* delicate satire. Coming, Affie?'

'I will be there directly,' said Affie. He was watching Mouse crawling on my arm.

Bee said, 'Where do you live, Affie?'

Without taking his eyes from Mouse, Affie said, 'My father and I are staying at the International Hotel.'

Bee flapped her hand at Mark Twain. 'You run along, Mr. Twain,' she said. 'I can show Affie the way.'

Mark Twain tipped his hat and exited the premises.

Bee hooked her arm in Affie's. 'Come along, then. It is almost eleven.'

Affie looked at Mouse. Then he looked at me. 'May I come by later and examine your specimens?' he asked me.

'Sure,' I said with a shrug.

Bee tugged Affie's arm and together they exited the premises.

Ping stood up. 'I cannot believe you do not wash in four month,' he said. 'Come! I take you to my uncle's bath house.'

I tipped my chair back and put my feet on my desk. 'It is a free territory,' I said. 'I reckon I will decide when and where to bathe.'

Ping narrowed his eyes at me. Then he exited the premises, banging the door as he left.

I raised my left arm & twisted my head so I could sniff my armpit. Yup. I smelled pretty ripe. But it was not as bad as a skunk.

And at least nobody would take me for a gal.

At that moment, the door of my office opened and two strangers in hats and long coats stomped in. Their boots left muddy footprints.

Through the open door I saw their horses tied to one

of the posts that held up the awning of the boardwalk.

'May I help you gentlemen?' I took my feet off the desk and sat up straight.

'You bet you can help us,' said the taller of the two men. He had a flat-topped gray hat on his head and a bushy black mustache on his face and a Colt's Army Revolver in his hand.

He aimed his big six-shooter at my chest.

'Hands up!' he commanded. 'You are under arrest.'

LEDGER SHEET 4

I STARED DOWN THE BARREL OF THAT COLT'S revolver and slowly put my hands up.

'Why am I under arrest?' I asked.

'You are under arrest for working in a bogus Detective Agency!' said the man with the gun.

'I ain't working in a bogus Detective Agency,' I protested.

'Then what d'ye mean by this?' said the other man.

BANG!

He slammed a wooden shingle onto my desk.

It was upside down but I could see it was the sign from outside my door.

It had the words *P.K. Pinkerton, Private Eye. We Hardly Ever Sleep* painted on it along with a picture of an eye.

'Why did you take down my shingle?' I said.

'Because it ain't legal and it ain't authorized!' said the man with the gun.

The other man turned to him. In a Scottish accent he

said, 'This one's nay more than a bairn. I dinna believe he's in charge.'

'Get your pa!' commanded the man with the gun. 'We are going to throw him in jail for the rest of time!'

I said, 'I do not have a pa.'

'Then get your boss. The man you work for!'

I said, 'I do not have a boss. I am boss of myself.' I spat some licorice juice to make me seem tough, but my mouth was too dry & some of it dribbled down my shirt.

I wiped my mouth with my sleeve.

'HANDS UP!'

'Dinna shout, Ray,' said the Scottish one, putting a hand on his partner's arm. 'And put your gun away. He's only a bairn.'

The man named Ray uncocked his big revolver and lowered it. But he did not put it away.

The Scottish one turned to me. 'Will ye explain yerself, please?'

I took a deep breath & then I let it out slow. 'My name is Pinkerton and I am a detective,' I said, 'but I am not a *genuine* Pinkerton Detective.'

'Dang right you're not genuine,' growled Ray. 'You are bogus!'

'We're from the Agency,' the Scottish man said. 'If we had operatives here, we'd surely know.'

I was confused. 'Agency? Which Agency? Who are you?'

'We are the Pinkertons.'

'You are the Pinkertons?'

Ray stuck his revolver in his belt. 'Yup,' he said. 'We

are the Pinkertons. The *genuine* Pinkertons.'

I could not believe it. It was my dream to work for the Pinkerton Detective Agency.

I said, 'It is my dream to work for the Pinkerton Detective Agency. I know all about it. It is located in Chicago, Illinois. It was founded by Allan Pinkerton. A few years ago he thwarted an assassination attempt against President Lincoln—'

'Hang on a wee moment,' said the Scottish man. 'The Pinkerton Agency wasnae founded by Allan. It was founded by me!'

'It was founded by you?'

'Aye,' said the man. 'I set it up nigh on twenty years ago to protect passengers, goods and guards on trains and stagecoaches. Me brother didna come in with me till it was well established.' He turned to his partner. 'Everybody makes the same mistake,' he said. 'They all think wee Allan is the founder.'

'You are Robert Pinkerton?' I said.

'Aye, that's me. And this is Mr. Ray G. Tempest.'

I am usually inscrutable but I reckon my mouth was hanging open.

The man standing before me was the older brother of Allan Pinkerton, the most famous detective in the whole wide world.

He was also my long-lost pa.

LEDGER SHEET 5

FOR AS LONG AS I COULD REMEMBER I HAD THOUGHT my Pinkerton Railroad Detective pa was dead and gone.

My Indian ma told me he died bravely, defending a train against robbers. Later, I heard he died of being frozen to death in the Sierra Nevada mountains. Finally, I learned he was not dead after all, but alive and well and living in Chicago. That was why I had decided to become a detective: so I could join him in that far-off city.

And now here he was, standing before me & trying to shut down the agency I had established so I could become a detective worthy of his approval!

The folk here in Virginia have a word for that: *ironikle*.

'Come on, Robert,' said his partner. 'We'll get the sheriff to deal with this pygmy bogus detective.'

Ray G. Tempest turned to go and so did Robert Pinkerton.

My long-lost pa was about to walk out of my life again!

'Wait!' I jumped up out of my chair. 'Stop! I will burn my shingle. Only tell me: what are you doing in Virginia City? Maybe I can help!'

'None of your business what we're doing,' growled Ray. His hand was already on the door. 'You are no more important to us than a bug on a rug.' As if to demonstrate my insignificance, he spat on the floor of my office even though he was not chewing tobacco.

Jace had once told me not to ride straight at people with my questions, but to use a flanking manoeuver. I reckoned I had rid at them too straight.

Once again I cried, 'Wait!' I looked desperately around my narrow office. On the potbelly stove the coffeepot was steaming. I could smell its aroma. 'Would you like a cup of coffee?'

The two hesitated & looked at each other.

'It is fresh ground and fresh brewed,' I said, 'using water from a Patent Moulded Ceramic Carbon Filter made by F.H. Atkinson of London which they keep in the saloon across the street. The water here in Virginia is full of arsenic, plumbago and copperas,' I explained.

'Full of *what*?' said Ray.

'And cookies!' I held up the waxed-paper parcel. 'I have cookies! Fresh-baked oatmeal cookies.'

My long-lost pa took off the small plug hat he had been wearing. 'I willna say no to a wee cup of java,' he said. 'It smells mighty good.' He looked at his partner.

'Sure,' growled Ray. 'I reckon a fresh-baked cookie and a cup of brew is the least you can do for causing trouble.'

He closed the door & they both came back & sat down in front of my desk.

Hallelujah! Ping's theory was right. Fresh coffee *did* encourage people to linger. Bee's oatmeal cookies probably helped, too.

As I poured their coffee, I secretly studied Robert Pinkerton.

I had always imagined my pa would be tall, dark and good-looking, like Poker Face Jace. But the short man sitting before me was ordinary looking. With his slightly bulging brown eyes & slicked back brown hair & little mustache, he reminded me of an otter.

But I know that appearances can be deceptive.

He was a famous detective. Probably the best in the world.

Any moment he would deduce I was his long-lost daughter.

I saw my detective sign on the desk & nudged it forward a little to help him with his deductions.

I said, 'What brings you all the way from Chicago to Virginia City? You did not come just to shut me down, did you?'

'Course not,' said Mr. Ray G. Tempest, munching a cookie & looking around.

My pa sipped his coffee, which he took black with no sugar. (Just like me!) He said, 'We got reports of a couple of Reb Road Agents in the Sierra Nevada mountains.'

I said, 'By "Reb" do you mean Confederate? And by "Road Agents" do you mean robbers?'

'Aye. Their plan is to rob silver-carrying stagecoaches and send the money to General Robert E. Lee.'

I said, 'They must be the men who robbed the Wells Fargo stagecoach a few days ago.'

'A Wells Fargo stagecoach was robbed?' said Ray, sitting forward.

I nodded. 'Up by Strawberry, according to yesterday's newspaper. The Sierras ain't snowed in like us,' I added. 'Our blizzard was localized.'

'I dinna think it could have been them.' My pa glanced at Ray.

Ray shrugged. 'It might have been them,' he said. 'You got a description? Or a newspaper?'

'Yup,' I said. I fished around in my big oyster tin which I use for waste paper & found yesterday's Daily Territorial Enterprise. 'Page three,' I said, as they both scanned it. 'But it only says they were wearing butternut-colored uniforms and bandanas over their faces.'

'Goll dang, it *was* them!' cried Ray.

I said, 'So they are like Confederate Robin Hoods?'

'Those Reb Road Agents ain't no dang Robin Hoods,' said Ray G. Tempest. 'They— Goll DANG!' He jumped up so fast that his chair toppled backwards. 'What is that?'

He was pointing at my shelf. Mouse was walking near my glass-fronted butterfly tray.

I said, 'That there is Mouse, my pet tarantula.'

'No, not that. *THAT.*'

I said, 'My butterfly tray?'

'Yes!' He took a step back. 'I hate them things.

Get it away!'

I stood up & scooted my butterfly tray right down to the end of the shelf.

'Further away,' he said. 'Those things give me the fantods.' He was wiping his forehead with his handkerchief. His face had gone pale.

I carried my glass-fronted butterfly tray to the back of my shop & put it out of sight behind the counter.

When I got back to my desk, Ray G. Tempest was standing behind the chair, putting it upright. I could see his hands shaking.

'Why don't you like butterflies?' I asked.

'He doesna like the beasties' wee feelers and flapping wings,' said my pa. 'Nor their zigzag manner of flying.'

'Had a bad experience when I was little,' muttered Ray. He took a flask from his coat pocket and drank from it. 'Tooth elixir,' he said by way of explanation. 'My tooth is panging me something awful.'

'Would you like another cup of coffee?' I said.

'Nah,' he said, putting away his flask. 'I'm gonna ride on down to find a livery stable and a hotel. And maybe some clove oil for my tooth.' He wrinkled his nose. 'Besides, something stinks in here.'

'Which hotel are you staying at?' I said quickly. 'The International?'

'Is that a good one?'

'Best in town,' I said. 'The Flora Temple Livery Stable is just a few doors along from it. If you turn right out my door and go three blocks north you can go in the B Street entrance of the International.'

Mr. Ray G. Tempest snorted. 'Only if my boss here deems a room there worth the expense. He is a notorious skinflint. See you at the livery stable, Robbie?' he said to my pa.

'I'll be there directly,' said my pa. 'Just finishing my brew.'

Mr. Ray G. Tempest exited the premises, taking my Detective shingle with him.

Heart thumping, I turned to my pa.

Should I reveal my true identity?

But he was a Detective. Probably the best in the world.

I reckoned I should give him a few more clews & let him deduce it himself.

He had opened his greatcoat & was now fishing around in a pocket. I noticed a little brass button on the lapel of his jacket. It said PINKERTON RAILROAD DETECTIVE in bumpy letters.

'I have a button just like that,' I said. 'Just like the one on your lapel.'

'Do ye?' He took a match out of the jacket and sparked it on the bottom of his boot.

I thought I should give him another clew. 'My Indian ma gave it to me,' I added. My heart was thumping hard. 'She was Lakota Sioux.'

'I guessed ye had a wee drop of Injun blood,' he remarked, holding the lit match to the bowl of his pipe.

I thought, 'How is it possible he does not recognize me? I'd best give him a real big clew.'

I said, 'My pa was a Pinkerton Railroad Detective, too.'

This last statement seemed to startle Robert Pinkerton to his feet. He had Expression No. 4 on his face – Surprise.

I stood up, too, my heart thumping. I thought, 'He has finally put two and two together. At last he has realized that I am his long-lost daughter.'

But I was wrong.

'Dang!' he said. 'That java has done the trick. I need the jakes!'

I stared at him. 'You what?'

'I need an outhouse!' he said. 'My bowels have been out of fix and I have been bunged up for a week. But now I am ready, willing and able. Can ye tell me where is the nearest wee privy?'

'Behind this building down the slope,' I said.

'Much obliged,' he said, touching the brim of his silly putty-colored plug hat.

And with that he ran out of my office.

As I watched the door shut behind him I tried to swallow, but my throat felt too tight.

I thought, 'My long-lost pa was sitting less than a yard away from me with my name right there on the shingle. I gave him three big clews but he failed to recognize his own flesh and blood, viz: ME. He must be the worst detective in the world.'

Then I thought, 'Maybe my original ma just met him once or saw him from afar and told me a big story.'

And finally, 'That would mean that Robert Pinkerton is not, and never was, my pa.'

LEDGER SHEET 6

MY HOPES HAD BEEN RAISED TO THE HIGH HEAVENS
and then dashed to earth. I felt mighty low & needed to
think. Also, I needed advice.

When I am low & need to think, I ride my mustang
pony, Cheeya.

When I want advice, I go to Poker Face Jace. He is the
only person in Virginia City who guessed I was a girl.
Jace knows people better than anybody I ever met.

I found Cheeya in his stall down at the Flora Temple
Livery Stable on C Street. He greeted me happily for I
had not had the opportunity to take him for any rides
during the blizzard.

It was about 11 o'clock when I saddled him & set out
on muddy C Street towards Geiger Grade & Steamboat
Valley. The warm sun was making everything steam
and sparkle but it still had not dried that bog of a road.
Just outside of town by the toll gate, a quartz wagon was

stuck in the mud and had caused a log jam of wheeled traffic. But the side of the road was fine for horses so Cheeya & I carried on down beside gurgling rivulets of snowmelt. We soon had the road to ourselves.

I reached Jace's ranch at the foot of the mountain about an hour later, at noon. I saw him right away. He was standing by the fence of his corral with one foot up on a rail & smoking a cigar. He was wearing a long black duster coat & watching his pal Stonewall break a mustang mare.

When he saw me riding up, he turned and touched his flat-brimmed black hat with a gloved forefinger. Jace always wears black.

'Howdy, P.K.,' he said. 'Road from Virginia open?'

'Just horse traffic,' I said. 'I reckon stages and wagons tomorrow.'

Jace nodded & turned to face the cookhouse. 'Tim!' he called. 'Bring two cups of black coffee?'

A Celestial appeared in the cookhouse door. 'Yes, boss!' he said and waved at me.

I waved back & swung down off Cheeya & left him near the water trough with his reins dangling. I walked past a few pecking chickens to the corral & I climbed up to the third beam of the fence so my head was level with Jace's.

'Howdy, P.K.!' called Stonewall from inside the corral. He is a big, scary-looking man with a soft heart.

'Howdy, Stonewall,' I replied.

The noonday sun was warm enough to make water

drip from the eaves of the barn & cookhouse & ranch house. The air smelled of wood smoke & horses & hay & Jace's cigar & fresh coffee as Tim Yung came out & handed me a cup.

The enamel tin cup was hot, but I was wearing my butter-soft buckskin gloves that Jace had bought me for Christmas. They had a 'zigzag' design on them in red & blue beads.

Four months ago I spent Christmas with Jace and Stonewall. On Christmas Eve, we sat in the parlor by the fire and Jace read *A Christmas Carol* by Mr. Charles Dickens & Stonewall cried.

The next morning we exchanged presents and that was when Jace gave me the buckskin gloves. I am partial to zigzags & I love those gloves.

'What brings you here today?' said Jace, sipping his coffee. 'Not that I ain't glad to see you,' he added.

I said, 'About two hours ago a couple of Pinkerton Detectives came into my office. They are after those Reb Road Agents who have started robbing silver-laden stagecoaches to help fund the rebellion. One of the Detectives was Allan Pinkerton's older brother, Robert.'

Jace turned so quickly that he slopped some coffee from the cup. 'Your pa,' he said. 'He found you.'

'Yeah,' I said. 'Only he did not recognize me.'

'Did you tell him who you are?'

'Nope. Him being a detective, I thought he should recognize his own child sitting two feet away.'

'Maybe he does not know you are alive.' Jace blew

cigar smoke down. 'Maybe you are the last person he expects to find out here. You sure it is the right Robert Pinkerton? I seem to recall reading that Allan has a son called Robert. Maybe it is the son you met, not the brother. Or maybe it is another Robert Pinkerton altogether.'

'He is the right one,' I said. 'But I am thinking maybe my original ma lied to me. Maybe she found that button and made up a big story.'

Jace smoked in silence for a few moments. Then he said, 'There is one sure way to find out. If he is your pa, then he will know what P.K. stands for.'

'Dang!' I said. 'You are right. I did not think of that.'

I had always called myself P.K., but even I did not know what those two initials stood for on account of my Indian ma could not remember the Christian names my pa had given me. I had confessed that secret to Jace one night last year when we were playing cribbage.

The only person in the whole world who knew what those initials stood for was the man who gave me my Christian names: my Pinkerton pa.

Something occurred to me.

I said, 'A person could *pretend* to know what the P and K stood for and invent two names and I would be none the wiser.'

Jace puffed for a spell & then said, 'But a person would not make up two names because nobody knows that *you* don't know what the P and the K stand for. In the whole world, only you and I know that fact. Unless you have told someone else,' he added.

'I ain't told nobody but you,' I said.

He sucked in smoke & blew it down. 'Course, there is another explanation for why he did not recognize you.'

'What would that be?'

Jace turned to face me. 'Your hair is greasy, your skin is grimy and your teeth are black. You stink to high heaven and I would not be surprised if you are lousy, too. If I had a long-lost daughter, I would not expect her to look and smell like you.'

'I ain't *that* bad.'

'Yes, you are. And you ain't getting better.' Jace used his cigar to point towards the line of hazy green trees that marked the course of a brook. 'See that steam puffing up from behind those cottonwoods? That there is Steamboat Hot Springs. There is a hotel and bath house there. For a dollar you can get a private room with a tub and soak in hot mineral water.' He reached into his pocket and pulled out a silver dollar. 'There is a good barber named Fritz who will trim your hair and your nails.'

I turned away from him. 'I don't need your money. I got plenty.'

'Then take this.' He reached into his coat pocket and brought out a round porcelain box. It said CHERRY TOOTH PASTE on it. 'Buy a tooth brush when you get back to Virginia,' he said, 'and use a little dab to polish your teeth after you eat. It might not be too late to get the black off. I reckon it is only licorice. Then go pay your pa a visit and see if he don't figure out who you are.'

A passel of emotions all jumbled in a bunch in my throat, the strongest of which was anger.

'I do not want to dress like a dam girl,' I said from between gritted teeth. 'I goddam despise dressing like a goddam girly-girl.'

'Nobody says you have to dress like a girl,' he said. 'Just clean yourself up. And it wouldn't hurt to modify your cussing, neither.'

I shoved the tooth-paste box in the pocket of my blue woolen coat & jumped down off the corral fence. Then I stalked over to Cheeya & swung up into the saddle.

'P.K.?' said Jace as I rode by.

I reined in Cheeya and looked over at him.

'You are becoming a woman,' he said, 'whether you like it or not. '

'Well, I goddam *hate* it!' I said, and galloped off without another word.

LEDGER SHEET 7

I WAS NOT SO MUCH MAD AT JACE AS I WAS MAD AT Mother Nature for changing me into a gal. I rode Cheeya hard until I cooled off a little. Then I turned him around & rode over to the hotel at Steamboat Springs like Jake had suggested. I had a private bath in a stone tank full of hot & sulfurous water from right out of the ground. After that I got my hair cut by Fritz the barber. I told him about the Cherry Tooth Paste & he sold me a small Tooth Brush & showed me how to brush my teeth. He left me to it & I stood in front of the mirror & spent about 10 minutes brushing my teeth & spitting into his basin. I used up about half the Cherry Tooth Paste that Jace had given me. I was amazed that my teeth went from black to white in no time.

When I got back to Virginia City it was 5.30 o'clock and starting to get dark. I stabled Cheeya & went straight to the International Hotel & asked for Mr. Pinkerton's room.

I intended to present myself to my pa all cleaned up and see if that spurred his memory.

But the clerk said they had no Pinkertons registered.

I reckoned my pa and Ray had decided to stay in a cheaper place, but it was now dark & almost dinner time, so I walked back to my boarding house up on B Street.

Mrs. Matterhorn currently has five boarders, including me.

She would be riled if she knew I was a gal as she only takes male boarders & has rules against any females even visiting the house.

As I came in, the other boarders were just sitting down to supper. I started to go into the dining room, but Mrs. Matterhorn gripped my upper arm & hauled me back out into the hall and looked me up & down.

'Good to see you cleaned yourself up,' she said to me after close scrutiny. 'When I went to make up your bed today I found your sheets to be filthy. Also, did I see a *bloodstain* on them? You know the rules here, don't you?' Her eyes were narrowed at me.

'I hurt my knee a few days ago,' I lied. 'It bled a little but it is better now.'

Her eyes were still narrowed into Expression No. 5 - Suspicion. 'Well,' she said, 'I changed the sheets and that means I will have to send *two* sets of yours to the Chinaman on washday. I will want extra pay for that. Two bits.' She held out her hand, palm up.

I fished a quarter out of my pocket & gave it to her.

Then I went in & sat down at my usual place. The other boarders noticed I was clean & made me the butt of their jokes for a spell, but they are always joshing me so I ignored them as usual.

Mrs. Matterhorn is a bully cook, with one of the best front yards in Virginia City. It is full of beans & squash & onions, and even a watermelon patch.

But I was not as hungry as I usually am & went up to bed without even tasting the chocolate layer cake, which is my favorite.

That night I had a bad dream.

In my dream I was riding on top of a stagecoach. I was sitting next to Robert Pinkerton, who was driving. My foster ma and pa and my original Indian ma were down below, riding inside. We were high on a winding mountain road & going too fast when something spooked the horses & they started to go over the edge of the precipice and we were falling & falling & falling & everybody was screaming, even me.

I woke up to a strange squealing sound, like a little animal caught in a trap. I realized it was me.

I lay there in a cold sweat with my heart pounding like a quartz mill stamp.

It was about 3 am, the time of night Ma Evangeline used to call the Hour of Bleak Thoughts.

There was a knock on my door.

'P.K.?' said Mrs. Matterhorn. 'You got a gal in there?'

'No, ma'am,' I said. 'There is just me. You can come in and see for yourself, if you like.'

'That won't be necessary,' she said. 'Just try to keep the noise down.'

I heard her footsteps going away.

I did not fall asleep for a long time, for I was plagued by many Bleak Thoughts.

When I woke up the next morning I could tell right away that I was too late for breakfast.

I splashed some water on my face and dressed in my normal clothes. When I went downstairs, I noticed Mrs. Matterhorn standing in the hall & watching me with narrow eyes & folded arms.

As I started along the boardwalk towards my office, I still felt low from my stagecoach-going-over-a-precipice nightmare. I was still thinking those Bleak Thoughts.

I thought, 'I am sure that Robert Pinkerton ain't my pa.'

Then I thought, 'Is there even any point in me learning to be a Detective?'

And finally, 'Why am I even alive?'

I slowed to a halt & stood there pondering the meaning of my existence. I had almost sunk into the Mulligrubs – which is a kind of bad trance – when I caught a glimpse of a man in a putty-colored plug hat standing on the boardwalk outside my office.

It was Robert Pinkerton.

I did not know what to say to him, so I said nothing.

I turned the handle & was surprised to find the door locked, as it was after 10 o'clock.

I said, 'What have you done with Ping? Have you thrown him in jail?'

He said. 'Who is Ping?'

I remembered I had been alone when he and Ray had burst into my office.

I said, 'Ping is my partner.'

He said, 'I have not seen him.' Then he added, 'Ye look different today.'

'I have been to Steamboat Springs,' I said, 'where I was bathed, manicured, trimmed and deloused.' I unlocked the door and went into my cold & empty Detective office.

He followed me in.

I could not think what he was doing there.

'What are you doing here?' I asked him.

He stared at the floor. 'Ye must think me a wretched detective.'

I said, 'What do you mean?'

He glanced quickly up at me, then looked down again. 'Thirteen years ago,' he said, 'I was in the Black Hills of Lakota Territory. I was riding shotgun, as they say, for a stagecoach plying back and forth between Chicago and Fort Laramie.'

I looked at him sharply. He had taken off his putty-colored plug hat and was turning it in his hands. He was still staring at the floor.

'I met an Indian lassie of about seventeen.'

Hope leaped into my throat. Could it be that he was my pa after all?

Robert Pinkerton said, 'She was bonny and brave and I succumbed to her charms. Her name was Squats on a Stump. Nine months after we met, she popped out a wee lassie and called her Glares from a Bush.'

I started to tremble. My ma had named me Glares from a Bush and only about six living people in the Whole World knew that fact. Not many people know that I am a girl, neither.

He added, 'Of course, I was the one who chose my daughter's Christian names.'

Everything went real quiet of a sudden, like someone had stuffed lint in my ears. I could not hear the thud of the quartz mills nor the tinkle of piano music from the saloon nor even the tromp of footsteps on the boardwalk outside. All I could hear was a kind of high-pitched singing, like a bat. Or an angel.

I remembered what Jace had said the day before: *There is one sure way to find out. If he is your pa, then he will know what P.K. stands for.*

I took a deep breath & said, 'What were your daughter's Christian names?'

'Prudence Kezia,' he said, without hesitation. 'Prudence Kezia Pinkerton.' His voice was kind of thick-sounding and his eyes were swimming with unshed tears. 'Yer name is Prudence Kezia and ye're me own wee lassie.'

Then he did a surprising thing.

He stepped forward & put his arms around me & held me tight.

I gave a start, as I do not like to be touched.

But after a moment I found I did not mind being held in a strong bear hug of a long-lost pa who had finally found his child. He rocked gently from side to side & one of his buttons pressed into my cheekbone & the woolen cloth tickled my nose. The coat smelled strongly of Lucy Hinton tobacco smoke & faintly of camphor. I felt safe & protected.

Tears welled up in my eyes, willy-nilly.

They were tears of happiness.

BANG!

The loud report of a gun made us jump apart.

Ping stood in the doorway with a smoking pistol in his hand.

It was a little two-shot Deringer but it took those big .50 caliber balls.

I did not even know that my Celestial pard packed a pistol. But apparently he did.

Ping had fired the first shot into the ceiling. Now he lowered his arm so the remaining ball was aimed right at my pa's heart.

'Make one move to hurt P.K.,' he snapped, 'and I shoot you dead!'

LEDGER SHEET 8

I WAS 'OVER THE MOON', OR AT LEAST 'OVER VIRGINIA City'.

I had explained to Ping that the man hugging me was my long-lost pa. Ping had apologized & had put away his piece. Now my pa and I were climbing Mount Davidson on account of Virginia is awful crowded & he thought a hike up that barren mountain would afford us a chance to talk without being interrupted and/or overheard.

As we ascended, my long-lost pa told me his life story.

He told me how he had been shipwrecked off Newfoundland on his way from Glasgow, Scotland to Chicago, Illinois.

He told me how in the early days he had first established an agency to protect stagecoaches and then trains. But later he wanted to help the Poor & Oppressed.

He told me how his younger brother Allan had become his partner after exposing a counterfeiting ring at a place called 'Bogus Island' near Chicago, Illinois.

'Bogus island?' I echoed. 'Was it not a real island?'

'No, it was a real island. They called the island "Bogus" on account of the fake money produced thereon. Wee Allan is a good detective. Maybe even better than me, who didnae even recognize me own wee lassie.'

My Pinkerton pa was good at telling about his many & varied adventures. He was good at mimicking other people's accents & voices. I was entranced by his tales of helping the Poor & Oppressed & fighting Grizzlies & catching Desperados & taking Slaves to Freedom on the 'Underground Railway' just like in *Uncle Tom's Cabin* by Mrs. Harriet Beecher Stowe.

My pa told me how he caught a bad chill when coming back from Canada after one such trip & how it took the stuffing out of him. After that, his 'wee brother Allan' took over the day-to-day running of the business and my pa mostly sat behind a desk.

Even though he was not tall and handsome like Poker Face Jace, but short and otter-looking, I was proud of my Pinkerton pa, now that I knew of his exploits.

I thought, 'If I could go back to Chicago with him to be a proper Pinkerton Detective, then I would be happy.'

We had just reached the summit of Mount Davidson where a tattered flag fluttered bravely on a 20-foot flagpole.

Pa was breathing hard and sweating a little. He took out his handkerchief and pressed it to his forehead. I observed it had the initials C.P. on the corner.

I pointed at the handkerchief. 'Who is C.P.?'

He looked at the handkerchief & frowned. Then his brow grew smooth again & he nodded. 'Ye will make a good detective,' he said. 'Ye are mighty observant.' He looked west towards the jagged snow-tipped mountains called Sierra Nevada. 'C.P. stands for Caroline Pinkerton,' he said. 'My wife.'

'You are married?' I asked. He had not mentioned that once in our 2-hour hike up the mountain.

He nodded. 'We married young, in Glasgow, Scotland. She sailed with me. She has been my wife nearly thirty years.'

I swallowed hard. 'Then you never married my original ma?'

He was concentrating on folding up his handkerchief again. He shook his head.

I felt the heat rising right up from my feet until my face felt like it was on fire. 'Do you have children?'

'Aye,' he said. 'Four big laddies.'

I swallowed again, but could not get rid of the bunch of emotions in my throat.

'So I could probably never go back to Chicago with you, could I?'

He shook his head. 'I dinna see how.'

We both stared out at the mountains.

Although I stood on a peak nearly 8000 feet high, I felt lower than I had ever felt.

As I looked down, I saw a tiny stagecoach far below. It was heading north on the road from Steamboat Valley to

Marysville via the Henness Pass.

I said, 'There is a stagecoach on the road from Steamboat Valley to Marysville via the Henness Pass.'

He said, 'By God, I have just had a gallus plan! If it succeeds I might be able to take ye back to Chicago with me! As an operative, mind ye, not me daughter.'

I was confused. I said, 'What is a gallus?'

He said, 'Gallus means "bold". Would ye be willing to help me and Ray catch those Reb Road Agents?'

I said, 'You bet!'

He told me his Plan.

It was a good one, full of danger & excitement & a trip across the Sierra Nevada. If it succeeded, I would be able to go back to Chicago with him and work as an operative for the world-famous Pinkerton Detective Agency.

There was only one problem. Pa told me that it was absolutely necessary that from that moment on, I dress like a girly-girl.

I scuffed at the ground with my moccasin. The last thing I wanted to be was a girly-girl. But going to Chicago with my real pa was my dream.

Somewhere in the sagebrush behind me, a quail called out, 'Chicago! Chicago!'

That clinched it.

I took a deep breath & nodded.

'All right, Pa,' I said. 'For you, I will try to be a girly-girl.'

TWO HOURS LATER, AT 4 O'CLOCK, I WAS STANDING IN front of a full-length mirror in Wasserman's Emporium wearing a balloon-sleeved, puffy-skirted merino-wool dress of a vivid yellow color.

Pa had told Ray G. Tempest our 'gallus' plan & Ray had liked it so much that he had gone to get us an appointment to meet with the owner of the Overland Stage Company as soon as possible. We had to act quickly as the road out of Virginia would soon be passable for stagecoaches and the first silver shipments would be double-sized.

Mrs. Wasserman had shown us three made-up dresses in the store. The one I now wore was the closest to my size & also the most girly.

It was mainly yellow, but had a kind of bib & cuffs & a waistband & pleated hem all in grass green. There were some green tongue-shaped flaps hanging down from the waist that the storekeeper called 'flounces'. I was also wearing my black wig with ringlets and my pink poke bonnet that I use for my 'Prim Girl Disguise'.

I said, 'I look like an Indian brave who has just massacred a little white girl and dressed in her clothes, scalp and bonnet for a hideous jest.'

'Oh, pshaw!' said my pa. 'It ain't that bad.'

'Try smiling,' said Mrs. Wasserman, who had just returned with some girly undergarments.

I turned to them & bared my newly whitened teeth.

They both took a step back.

'Ach! That is mair a grimace than a smile,' said my pa.

'You look like a wolf trapped in a hole,' said Mrs. Wasserman.

I stopped smiling.

Mrs. Wasserman said, 'I believe part of the problem is that bonnet. You can't really see her face. Just those glittering black eyes and gleaming teeth.'

'Ye're right,' said Pa. 'We need to see that bonny wee face.'

Mrs. Wasserman reached up to a shelf & brought down a bonnet. It was tall rather than deep, and made of yellow straw. It had two yellow flowers on top and a kind of yellow sash that poked through the straw to tie under your chin.

'This is the new style Skyscraper Bonnet for May,' she said. 'Some folk call it a "lighthouse bonnet". It is all the fashion. Go on. Try it.'

I took off my poke bonnet and put on the lighthouse bonnet.

'Why, there!' said Mrs. Wasserman, adjusting one of the flowers on top. 'It suits you down to the ground.'

Instead of hiding my face, it framed it.

'There's me bonny wee lassie!' said Pa.

But I could not bear to look & had to avert my eyes. Pa was nodding happily & turning his putty-colored plug hat in his hands.

Among some other men's hats on a shelf, I saw a hat with a flat top and a flat brim like Jace's, only it was brown not black. 'How much is that hat?' I asked Mrs. Wasserman.

'That one is ten dollars,' she said, 'on account of it is real beaver felt.'

It looked like a regular hat to me, but when Pa tried it on it made him look fine, and not a bit silly.

'It makes you look fine, and not a bit silly,' I said. 'I will buy it for you.'

'Ach, nay. I cannae let ye do that.'

'Sure you can. I have plenty of money at Wells Fargo & Co. just across the street.' I pulled out my medicine bag and took out some gold eagles. Because the dress was already made up and store bought, it was more expensive than I thought it would be. So was that lighthouse bonnet. What with buying those things & new undergarments & my pa's new beaver-felt hat, I would have to pay another visit to Wells Fargo & Co. in the near future. But if it could help me catch those Reb

Road Agents and earn me a place in Pa's Agency, then it was worth it.

'Let me just alter your frock,' said Mrs. Wasserman. 'Come with me. It will only take five minutes on my new Singer Sewing Machine.'

I went into a back room with her. She had one of them new Singer Sewing Machines that looks like a giant black ant with a wheel on its backside. She also had two dressmaker's dummies in there: one was wood & the other was papier-mâché. She made me stand still while she put pins in my dress & made me take it off & stand in chemise & bloomers.

She put the dress under the metal ant's nose & used her feet to make it take little sips of the cloth with its needle tongue. When she brought it back out, why, there was a new seam! Now the dress fit perfect.

When I came back into the shop, I saw Ray standing by a window with my pa. They were at the far end of the shop smoking & talking. They had their backs to me, but I have excellent hearing.

I heard Ray say, 'It's a perfect plan; better than we could have imagined.'

They must have heard my tippy-tappy boots for they turned to look at me.

'There's me wee bonny lassie!' said Pa. 'Guess what? Ray is just back from the Overland Stage Company. We have a meeting with the owner tomorrow morning at ten o'clock. Come closer.'

I went over to them, feeling awkward in my yellow

balloon sleeves & puffy skirt & flounces & furbelows & lighthouse bonnet.

'Her walk ain't quite right,' said Ray, blowing smoke down.

To me, Pa said, 'Try to walk like a lady and not stride forth like an angry teamster.'

I took little tripping steps & held my arms straight down by my sides with wrists bent so my palms faced the floor.

Ray shook his head & blew more smoke down. 'You have come up with a bully plan,' he said, 'but she has got to be a dam sight more convincing than that, or the owner of the Overland Stage Company will never buy it.'

LEDGER SHEET 10

I WAS FACING THE BIGGEST CHALLENGE OF MY career as a detective. To act like a convincing girly-girl.

It was vital to our Plan.

Even dressed in the girliest dress west of the Rockies I was not convincing.

Pa smiled at me through a cloud of his own pipe smoke. 'Don't ye worry,' he said. 'I will teach ye to walk and talk like a lassie in no time. It is still afternoon, but what do ye say to an early supper at Almack's Liquor & Oyster Saloon? They tell me it is the best restaurant in town.'

My stomach growled, for I had eaten nothing all day. 'All right,' I said. 'But only oysters. No liquor.'

'Of course no liquor!' said Pa. 'I am teetotal.'

'Well, I ain't teetotal,' said Ray, 'and I need a few stiff drinks. So I hope you don't mind if I dine elsewhere. I will see you both tomorrow at the offices of the Overland Stage at ten o'clock sharp.'

He exited the shop while I paid Mrs. Wasserman what I owed her.

As my pa and I emerged into the late afternoon sunshine and set out south on the C Street boardwalk I felt kind of queasy in my stomach.

I had worn a girl's disguise before but I always had a poke bonnet to hide my face. That lighthouse bonnet made me feel exposed, especially in the bright afternoon sunshine. Also a ruffle at the back itched my neck.

Pa took my left hand and tucked it firmly under his right elbow.

'This is how a respectable lassie walks with her escort in Chicago,' he explained. 'That is to say, a wife with her husband, a sister with her brother, or a daughter with her pa.'

I nodded and dutifully hung on to the crook of his elbow.

There was a line of people waiting outside the office of the Cal Stage Company. I reckon they were waiting to buy tickets now that the stage would soon be running again. I noticed Mr. Sam Clemens AKA Mark Twain, standing there with his friend, Clement T. Rice AKA The Unreliable.

I did not want to be recognized so I hung my head.

'Head up,' whispered Pa. 'Gracious expression.'

'I only have one expression,' I said. 'Inscrutable.'

'That will do at a pinch. But lift your head.'

We were past the line of people, so I lifted my head.

'Don't stomp,' whispered Pa.

'I cannot help it,' I said. 'These dam boots are so noisy.'

'Walk on the balls of your feet,' said Pa. 'That is, the front part. Take two wee steps instead of one big one. And ne'er blaspheme.'

I tried walking on the boardwalk in little tappy steps without blaspheming.

I hated every step.

I missed my silent, butter-soft moccasins.

I missed my shielding slouch hat with the black felt brim I could pull down low against the slanting sun.

I missed my pockets, and the comforting weight of a gun in one of them.

Almack's Oyster & Liquor Saloon was only two blocks south so I sent up an arrow prayer that I would not meet anyone known to me. If Sam Clemens and his friend were leaving town on account of a 'delicate satire', how would the townsfolk treat me when they discovered I had been pranking them for over half a year?

Then I saw Bee Bloomfield and Affable Fitzsimmons walking arm in arm straight towards us.

I wanted to dive behind a nearby barrel.

I wanted to squeeze underneath the boardwalk.

I wanted to do anything to get me out of their path.

When I thought Pa wasn't paying attention, I made a sudden lunge towards the swinging doors of the nearest saloon. I almost got away but Pa caught me & reeled me in & clamped my hand between his arm & his side. There was no escape.

I lowered my head as Affie and Bee approached, and

tried to make my black ringlets hide my face.

We were almost past them when I heard Bee's voice. 'P.K.? Is that you?'

I made as if to keep walking but my pa stopped & turned to face them & touched the brim of his new brown hat made of beaver felt. 'Good afternoon,' he said in his Scottish burr. 'Are ye friends of my daughter Prudence?'

'Pinky,' I mumbled, keeping my eyes firmly on their feet. 'Please call me Pinky.' Bee was wearing her little white button-up boots and Affable had exchanged his canvas shoes for sturdy brogues.

'Daughter?' cried Bee.

I took a deep breath and looked at her face. She was staring at me with Expression No. 4 – Surprise.

Then her face relaxed & she said, 'Oh, you are in *disguise*!' Abruptly she clapped both hands over her mouth.

Affable was staring at me, too. His eyes looked extra-big behind his spectacles. 'You are the same P.K. Pinkerton who collects bugs and butterflies?' he said.

'Shhh!' hissed Bee in a barely audible voice. 'He is *in disguise*.'

'Pinky is not in disguise,' said my pa in a mild tone. 'We thought it time to let the world know that Pinky is a lassie.'

'A lassie?' said Bee with a frown.

'A lassie?' said Affable, wide-eyed.

'Aye! That is to say, a girl. She always has been and always will be. Only she has finally decided to admit the fact and "come clean". By the way, I am her father, Robert Pinkerton.' He gave a little bow.

'Of the world-famous detective agency?' Affie extended his hand. 'Honored to meet you!'

My pa smiled & nodded & shook his hand.

'You're a girl?' squeaked Bee. She was staring at me with eyes as round as banjos.

I nodded & felt heat rise up into my face. My throat was tight. I did not know what to say.

'But I . . .' said Bee. 'I wanted to . . . I almost . . . Oh, you *creature*!' I saw her nostrils flare, which usually means someone is going to wallop you. I reckoned I deserved it so I braced myself & closed my eyes.

Sure enough, Bee Bloomfield slapped my face.

LEDGER SHEET 11

AFTER BEE SLAPPED ME, SHE TURNED & RAN through the crowd back the way she had come.

'Why did she strike you?' asked Affable, looking after her retreating bonnet.

I stared at the boardwalk. 'She had a bad habit of trying to kiss me,' I said. 'I reckon she is mortified to learn I am a girl.'

'I will attempt to console her,' said Affable. He touched his hat & turned & followed her.

As my pa and I resumed our perambulation along the boardwalk I clenched my jaw. All my fears were coming to pass. My friends felt betrayed by my secret, that was no longer a secret.

If my deception had caused a prim and proper girly-girl to strike me, how would my less demure friends react?

I wished I could put on my beloved buckskin trowsers & pink flannel shirt.

I stopped dead. 'Where are my buckskin trowsers and flannel shirt?' I asked my pa. 'I took them off at Wassermann's.'

'Those greasy old things?' said Pa. 'Why, Ray and I tossed them on a bonfire out back of the livery stable while you were getting alterations.'

I was too stunned to reply.

Then my pa stunned me some more: instead of crossing over to Almack's, he turned right. He was taking me up steep & muddy Taylor Street.

'Where are we going?' I said. 'Almack's is right back there. It is kitty corner across C Street. Ain't we going to supper?'

'I thought it would be good for us to preserve this special moment with an ambrotype,' he said. 'Before the sun sets.'

He was taking me to Isaiah Coffin's Ambrotype & Photographic Gallery right next door to my office! That meant Isaiah would find out I was a gal. So would Belle Donne. So would Ping, the person I most dreaded telling.

'No!' I cried, digging in my heels.

'But I want to send a photographic image to my brother, when I tell him about you,' said my pa.

Reluctantly, I undug my heels.

The sun had not yet dropped behind Mount Davidson when we reached Isaiah Coffin's Ambrotype & Photographic Gallery. The little bell over the door gave a familiar tinkle as we came into the empty studio.

'They ain't here,' I said, tugging his arm & backing up. 'Let's go. We can try tomorrow.'

'Nonsense,' said my pa. 'The door was unlocked and the sign said OPEN. Hello?' he cried. 'Anybody here?'

There were some muffled noises from the storeroom where the proprietor has various costumes & also a small laboratory in a cupboard. After about a minute Mr. Isaiah Coffin emerged, putting on his frock coat. Despite his grim-sounding name, he is a good-looking man with fair hair, symmetrical features and a billy-goat beard. I observed his cheeks were pinker than usual.

'Excuse my disarray,' he said, 'but I was developing— Zounds!' He stopped with his arm half in one sleeve and stared at me, open mouthed. Then he closed his mouth & resumed putting on his coat.

'That is to say: good afternoon, sir! Good afternoon, *little girl*. May I help you?'

'We'd like ye to ambrotype us,' said my pa. 'My name is Robert Pinkerton. I believe ye know my daughter, Prudence Kezia?'

Mr. Isaiah Coffin's gray eyes opened wide in Expression No. 4 – Surprise. 'Prudence Kezia?'

I nodded.

He narrowed his eyes. 'Prudence Kezia?' This time his face wore No. 5 – Suspicious or Thinking.

I sighed. 'Yes.'

Finally his face showed No. 1 – a Genuine Smile. 'Prudence Kezia?'

I sighed again. Deeply. 'Yes.'

'Sacray blur! You have confounded us all! For over half a year you have pulled the proverbial wool over our eyes.'

'Who has pulled the wool over our eyes?' said a feminine voice, and Miss Belle Donne came out of the same storeroom from which her husband had emerged. Yes, the prim & proper English photographer and the pistol-packing Soiled Dove were now man & wife, though she retained her stage name.

She was prettily attired in a dark-blue silk outfit with flounces & furbelows. Her cheeks were also pinker than usual and her bodice was buttoned wrong near the top.

'Vwa la!' said Isaiah Coffin to his wife. He flourished his hand at me. 'It transpires that P.K. Pinkerton is one of the weaker sex.'

'Ha, ha!' said Belle. 'That is rich.'

'Go on, Prudence,' said my pa. 'Tell her.'

I hung my head. 'It is true,' I confessed. 'I am a gal.' I shot a glare at Isaiah Coffin. 'But I ain't weaker, dam it!'

'Prudence,' said my pa with an admonishing tone. 'Didn't I tell ye not to blaspheme?'

'I meant a mill dam,' I said.

'Why, you cunning little vixen!' cried Belle, narrowing her eyes. She came close to me & circled round me & took my chin to turn my head this way & that. Finally she prodded my chest with a hard forefinger.

'Outch!' I cried.

'Dang!' cried she. 'You *have* been pulling the wool

over our eyes. The merino wool!' Then she laughed & clapped her hands. 'Oh, but this is bully news! I must tell everybody I know and have ever met.'

'No!' I cried. 'Don't!'

Too late. She was out the door.

By the time Isaiah had stood me and Pa up against his new painted backdrop of a Greek Temple & put our heads in iron vise-like contraptions to keep us from moving – lest we make the image blurry – a whole passel of people had gathered outside the shop and were peering through the window at us.

I stood there in humiliation – the back of my lighthouse bonnet gripped by iron pincers – and watched the townspeople of Virginia City watch me.

I saw my lawyer, Mr. William Morris Stewart, a lofty man with a beard the size of a sage-brush whose office was right across the street. He had obviously been doing business with Joe Goodman, the young owner of the Daily Territorial Enterprise newspaper, for he was there, too. Stewart and Goodman had both helped me in times past, but now they were staring at me with Expression No. 4.

Doc Pinkerton (no relation) appeared beside them. He had once offered to adopt me. I wondered if he would have made that offer if he had known my sex.

I noticed Titus Jepson, who had lost the tip of his pinky finger on account of me, but had promised to feed me in perpetuity. His Mexican waiter Gus was there, too, and several regular customers known to me by sight. They were all staring at me with banjo eyes & open mouths & shaking their heads in disbelief.

I felt a dribble of sweat tickle my backbone as Isaiah Coffin made a few last adjustments to his camera.

'Compose your faces,' he commanded. 'Look into the lens, and do not move! The sun will be gone in a moment.' Then he took a black disc from the front of the camera. I kept my eyes on the front of the camera but that did not stop me spotting the person I dreaded seeing most: my partner Ping.

Belle Donne was beside him, gesturing & talking in an animated fashion. But he was taking no notice of her. He was glaring at me with his arms folded across his chest & the scowliest scowl I had ever seen. He was mouthing something, too. I am good at lip-reading but I could not tell what he was saying. I reckoned he was cussing in Chinese.

Finally Ping turned and stalked off.

I wanted to run out of the studio & go after him to explain, but my head was in the jaws of that vise & also I was too ashamed. Of all people, I should have told him sooner, for he was my business partner.

I hoped he would not stay riled at me forever.

More people had come and were jostling at the window to see. They had stopped staring & were now laughing & pointing & shaking their heads. I felt my cheeks go hot.

When Isaiah released us from the gripping vises & said we could go, I wanted to go out the back way. But Pa said I must hold my head high and be seen as his daughter, so he made me leave by the front door, holding his arm in a girly fashion.

As we pressed through the gawping & grinning throng I heard people say, 'Is it true? Have you really been a gal all this time?'

I kept my head up but squinched my eyes shut. I clung onto Pa as he led me through the clamoring crowd.

I knew it was vital to our Plan that I act like a girly-girl, but I hated it.

I thought, 'Pa had better take me back to Chicago when we have solved this case, for I will never be able to face the folk of Virginia City again.'

LEDGER SHEET 12

MY SPIRITS REVIVED A LITTLE WHEN PA TOOK ME TO Almack's Oyster and Liquor Saloon down on C Street. We were shown to a high-tone dining room at the back.

It had tables around a polished square of wooden floor with a big chandelier overhead. It was now dusk and there were candles giving a soft, golden light.

The tables had heavy white tablecloths & silverware & crystal goblets.

A high-tone waiter in black and white led us to a table for two. He pulled out a velvet chair for me.

When I slumped down on it, Pa rolled his eyes.

He showed me how to sit with ankles crossed and Good Posture.

He told me to take off the little white gloves he had made me buy.

Then he ordered a bottle of Best Champagne. (Ma Evangeline had made me promise never to drink liquor but my Pinkerton pa said the bubbles meant it didn't count as liquor, and he was teetotal so he should know.)

The bottle of Best Champagne made a pop when the waiter opened it & it spurted out some white foam. Pa tried to catch it in one of the glasses and he laughed when it soaked his new shirt cuff. (I had bought him a new shirt to go with his hat.) The waiter dabbed Pa's damp cuff with his waiter-napkin & then poured the champagne into special glasses that were flat & round & shallow. I was entranced by the pale-gold liquid. It had about a hundred tiny silver bubbles all swimming up in strings that never ran out.

I downed mine in one, like I have seen folk do with whiskey in a saloon, but I had a bad coughing fit on account of the bubbles & coldness.

'Sip, for the love of God,' hissed my pa, as he refilled my glass. 'Sip!'

I sipped.

It was sweet & fizzy & made my heart rise up in my chest like a little hot air balloon in the blue sky.

It was the bulliest beverage I had ever tried.

There were 3 forks & 2 knives & a passel of little spoons on my place mat. Pa told me to start with the outside utensils and work my way in.

Pa ordered a fancy five-course meal. It was tasty food but I would have enjoyed it more if Pa had not kept telling me what not to do.

He told me not to hunker down like a vulture over its prey, but to sit up straight.

He told me not to slurp my soup, but to make my spoon like a boat.

He told me not to tip the oysters out of their half-shells straight down my open throat, but to use a special fork.

He told me not to use the horseradish to glue the peas to my knife.

He told me not to lick the last of the strawberry blancmange off my plate.

After all five courses, the waiter brought two china cups of black coffee and a plate of fancy little marzipan cakes called *petits fours* which are pronounced Putty For. Pa taught me to crook my little finger while sipping coffee and he challenged me to eat one of the marzipan cakes in ten tiny mouthfuls. I just about managed to do both those things.

About this time two men with fiddles started playing toe-tapping music. A few couples got up & began swirling around the little bare space which was a dance floor. The music was bully & it might have entranced me but Pa wanted to teach me how to make Small Talk.

Small Talk is where you talk about the weather & other genteel things but never about how a Methodist preacher & his wife found you on the Great Plains by the grave of your massacred Indian ma or how they adopted you & taught you reading & writing & scripture and brought you to Nevada Territory before they too got massacred.

By and by Pa allowed me to tell my story but he made me do it without the cussing or scalpings.

Then he let me tell him about some of the crimes I had solved. By now he had stopped telling me not to cuss nor mention blood. He just listened with his mouth half open. I reckon he was entranced.

I was telling Pa how I had vanquished a beautiful but murderous widow named Violetta de Baskerville when he stood up sudden-like and offered his hand.

'What are you doing?' I asked.

'I am going to teach ye to dance,' he replied.

'Do I *have* to learn how to dance?'

'Aye,' he said. 'A young lady needs to know how to dance. If ye are to be a Pinkerton operative, ye might have to do lots of it. Put on yer wee gloves and hold up yer right hand,' he said. 'Like ye're taking an oath in court.'

Part-Indians like me cannot take oaths in court but I held up my right hand anyways. He took it & pulled me to my feet & put his arm around my waist. I usually do not like to be touched but I did not mind it too much as he was my pa. He showed me how to move my feet by moving his own.

I could not do it.

'Keep trying,' he said. He smelled of Lucy Hinton tobacco & coffee & musky hair balm. It was a nice smell. I kept trying.

I could not master it.

'They are playing a dance called a Schottische,' he said. 'It is from Scotland. It is our slower version of a polka.' He was smiling & not getting impatient with

64

my clumsiness & stupidity. Concentrating on the steps prevented me from slipping into a music trance and I found my pa looked like a friendly otter again. I did not mind dancing with a friendly otter.

I kept trying to get it.

I almost had it.

I finally got it!

One moment I was stepping on my pa's new shoes & the next we were dancing! I could do it. Even in my silly button-up boots, I could do it!

We were spinning & trying not to barge the 2 other couples & our feet were twinkling & the fiddlers' faces whirled past wearing No. 1 smiles. Finally the music stopped & everyone laughed & clapped & fanned their faces.

When my pa went out back to use the outhouse, I almost plonked down at our table but remembered just in time and sat with ankles crossed and Good Posture.

I finished the champagne in my glass. I felt like all the little bubbles were lifting me up from inside.

Suddenly Jace was sitting opposite me.

'P.K.,' he said, 'what do you think you are doing?'

'Jace! What are you doing here?' I said. My words came out a mite slurry.

He looked at me through a cloud of cigar smoke. 'News reached me a couple of hours ago. People ain't happy that you have been pranking them for seven months. Why are you dressed like that? Folk will think you are mocking them.'

'What is wrong with this?' I said, looking down at my yellow and green frock. I could hear my voice was too loud. The room was tilting a little.

'Well, that color don't suit you, for one thing,' he said.

'You think Magenta would be better?' I said. 'Or maybe Solferino? Like what Violetta wears?'

(Violetta de Baskerville was the beautiful but deadly widow I had been telling my pa about. She was partial to fashionable shades of purple. She had tried to get her claws into Jace a few months earlier, but I had saved him from unholy matrimony & sent her packing to Frisco.)

He turned his head to blow smoke away from me. 'I ain't saying you should dress like Violetta,' he said. 'Though any dress in her closet would suit you better than what you are wearing now.'

It stung me when he said that but I was sure my face showed no emotion.

'This is the way my pa likes me to dress,' I said, lifting my chin.

'Yeah,' said Jace. 'I been watching you and your pa.'

'Well, he is going to take me to Chicago and I don't care what you think.'

Jace stubbed out his cigar even though it was only half smoked. 'All right then. I didn't come to talk ladies' fashions. I just came to try to help. But it looks like you don't need advice. Good luck in Chicago.'

'Who was that?' said Pa, coming up to the table.

I looked at Jace's retreating back. 'Just an old client,' I said.

'I have had a wee notion,' said my pa.

'What?' The champagne in my stomach had gone sour.

'I have decided to adopt ye.'

'What?' I said again. There was a high-pitched ringing inside my head.

'I'm going to adopt ye. Tomorrow morning first thing, if ye will let me.'

'But,' I said, 'what about your wife?'

He shrugged. 'I'll tell Caroline that ye're an orphan. I know she'll learn to love ye. And ye'll be a bone fide Pinkerton. Now gissa hug.'

I stood up and let him embrace me in a strong, firm bear hug. Through the muffling sleeves of his jacket against my ears I heard a lady say, 'Aw, ain't that sweet. A pa hugging his daughter.'

I knew I should have felt happy, for my dearest dream was about to come true.

But for some reason I only wanted to blub.

Dang my changing body!

LEDGER SHEET 13

'**Good morning, Miss Pinkerton!**' **snapped Ping** the next day. 'You late.'

It was only a quarter past 9.00 but I let that pass. He was sitting in *my* chair behind *my* desk. I also let that pass.

'Happy May Day,' I said. (It was Friday the 1st of May.)

Ping scowled at me. 'That is stupid hat.'

I was wearing my new lighthouse bonnet with its silk flowers & sash & ruffles. And also my daffodil-yellow, merino-wool dress with only one petticoat so it was not too puffy.

His words stung me but I pretended not to care.

'I don't care,' I said. 'This get-up is vital to a gallus plan of my pa's devising.' I held up my new adoption papers. 'Also, I have just been down to the recorder's office with my pa and I am now a genuine Pinkerton detective and no longer bogus.'

'I think you *very* bogus,' said Ping. He rose up from my chair & stood with folded arms. 'You lie to me. All this time.'

He stood facing me with the desk between us as if he was the Detective and I was the Client. He wore his smart gray worsted suit with the white shirt & jade silk cravat & he smelled faintly of jasmine soap or hair tonic. His black hair was very clean & shiny. When he wore his suit he tucked his long pigtail in the jacket so it looked like short hair.

For the first time it struck me that he was good-looking, even handsome.

He said, 'Why is our account at Wells Fargo one thousand dollar emptier than two days ago?'

I said, 'When I got home last night I found that Mrs. Matterhorn had heard about my being a gal and evicted me from my boarding house. I had to take a suite at a hotel.'

He said, 'What hotel?'

'The International.'

'Why suite?' His black eyes almost sparked with fire.

'So Pa and Ray can stay there, too, in their own rooms. They were lodging at a cheap boarding house down on D Street.'

He said, 'Suite at International for how long?'

I said, 'Only one night.'

He said, 'That is not thousand dollar.'

I said, 'I had to buy some new clothes.' I felt my face grow hot. Dang my body for betraying me!

'Those clothes?' He looked me up and down. His nose wrinkled on one side. Expression No. 3 - Disgust. 'Anything else?'

I said, 'I had to pay a clerk upwards of two hundred dollars to get these adoption papers cleared extra quick.'

'Anything else?'

I said, 'Five-course dinner at a high-tone restaurant last night.'

He looked at me, his arms still folded across his chest.

'With champagne,' I admitted.

He said, 'Fool! Do you forget we are partners? I handle business side. You should have check with me first.'

'I should have checked with you about getting adopted?' I said.

'Yes!' he said. 'If anything happen to you then he get all your money.'

'And if anything happens to *him*, I inherit a fifth of his wealth.'

'He wealthy?'

I shrugged. 'I reckon.'

'Then why you pay for hotel, clothes, dinner, champagne and adoption bribe?'

'Bribe? What do you mean "bribe"?'

'You pay extra to rush something through, it is called "bribe".'

I said, 'It was not a bribe. I had to pay two hundred to the clerk to get these adoption papers cleared extra quick. My pa keeps the accounts for the Pinkerton Agency and he says they are very strict on expenses.

But I know they are rich. They are a famous detective agency. They are world-renowned.'

'That does not mean they have money in their coffers.' Ping's scowl deepened.

'If we catch those Reb Road Agents,' I said, 'There will be a big reward. Two percent of whatever we recover. Pa said the stolen money might be as much as five hundred thousand. So our cut would be ten thousand dollars if we catch them.'

He said, 'If.'

I said, 'Did you see our shingle is up again? We are back in business.'

He said, 'I not sure I want to be partner with liar.'

I said, 'I ain't a liar.'

He said, 'You should have trust me. I do not care if you boy or girl. I only care about success of business.'

I said, 'You do too care if I am a girl. Would you have worked with me if you'd known?'

'Yes,' he said. But for the first time his gaze slid away.

I said, 'You only care about money.'

He said, 'A business with no money will not last long. Look.' He opened a ledger book on the desk. It was a proper ledger book with numbers and dates meticulously recorded. It had all our income from the seven months we had been doing business.

'Before you take out that thousand dollar,' he said, 'our balance was good. Nearly four thousand. Now it is only this.'

He pointed at a column on the ledger book & I looked.

I saw the remaining balance in the Pinkerton strongbox was $2,784.20

He said, 'I want fifty percent.'

I said, 'Beg pardon?'

He said, 'I do not want to work with lying female.'

'You just said it didn't matter if I was female.'

'Female does not matter. Lying does.'

I was flummoxed. I did not know what to say. I had not thought Ping would be this riled at me for deceiving him.

He re-folded his arms across his chest. 'You soon go back to Chicago with your pa, correct?'

When he said that, I felt a mite queasy, like when I stand too close to the edge of a precipice. I would be abandoning my life as I knew it, but Chicago was my dream. I had to make that leap of faith sometime.

'Yes,' I said. 'I will be going to Chicago.'

'Then split business assets fifty-fifty,' Ping said.

The whole room seemed to swell and then shrink back again, as if *it* had taken a deep breath, not me.

He said, 'You still have those feet of Chollar Mine which bring you about one fifty a month. They are yours. Good income. Do not sell them.'

'All right,' I said. 'We will go to the bank right now, and I will give you your half of the money.'

He said, 'I could also ask you to pay back thousand dollar you just spend, so we could split that, too, but if you sign over deed of this office to me, we will call it even.'

'You want this office?'

'Yes, I want this office. After you go, I rename business Pingerton Detective Agency.'

'Pingerton? As in Ping?'

He nodded curtly.

'That is clever.' I looked around the narrow room with its shelves & desk & chairs & sky window & wood-burning stove & the branch with butterfly chrysalises & the hat-tree & the counter at the back & the door to the little storeroom/bedroom where I had lived for a month or two before moving to Mrs. Matterhorn's. I felt a bunch in my throat but I swallowed it down.

'All right,' I said.

I do not usually like to be touched but this was important so I spat on the palm of my right hand and held it out.

Ping spat on the palm of his right hand and we shook.

Then we went down to Wells Fargo & Co. and apart from the necessary yesses and noes required to get a clerk to withdraw $1,392.10 in gold from my strongbox and hand it over to him, we did not speak another word to each other.

I left the bank without saying goodbye, for it was almost ten o'clock.

I had somewhere to be.

THE VIRGINIA CITY OFFICE OF THE OVERLAND Stage Company was noisy & crowded. It smelled of spittoons & sweat & cigars. Pa and Mr. Ray G. Tempest were standing behind a counter and I was standing behind them. It was just past ten o'clock. We were waiting to see the owner so we could tell him our clever Plan.

Behind me, a woman's hoop skirt nudged me up against Pa so that his brown woolen greatcoat tickled my nose. Now that the road out of Virginia was passable, there were a lot of folk wanting tickets for the stagecoach.

'We have an appointment with Mr. V.V. Bletchley,' said Ray to someone on the other side of the counter. 'We are Pinkerton detectives.'

'I will see if he is ready for you,' said an Irish accent.

I could not see over the counter, so while we were waiting, I read a sign on the wall:

OVERLAND COMPANY RULES
FOR STAGECOACH PASSENGERS

1. Do not jab people with your elbows or jostle them with your knees.

2. Do not talk to other passengers if you have not been introduced.

3. Do not discuss Politics or Religion.

4. Do not wear strong-smelling toilet water or pomade.

5. Do not smoke a strong-smelling pipe or cigar.

6. If you must spit or vomit, do so out of the window. (On the leeward side.)

7. Do not stare fixedly at the other people in the stagecoach.

8. Do not drink whiskey or other spirituous beverages.

9. Do not lean upon your neighbors when sleeping.

10. Do not point out where murders, robberies and/or grisly stagecoach crashes have occurred.

11. Do not discharge firearms. The noise might upset the passengers & spook the horses.

12. If the team runs away, sit still and take your chances. If you jump, nine out of ten times you will get hurt.

It was that last rule that worried me the most, on account of my stagecoach-going-over-a-precipice nightmare. If Mr. V.V. Bletchley liked Pa's idea, I would soon be sitting atop a stagecoach. I wondered, if something spooked the team, would I be better off jumping or sitting still?

An Irish accent broke into my thoughts. 'Mr. V.V. Bletchley will see you now. Please follow me.'

'Remember, Pinky,' whispered my pa, 'it is important ye act like a girly-girl.'

I followed Pa and Ray around the counter. I practised taking dainty half-steps. We went past some desks and along an echoing corridor. The clerk opened a door and stood back to let us enter.

I followed Pa in & was about to close the door with a backward kick but remembered just in time & gently closed it with my gloved hand instead.

'Please be seated, gentlemen,' said a plump man behind a desk, without looking up. He had some .36 caliber balls & powder & lint & caps laid out on the blotter of his desk & he was loading a revolver. I observed it was a Colt Pocket Navy. It is like the normal Navy only it has a shorter barrel and the cylinder holds five balls, not six.

There were two chairs in front of the big maple desk and a small red velvet stool over by the window. My pa brought the stool and set it between the chairs and we all sat down with me in the middle.

The man still had his head down as he concentrated on putting little brass caps on nipples. I could see he had a few strands of black hair pasted over his bald head.

At last he finished loading his five-shooter & looked up.

I sometimes find it hard to remember people's faces and names, which can be a handicap when you are a detective, but Mr. V.V. Bletchley's face and name would be easy to remember. His cheeks were blotchy, which sounds like Bletchley.

'Who is this?' he said when he saw me sitting between the two operatives. His voice sounded clotted & thick, like porridge.

'This is me wee lassie,' said Pa. 'Say hello, Prudence.'

'How do you do?' I said in my little-girl voice. I half rose from my stool to make a curtsy.

'Charming,' said Mr. V.V. Bletchley. 'Her mother must have been quite lovely. Mexican, I'd guess, like my wife. And who are you?'

'I am Robert Pinkerton, founder of the world-renowned Pinkerton Detective Agency. This here is Ray G. Tempest, one of our finest operatives.' They both opened their greatcoats to show the detective buttons on their coat lapels. Mr. V.V. Bletchley's eyebrows went up.

'Pinkertons!' he exclaimed. 'What are you doing this far west?'

Ray said, 'We are on the trail of some "Reb Road Agents" who have been robbing stagecoaches in Utah Territory. They have recently moved their base west to the Sierra Nevada mountains. '

'I've heard of them,' said Mr. V.V. Bletchley.

Ray said, 'We believe they will be lying in wait for your next silver shipment to Sacramento.'

'Where did you get this information, sir?' Bletchley's blotchy face had gone a shade lighter.

'We cannot reveal our source, as it might endanger the life of one of our undercover operatives,' continued

Ray. 'But we have an idea of how to safeguard the silver and hopefully catch those bandits.'

'Gentlemen,' said Bletchley, 'you have my full attention.'

'A stagecoach leaving Salt Lake City was robbed last month and a female passenger gave us valuable information about these so-called Reb Road Agents,' continued Ray. 'She said the only thing they stole from her was a kiss, on account of they do not rob stages with women nor children, but only those carrying gold and silver and Fat Cats. The woman's little girl was on the stage with her and one of the Reb Road Agents bounced her on his knee. He said they would not harm a hair of her head as they both had little girls of their own.'

'I was not aware of that incident,' said Bletchley. 'Nor of their fondness for women and children.'

'This is our plan,' continued Ray. 'We suggest a trap. Put your best driver and your fiercest-looking conductor on top of a vehicle well-suited for transporting valuables. However, instead of silver it will hold your bravest guards. The bandits will see that heavy-laden coach and naturally assume it carries the big silver shipment. When they tell you to "stand and deliver", your guards will spring forth and apprehend them. No passengers will be hurt, no silver stolen. As those Reb Road Agents are being clapped in irons,' he concluded, 'the genuine silver shipment will pass by on a second stagecoach, which will appear to be a harmless passenger stage.'

Mr. V.V. Bletchley pursed his lips. Then he nodded.

'That is a bully idea,' he said. 'Simple yet effective. Let me put it to one of my drivers and one of my conductors.' He struck a little brass hand bell on his desk: *ding!*

The clerk came in.

Bletchley said, 'What drivers and conductors have we got available at the moment?'

'Almost all of 'em,' said the clerk. 'Blue, Calloway, Prince and Burns. Oh, and Dizzy just came in.'

'Send in Blue and Dizzy.'

While we waited, Bletchley turned to me. 'I would offer you coffee but it is cold and black.'

I was going to say that cold and black was my preferred method of drinking it but I remembered I was supposed to be a girly-girl so I replied, 'I will be grateful for it, however it comes.'

Bletchley stood up, went to a sideboard, poured black coffee into a china cup with matching saucer & put it on the desk before me.

I lifted the cup to my lips, careful to keep my little finger crooked as I took a dainty sip.

Mr. V.V. Bletchley went back to the sideboard. 'Whiskey, gentlemen?' he said, lifting a cut-glass decanter half full of amber liquid.

'I dinna drink,' said my pa.

But Ray nodded. 'I ain't teetotal. I will have one.'

As Bletchley was pouring whiskey the door opened and two men came in. One of them was known to me on account of he was an albino with skin as white as a corpse's & a stubbly snow-white beard & little round dark-blue goggles. Folk hereabouts called him 'Icy' because of his icy skin color and his initials, which are I.C.

I like people with such distinctive looks; I do not forget them like I do ordinary people.

The man who followed Mr. Icy Blue into the office was unknown to me. He was short & tubby with a snub nose and stubble on his chin. He wore a floppy gray slouch hat with the front brim folded back & pinned to its dented crown. His faded flannel shirt showed me a glimpse of his undergarments where some buttons were missing at the belly.

When he saw me sitting there he snatched off his hat & sucked in his gut. 'Beg pardon, Miss,' he said. 'I do not mean to exhibit my unmentionables but my dinner done popped the buttons of my shirt.'

Mr. V.V. Bletchley pointed to the man with blue goggles. 'Mr. Isaac C. Blue here is a conductor.' To me he said, 'The conductor is what you might call the captain of the stagecoach, for he takes charge of the passengers & goods and protects them with his shotgun. For that reason the conductor is often called the "Shotgun".'

I knew all this but I was pretending to be a girly-girl so I just nodded politely and tried to make my eyes big & round.

He smiled at me and then pointed to the tubby man. 'Mr. Davey Scrubbs there goes by the name of "Dizzy". He is one of our best drivers. Sometimes we call the driver the "Whip" because of the big black whip they hold.'

'They call the whip a "black snake",' explained Dizzy.

'And whipping the horses is called "blacksnaking".'

I covered my mouth with both hands, the way I had seen Bee do sometimes. 'Does it hurt the horses?' I asked in my girly-girl voice.

'Nah!' chuckled Dizzy. 'It only makes a loud crack, like a gunshot. That is what gets 'em running. A good "Whip" will not even touch them horses,' he added.

'Dizzy,' said Mr. V.V. Bletchley, 'what would you say if I asked you to take the big silver shipment over the mountains to Sacramento this very afternoon and put it on the steamboat to Frisco?'

Dizzy was so surprised that he swallowed his chaw of tobacco. He coughed & then stood up a little straighter. 'You never asked me to do that before, boss,' he said. 'I would not like to be responsible for that much silver. You know I cannot shoot worth beans.'

'You don't have to worry,' said Ray. 'One of us will be your conductor and ride shotgun with you, and the other will ride close by for extra protection, just in case. But you probably won't even see the Reb Road Agents as the decoy stage will be a few miles ahead of you.'

'Decoy stage?' said the albino with blue goggles.

'Just so,' said Bletchley, turning to him. 'Would you be willing to take a coach full of armed men in order to apprehend those robbers lurking up in the Sierra Nevada?'

Icy nodded. 'I would relish the chance to meet those varmints,' he growled. 'I am ready to send those goddam Road Agents to h-ll.'

'I thought as much,' said Bletchley. He smiled at Dizzy. 'So you see? There should be no danger. Icy here will be the bait so you can drive your coach full of silver right on past those Reb Road Agents as he is clapping them in irons.'

'But what if they miss spotting that decoy coach and spy me in a low-slung coach all groaning with silver?' said Dizzy.

Pa said, 'We have thought of that. We have an ace in the hand: my wee daughter Prudence!'

Mr. Bletchley looked at Pa and then at me. 'What do you mean?'

Ray said, 'Like we told you, we know that those Reb Road Agents have a soft spot for little girls.' He turned to Dizzy. 'Therefore, we intend to get Prudence here to pretend to be your young niece and ride atop the stagecoach in a prominent position.'

'What, sir?' cried Bletchley. 'You would put your own child at risk for the sake of a little silver? Why, that is monstrous! I could not live with myself if a hair of this sweet little girl should be harmed. I cannot believe you would be willing to put her in danger.'

I looked at Pa and he looked at me.

I was not sure exactly what had just happened but I think it was this: I had girly-girled myself right out of a job!

LEDGER SHEET 15

Mr. V.V. Bletchley had squashed my pa's plan of using me to convince Reb Road Agents that our coach could not be transporting silver. It was too 'gallus'.

But Pa did not give up. He tried a 'flanking manoeuver'.

'Sir,' he said, 'Have ye heard of a certain P.K. Pinkerton, a private eye operating on B Street?'

'Everybody's heard of him,' said Mr. V.V. Bletchley. 'He exposed a murderer last year and vanquished a bothersome outlaw, name of Whittlin Walt, back in September, even though he is just a kid.'

Pa put his hand on my shoulder. 'This, sir, is P.K. Pinkerton!'

'What?' said Mr. Bletchley. 'You are claiming your half-Mexican daughter is the half-Injun Private Eye who has been working in this town for the past seven months?'

'Aye,' said my pa. 'The P.K. stands for Prudence Kezia.'

'And I ain't half Mexican,' I said in my normal voice.

'I am half Sioux Indian.'

Bletchley shook his head slowly, like a boxer who has been punched one time too many. Then he looked at me.

'*You* are P.K. Pinkerton?'

'Yes, sir! You can call me Pinky.'

'Pinky is a master of disguise,' said my pa, 'and skilled with all kinds of firearms. She will be perfectly safe, else we would not have suggested it. Her visible presence virtually guarantees the safety of the silver-coach.'

Mr. Bletchley looked at me. 'Ain't you afraid?'

I must confess I *was* a little afraid on account of my stagecoach-going-over-a-precipice nightmare, but I knew my inscrutable features would not betray me.

I sat a little straighter. 'No, sir! I have been shot at, chased down a mine, sucked at by quicksand, almost buzzed in half and nearly froze, too, but I was never scared. I can shoot a gun and I can make a fire. I can ride a pony with or without a saddle.'

'Although of course she won't be riding a pony,' said my pa. 'She will be sitting up on top of the stagecoach for all to see.'

'You sure you want to do that?' Dizzy asked me. 'You know those stages can be awful jouncy. I would hate anything to happen to a purty li'l thing like you.'

'I am sure,' said I.

Dizzy shrugged & nodded, but Bletchley was looking at me with lips like a trout. Poker Face Jace said if someone purses their lips it means they are pondering something & have not yet made up their mind.

Through the open window of the stage office came the smell of sage-brush & the sound of some quail. They were urging me to go to, 'Chicago! Chicago!'

I could also see an outhouse.

'Well, Mr. Pinkerton,' said Mr. V.V. Bletchley at last. 'I concede it is a bold plan, but I am afraid I cannot allow it. I will not risk harming a hair of this dear little girl's head!'

'H-ll!' I said. 'It ain't even my hair! It is a _____ wig.' (Here I used a strong adjective.) I pulled off my lighthouse bonnet & wig in one swift motion and plunked them on the desk before Mr. V.V. Bletchley.

Then I snatched up his freshly-loaded Pocket Navy and – before anyone could object – I cocked it, aimed & fired five shots in quick succession through the open window.

Bang! Bang! Bang! Bang! Bang!

Through the cloud of white gun smoke we all saw the door of the outhouse fly open. A miner dashed out. He was gripping a copy of the Daily Territorial Enterprise newspaper in one hand and the waistband of his trowsers in the other.

'Why, lookee there,' wheezed Dizzy, as the gun smoke cleared. 'That little gal made that crescent moon into a full one!'

I nodded with satisfaction & blew away a coil of gun smoke issuing from the barrel. I had used the five shots to make the semi-circular moon-shaped vent into a circle.

'Goll darn!' exclaimed Mr. V.V. Bletchley. 'You sure can shoot. Well, that puts a whole new light on the matter.'

Here I noticed that Mr. Icy Blue had pulled the goggles up on his forehead so he could see better. Now he was watching me with his arms folded across his chest and his pale eyes narrowed.

It was like he was waiting for me to do something more.

I quickly set about reloading the five-shooter. They were all watching me but I was not nervous. Everything I needed was right there on Bletchley's blotter. I used his powder flask to drop a measure of black powder into each chamber & then added a piece of lint & then dropped in a .36 caliber ball & used the built-in rammer to jam it in real good. Finally I put caps on the nipples at the back of the cylinder.

When I finished reloading, I handed the revolver back to Bletchley, butt first.

Out of the corner of my eye I saw Mr. Icy Blue give a little nod and replace his goggles over his eyes. I felt I had passed a test.

'Well,' said Bletchley. 'I do believe I have changed my opinion of your daughter!' He put the pistol in his drawer & looked at Pa. 'I think your plan might work after all.'

Dizzy scratched his belly and frowned. 'I don't rightly understand the Plan,' he said. 'Can you 'splain it again?'

Bletchley turned to him. 'As I see it, these detectives are suggesting that you let the little girl and one of them ride up on top with you in shotgun position. The silver will be inside your coach. We will hide it under mailbags, as we got so many of those still left to deliver. But a decoy coach will set out first. It will appear to be carrying silver, but when the Reb Road Agents hold it up, half a dozen of my men will jump out and arrest them. Then you and the silver will ride on past to Sacramento in perfect safety.'

'What is the point of that li'l gal, again?' asked Dizzy.

'To make your coach look harmless and ambling.'

'All right, then,' said Dizzy after a moment. 'If you are sure you want to entrust so much silver to my care, I reckon I will do it.'

That is what he said, but I could tell from his feet pointing towards the door that he was not happy.

'Blue?' said Mr. Bletchley. 'You all right with our plan? Can you rustle up five or six men for the decoy stage?'

'Dam right,' he growled.

'And you, Miss Pinkerton?' said Mr. V.V. Bletchley, turning to me. 'Are you absolutely, positively certain you want to do this?'

I set my wig & hat back on my head, looked at my beaming pa & nodded firmly. 'You bet!'

LEDGER SHEET 16

EVERYTHING HAPPENED REAL FAST AFTER THAT.

Within an hour we were standing in a dim livery stable, watching half a dozen heavily armed men climb into a sturdy stagecoach.

Once in, they pulled down the leather shades. Then Icy Blue & his driver climbed up into the box.

'How does that look?' said Mr. V.V. Bletchley to us.

'Looks good,' said Dizzy. 'Looks like we got something to hide.'

I agreed & looked at Pa to see whether he did, too, but he was busy adjusting the saddle on a big gray gelding.

'Off you go then,' said Mr. V.V. Bletchley to the first stagecoach. 'And good luck to you! You catch them Reb Road Agents.'

Icy Blue raised his shotgun and his driver flicked the reins & said, 'Hee-yah!'

The decoy coach was away!

Pa swung up into the saddle of the gelding. 'I hope to see ye pass us on the road,' he said, 'as we clap those bandits in irons.'

'Pa!' I cried. 'Ain't you riding shotgun with us?'

'Not for the first wee stretch,' he said. 'Horses and Ray dinna get along so he'll ride with ye. But don't worry, me wee lassie. Once we've clapped those pesky Reb Road Agents in irons I'll ride with ye to Sacramento.' His eyes were brimming with tears like he was sad to leave, & he could not meet my gaze.

I confess I was disappointed. I had been looking forward to working with my pa on our first case.

'Fare thee well!' He touched his finger to the brim of his new hat. Still without looking at me, he turned his horse & spurred it & trotted after the departing coach. I saw his silhouette against the bright square of outside light coming in through the stable doors. Then the light kind of dissolved him & he was gone.

Mr. V.V. Bletchley, Dizzy and Ray were examining the second stagecoach.

I studied it, too. It was battered and old, with a faded vista of mountains painted on the door and gold trim that was almost chipped off.

Bletchley turned to me. 'She may look old and battered,' he said, 'but she was recently fitted with a new thoroughbrace and she can hold tons of silver. Come look.'

He opened a door and showed me how they had covered the floor of the coach with 78 silver bricks of varying shapes & weights all laid neatly side by side. He told me the 'ingots' were worth over 50 thousand dollars! As I watched, they piled some letter-sacks inside the coach to cover up the silver. Then they pulled down all the leather window shades so you could not see inside.

'What do you think?' said Mr. Bletchley, standing back. 'How does it look?'

'Not too good,' said Dizzy, scratching his belly. 'With the shades down, it looks like we got something to hide. Folk generally like to look out.'

'But if we open the shades then everybody will see we have no passengers.' Bletchley looked at Ray. 'You should have thought of that before.'

Dizzy scratched his armpit. 'Maybe Miss Pinky can ride *inside* the coach so people will glimpse her in the window.'

Ray shook his head. 'The whole point of her is to be conspicuous – that is, easily seen – so any lurking bandits will see a little girl and let you pass.'

I had an idea of how I could make a bogus passenger who would look real.

'I have an idea of how I can make a bogus passenger who will look real,' I said. 'Wait here!'

I ran out of the stable & pelted up to Mrs. Matterhorn's & plucked a head-sized unripe watermelon from her back garden & then hurried one block down to Wasserman's Emporium & bought Mrs. Wasserman's old papier-mâché dummy & also a velvet ladies' coat & also the biggest straw sunhat I could find. Then I whizzed back to the Overland Stage Co. livery stable.

'Where you been?' they all cried. 'It has been near half an hour.'

But when I wedged the dummy torso inside the stagecoach at the front & draped the purple velvet coat around her shoulders & stuck the watermelon on the dowel neck of her papier-mâché body & added that big sunhat to hide her green & yellow striped head they all said, 'Ah!', for my construction appeared to be a fashionable lady sitting in the best seat with her back to the driver & looking out the window.

We stood back to judge the effect.

'She is bully!' said Dizzy. 'Now it looks like a school marm, maybe with the other shades down to shield her napping pupils on their way back from a picnic.'

'Much better,' agreed Bletchley, puffing on a cigar.

'Good idea to use a watermelon for a head,' said Ray. 'Otherwise her hat would lie too low.' Then he spotted something & frowned & went closer to inspect her. 'Goll DANG it!' he cried, making us all jump. 'What is that on her hat?'

'Flowers,' I said. 'Just some old silk flowers.'

'No. That! Right there!' He was white as chalk.

I went closer and saw a silk butterfly among the flowers.

I said, 'That is a silk butterfly among the flowers.'

'Take the dam thing off!'

'It is not genuine. It is bogus.'

'I don't care! I told you before. Those things give me the fantods.'

I pulled the bogus butterfly off the hat-band & stuck it out of sight in my medicine bag.

'You best be going,' said Mr. Bletchley, looking at his pocket watch. 'Otherwise you will not have the protection of Icy and all those agents if anything goes wrong. They are nearly an hour ahead of you.'

Dizzy quickly clambered up onto the driver's box & so did Ray.

I was about to scramble up after them but then I remembered to be a girly-girl. I accepted Dizzy's hand and let him help me up via the wheel onto the lofty box seat. I took my place in the middle, with Dizzy on my right and Ray on my left.

'Ready?' Dizzy asked me.

I nodded.

Dizzy hooked his right foot around the lever beside the driver's box & pulled it back to release the brake. Then he flicked the reins & cried, 'G'lang! G'lang there, you sons of blanks!' To me he said, 'Pardon my cussing. Those critters won't pay me no mind lessen I blaspheme.'

'Good luck!' called Bletchley after us.

We emerged from the livery stable into the bright day. It was the first day of May. I was wearing my wig with its swinging black ringlets and my lighthouse bonnet with its silk flowers & sash & itchy ruffle at the back. It was warm so I only needed a light pink shawl over my daffodil-yellow dress. I had my black button-up boots & a yellow velvet drawstring purse around my left wrist. Pa had made me buy some little white cotton gloves but

I had replaced them with my beaded buckskin gauntlets. They were my lucky gloves.

As we went over the Divide – a kind of hump in the road between Virginia City and Gold Hill – I could feel the horses straining to pull the coach full of heavy silver ingots and letter-sacks. But as soon as they started heading downhill towards Silver City, the coach fairly flew along. I had to retie the yellow ribbon under my chin or my yellow lighthouse bonnet would have flown off into the atmosphere.

'Dang!' wheezed Dizzy. 'That silver is pushing them hard.'

I nodded and gripped the edges of the bench. The road was steep and curvy with precipitous drops onto jagged orange rocks. It was scary like my nightmare but also thrilling. My heart was pounding hard.

I wished Pa could be sitting beside me instead of Ray G. Tempest who kept taking secret swigs from his small flask.

Dizzy concentrated hard as we drove through Gold Hill & Devil's Gate & Silver City. The road was crowded but everybody made way for our thundering stagecoach. Ray flipped the toll-booth operators their coins and we fairly raced through. When the mountain finished and the road leveled out on its way to Carson, Dizzy kind of breathed a sigh and wiped his forehead with his faded bandana.

He glanced at me. 'You're awful quiet. You scared?'

I shook my head. 'I just wish my pa could have seen my clever ruse of using a dummy as a dummy.'

'I'll make sure he hears about it,' said Ray. He took a swig from his flask and then saw us looking. 'Tooth elixir,' he explained. 'My dam tooth is still paining me.'

We rode for a while without conversing. I strained my eyes to see Pa but he was too far ahead.

I noticed that Dizzy had a double-barreled shotgun in a kind of leather scabbard beside him.

'You ever been robbed?' I asked.

'Nope,' said Dizzy. 'Most local robbers know the boss don't trust me with big payloads so they let me alone.'

'That is why you are the perfect choice for this job,' said Ray.

We changed teams at Curry's Warm Springs Hotel where I had once stayed, but I did not see anyone known to me. Ray got himself a red bandana with a few drops of strong-smelling creosote on it and some ice chippings and he tied this around his head with the knot on top and his hat hiding it. This gave him some relief but made it hard for him to talk.

Our fresh team of six bay horses sped us through Carson City without stopping and my haunts of the previous winter flashed past. Soon we were out of town and racing along the flat road to Genoa with sage-brush and greasewood dotted plains either side and those barren, high-rising mountains to the southwest.

'Nice gloves,' said Dizzy.

He was admiring my buckskin gloves with the beaded zigzags that Jace had given me for Christmas.

'These are my lucky gloves,' I said.

'Lucky gloves, eh?' chuckled Dizzy. 'Then why don't you take the ribbons?'

'Beg pardon?'

'The ribbons. The traces. The reins. Go on! Take 'em!'

And before I knew what had happened he'd put the control of six powerful horses & $50,000-worth of silver into my hands.

LEDGER SHEET 17

DIZZY HAD PUT THE HEAVY REINS OF A SIX-HORSE team in my gloved hands. I was so startled I nearly fell off the coach.

I said, 'How can I drive a six-horse team if I am supposed to be personating a demure little girly-girl to fool the Reb Road Agents?'

Dizzy said, 'You can see there ain't nobody on this here stretch of road. Besides, those Road Agents are lurking up in them thar mountains not down here on the high plains.'

'Hey!' protested Ray. 'Ain't that dangerous?' He had been sipping tooth elixir from his flask and only just noticed I was holding the traces.

'Nah!' said Dizzy. 'It ain't dangerous. These horses know the road so well they could do it blindfolded.'

But I reckoned it *was* dangerous. I could feel the life energy of those six steeds whizzing up through the leather straps into my fingers & arms & spirit.

I felt scared and powerful at the same time. It was like flying on a rocking, creaking boat. Dizzy was right: the coach might look old & battered but that thoroughbrace – or whatever it was called – worked real well.

We hit a bump and all three of us flew about four inches up and came down bang!

'Yee-haw!' cried Dizzy.

'Dam!' swore Ray, but he was laughing.

Dizzy turned to me. 'Let it out!' he said. 'It ain't good to hold it in. It'll make you queasy. Go on! If you can't choke out a "yee-haw" then cuss like a miner or squeal like a gal.'

'Yee-haw,' I said. I was concentrating on driving & did not feel like yelling.

Dizzy looked at the sky. 'I thought I heard a squeak. Could it have been a bat?'

'Yee-haw!' I cried, a bit louder.

'Did you hear something, Mr. Ray?' said Dizzy.

Ray shook his head. He was grinning despite his toothache.

Using both my lungs I shouted, 'YEE-HAW!'

It felt good. Everybody laughed. Even me.

I only wished my pa had been there to share the moment.

Dizzy took a fresh chaw of tobacco from his trowser pocket & bit off a corner & folded up the plug in its paper wrapper. I was paying attention to the horses but out of the corner of my eye I saw that it was Blue Star brand chewing tobacco. I try to be observant about such things. Identifying tobacco is one of my special detective skills.

The road was running smooth through a flat marshy plain towards those great, jagged snow-topped mountains called the 'Sierra Nevada' which means 'Great, Jagged Snow-topped Mountains' in Spanish. There is a pretty little town called Genoa situated right at their foot with some oak trees & cottonwoods by a stream. We could see it a long time before we got there. Pa Emmet once told me that it used to be called Mormon Station until the Mormons all upped sticks and went to Salt Lake City. He said they renamed it Genoa after a town in Italy but they pronounce it different so people will not get confused.

'Dam,' said Ray. He took his flask from his pocket and tipped it upside down to show us his Tooth Elixir was all gone.

'You should get that tooth pulled,' said Dizzy. 'Any blacksmith will do it.'

Ray touched his cheek & winced. 'You mind if I lie down inside the coach?' he asked Dizzy.

'Course not! But you will have to lie on them hard leather letter-sacks.'

'I don't mind.' Ray tossed his empty Tooth Elixir bottle into the marsh on the left-hand side of the road. 'Pull up,' he said, 'so I can go down right now.'

I was still holding the 'ribbons', as they say.

'Pinky,' said Dizzy, 'you want to try slowing this rig?

You just—' he began, but I was already pulling back on the heavy reins.

'Whoa, you sons of blanks!' I hollered.

The team of six bay horses slowed & stopped right there in the road. They stood snorting & tossing their heads.

'Why, missy,' said Dizzy with his brown-toothed smile, 'you are a natural.'

Ray started to climb down.

Dizzy put a hand on his arm. 'Hold on, mister.' Dizzy looked at me. 'Now that we've stopped, what's the first thing you gotta do?'

'Foot brake?' I said.

'You got it!' He was nearest the brake so he used his foot to push the lever forward. I felt the coach turn from a living thing to a solid, unmoving object.

Once again, I wished it had been my pa sitting there beside me to be impressed by my skill at handling a six-horse team. But it was only Ray & he did not even seem to notice. He just climbed down off the box. I felt the coach rock a little as he opened the door & climbed inside.

'Shotgun?' came Ray's voice.

Dizzy and I both leaned to the right to see Ray's hand sticking out of the front window.

Dizzy took the double-barreled shotgun from its leather sheath beside the driver's box & handed it down. Ray's hand & the shotgun both disappeared back inside the coach.

'OK.' Dizzy released the brake & turned to me. 'To start up again you just give the reins a little flick and say "G'lang!", real firm-like.'

'G'lang! G'lang there, you sons of blanks!' I said, imitating Dizzy, and we were off again.

Little did I think I would be taking the reins in earnest and riding for my life in less than two hours.

LEDGER SHEET 18

WE REACHED GENOA ABOUT AN HOUR AFTER WE SET
out from Carson, for we had been going at a fair clip
through the sage-brushy desert and flat marshes. It felt
satisfying to have control of six powerful beasts and a
stage worth $50,000.

'I'd better take them there ribbons now,' said Dizzy,
'lessen someone sees a girl in black ringlets and a yaller
bonnet driving.'

As we pulled in front of a Livery Stable, the door of an
outhouse partly opened and a voice shouted, 'Be right
out!'

Dizzy pushed the footbrake forward & tossed the
reins to the ground. He stayed in his seat so I did, too.

It was now about 5 in the afternoon. We were in the
shadow of the mountains & it was chilly. I could hear the
throaty coo of a dove from the Genoa oak trees and in the
cottonwoods some birds were having a lively conversation.

Some folk standing in front of the General Store were also conversing & they hardly even glanced at us.

The hostler came out of the outhouse.

'Howdy, Dizzy!' he called up to us. 'I got a fresh team all ready for you. Little Ben?' A towheaded boy came out, leading a fresh team of six horses, all harnessed and strapped to their pole.

'That there wooden stick is called a "whippletree",' said Dizzy, pointing down at a kind of plank the hostler was releasing from the front of the coach. 'See there? The traces are all passed through and ready so you can go at a moment's notice if'n you want.'

'From what Icy said, I thought you would have been here sooner,' said the stableman as he led our team away from the coach.

'We was a mite delayed,' said Dizzy. 'How long ago did he come through?'

'Half an hour maybe,' said the hostler. He stopped to watch the boy fit the new team's whippletree to the front of our coach. 'No more than forty minutes.'

'Dang!' cursed Dizzy. He spat some tobacco juice onto the ground. 'Any other travelers pass by?'

'Just a man on a gray and three miners footing it,' said the stableman. 'Carson City Stage is due in around an hour. Evenin', ma'am,' he said to the window. 'Would you care to stretch your legs?'

When he got no response he shielded his mouth with his hand and whispered to Dizzy, 'Something wrong with that lady in there? She don't seem very friendly.'

'Why, Al,' said Dizzy, 'that lady is real friendly. In fact, she is so friendly that you could give her a kiss and she would not object.' He gave a wheezy laugh.

'Don't take no notice of Dizzy, ma'am,' said Al, tipping his hat at the open window. 'He can be rude and— Dang!' he leaped back as if bit by a snake. 'There is something wrong with her face. It looks like an unripe watermelon.'

'Hee, hee,' said Dizzy. 'It *is*. She is a dummy with a watermelon head. She is meant to mislead those Reb Road Agents into thinking we have passengers,' he added.

'You watch out for them,' said Al. 'Latest news is they was spotted between Yank's Station and Strawberry. They tried to rob a passenger stage but O'Riley started blasting at them with his scattergun and they skedaddled.'

Little Ben had hitched the new team to our coach. He handed Al the hostler the reins of the fresh team and led off the old team.

Dizzy spat a brown squirt of tobacco juice down onto the dirt. 'That stiff lady ain't the only one riding today,' he said. 'Got a Pinkerton Detective of our own in there, too. But I don't think those bandits will bother with us. Not after Icy & his men have got hold of them.'

'Well, God go with you!' cried Al the hostler, holding the bunch of reins aloft.

Dizzy took them and released the footbrake. 'Amen,' he said, and to the horses, 'G'lang! G'lang there, you sons of blanks!'

That fresh team pulled us along a flat, straight road at the foot of the mountains for a spell.

We passed Van Sickles Station, which is a white two-story wooden house with a grand porch and corrals & stables, all on its lonesome with those barren mountains rearing up almost perpendicular behind it.

I knew the road doubled back a few miles up ahead to become the Kingsbury Grade. I turned my head to search for Pa but I only saw a stagecoach coming down the mountain, not going up.

I said, 'I see a stagecoach coming down the mountain.'

Dizzy said, 'That'll be the Pioneer Stage from Placerville on its way to Carson and Virginee.'

We came to that sharp switchback & started to climb up the side of the mountain.

Dizzy was using his whip now, pulling it back & then flicking it forward to make it uncoil like a big black snake & crack like the report of a pistol right over the horses' heads. But he did not have to do too much blacksnaking. Those horses knew it would be uphill now but downhill on their way home so they pulled bravely.

As we got higher & higher I could see back the way we had come. Over to my right – to the east – I could see vast empty sky & far below a flat plain like a patchwork quilt of green & sage & buff & brown. The sight of that much sky and that far a drop made my stomach do a handspring and all the blood sink down to my toes.

If I looked almost straight down I could see the ribbon of a road with Van Sickles House & Stables looking like a little pair of white and brown dice. A humpy part of the mountain prevented me from seeing Carson City or even Genoa to the north. As we climbed it felt like my ears were getting fuller & fuller of cotton lint. Then something went pop and my head was empty & light.

We were now so high that it made me feel queer to look over the side. So I kept my gaze straight ahead.

Presently the Pioneer Stage from Placerville appeared around a bend. It was pulled by a strange-looking team of bays and grays. The three starboard horses (as Dizzy called them) were dark and the other three were light. Also, it had about six people riding up on top behind the Driver and his Conductor.

As they came closer both coaches slowed down a little. The driver was a slight man with a flat-brimmed hat and billy-goat beard.

'Evening, Dizzy!' he called.

'Evening, Hank!' Dizzy replied. 'Any sign of them Reb Road Agents?'

'Nope,' said the driver. 'Like we told Mr. Blue, we ain't seen 'em. Where's your conductor?'

'This little lady here is riding shotgun.' Dizzy gave a wheezy chuckle.

'You must have some weighty passengers in there today,' called the driver over his shoulder. 'Your team are struggling to pull it.'

'Dang!' swore Dizzy after the stage had gone past. 'I hope those Reb Road Agents ain't as perspicacious as that there Hank Monk.'

But as I will shortly relate, they were.

THE SUN HAD SET IN GENOA, BUT WHEN WE REACHED the top of the pass, why, there it was again, like an old friend. It was very low in the sky, lighting up some puffy clouds all red & purple & yellow. This fiery sunset was reflected in Lake Bigler, which some folk call Tahoe. It was so pretty it made my spirit want to fly up into those clouds like a hawk.

Dizzy tossed a coin to a toll-gate keeper. A few moments later he guided the puffing team of horses off the road & onto a muddy patch of ground in front of a couple of raw-plank buildings. There was a smell of wood smoke & stables.

'Is this Friday's Station?' I asked.

'Yup.' Dizzy reined in the team and we rocked to a halt. 'Wanna get down or can you last one more stage?'

'I need the jakes,' I said.

While Dizzy was helping me down, two men came out

of the shack. One had a little nose and a big mustache. The other had a big nose and a little mustache. Big Mustache went to get a fresh team and Little Mustache started undoing the whippletree.

When I got back from using the outhouse, Big Mustache was telling Dizzy how another California-bound stage had changed teams an hour before and a rider came by not long after.

'Dang,' said Dizzy. 'They are now a whole hour ahead of us. We'd best not dilly-dally.'

It was chilly up here with a breeze coming off the lake. The pine-scented air came cold into my chest & made me feel light-headed. I pulled my pink shawl around my shoulders. Then I remembered the coat I had bought for the dummy to wear. I went towards the coach.

Through the window, I saw that the dummy was leaning against the corner & her hat was down over her watermelon face, so it really did look like a lady was sleeping. That was good.

I gave a soft knock on the door and opened it.

Mr. Ray G. Tempest was lying on his back upon the bed of mailbags with his head back, his eyes closed and his mouth open. His hat & Dizzy's shotgun lay nearby on one of the other mailbags. I took the coat off the dummy & gave her my shawl instead & restored her to her former position.

Ray snored on.

I quietly closed the door of the stage and then put on the coat. It was a lot warmer than my shawl. Mrs.

Wasserman had called that coat a 'sacque' & told me it was the girliest coat she had & that it was the latest fashion. It was like a cape, only with sleeves, made of silk-lined purple velvet & white fur trim. When I put my gloved hands in the little slits at the front I discovered a hidden pocket.

One of the things I hate about dresses is that there are no pockets so the only place to put things is in a purse or similar. But now I had found a pocket in this sacque. Hallelujah!

I took my four-shooter out of my medicine bag & put it in the secret pocket along with a few spare cartridges. Then I let Dizzy help me back up into the box. He took the reins from Big Mustache, released the brake & we were on our way again!

My stomach growled so I opened my yellow drawstring purse which I had tied to the rail of the driver's box. I took out some beef jerky & shared it with Dizzy.

I noticed a wooden sign down by the side of the road. It said, *WELKOM TO THE STATE OF CALIFORNEE*. We had left Nevada Territory behind and were now in California, a state I had not heretofore set foot in.

The sun had set for good & dusk was gathering fast.

I said, 'Do you think the Reb Road Agents have held up the decoy stage yet?'

'I hope so,' said Dizzy. 'Soon it will be too dark to see. If they miss the decoy they might hold us up instead. We should of set out earlier.'

'At least they are an hour ahead of us.'

'Yup,' said Dizzy.

I said, 'When Icy Blue and his agents catch them, what will they do with them?'

'Why, clap 'em in irons and take 'em back to Virginee. Hopefully we will see them coming back this way, mission accomplished, at any moment.'

My spirits lifted. I might see my victorious pa soon & then he would turn around and ride to Sacramento with us and soon we would go to Chicago covered in glory.

'Want to see something awful?' said Dizzy, chomping his piece of jerky.

'Sure,' I said.

'See that bend we're coming up to? Scoot on over to the left and look down.'

I scooted over to the edge and looked down. As we came to a curve in the road I saw a steep slope tumbling down to a rocky gorge far below. My sharp eyes saw a wheel on the jagged gray rocks & some broken crates & then the worst thing of all: a smashed-up stagecoach and what might have been the bones of a horse. I could not be sure about the horse bones, for the light was fading fast.

'What happened?' I asked.

'Coach went off the road,' said Dizzy. 'Crashed on them rocks below. Happens more than people think.'

'Stagecoaches going over the edge and crashing on the rocks below?'

'Yup. That is why they never put glass in the windows. In case it breaks and cuts you to ribbons.'

'Were the passengers killed?' I asked.

'Only a couple,' he said. 'The others escaped with just a few broken bones and cracked heads.' He chuckled. 'Driver broke both arms. When they took the bandages off, he found one arm was an inch shorter than the other.'

I held out my arms.

I tried to imagine having one arm shorter than the other.

I could not do it.

We rode for a while without speaking. I tried to listen out for the sound of Pa and the decoy stage coming our way, covered in glory & with the Reb Road Agents in irons.

But it was hard to hear much above the noise of 24 thundering hooves & a creaky old stagecoach.

Soon it was so dusky I could hardly see the road.

I said, 'How do you light the road when it gets dark?'

Dizzy said, 'You don't.'

I said, 'Because there is an almost-full moon tonight?'

He said, 'Moon won't rise for an hour or so. But we don't use lights even when there ain't a moon.'

I said, 'How do you see in the dark?'

He said, 'You don't.'

I said, 'You drive in the dark?'

'Yup. Dark. Rain. Storm. Snow. You gotta remember that each team of six horses just goes back and forth over ten or twelve or fourteen miles at most. They know their stretch of road so well they could do it blindfolded. Why, some of the drivers just have a little sleep while they are holding the reins.'

'You won't sleep, will you?' I asked.

'Nosiree. Not with the chance of Reb Road Agents behind any pine and a crumbled road at any bend.'

'The road crumbles sometimes?'

'Yup,' said Dizzy. 'You got any more jerky?'

'Yes,' I said.

'Gimme,' said Dizzy.

He opened his mouth like a hungry bird and I fed him another piece of beef jerky.

I was glad of my gloves and velvet sacque for it was now cold.

We were going up a rising bend. Our fresh horses from Friday's were working hard. I looked over the edge and saw what looked like a sheer drop. The granite rocks far below were almost as jagged as the hundred black pine trees that poked up like needles. I did not want to look, but I could not tear my eyes away.

'Jumping Jesus!' said Dizzy.

'Beg pardon?'

Dizzy swallowed hard & cussed. 'Looks like we got ourselves company. Those Reb Road Agents must of let the decoy stage pass right on by. Here they are, all right: fixing to hold us up.'

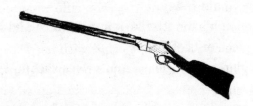

I HAD BEEN LOOKING OVER THE EDGE BUT NOW **I** turned to look ahead. Sure enough, there in the gloaming were two men standing either side of the road.

'Halt!' they cried, and both put up their hands, palm forward, in the universal gesture that means stop. They wore butternut-colored uniforms which meant they were Confederate soldiers, AKA Rebs.

I swore under my breath, using language unfit for publication.

Pa's Plan had failed.

'Don't cuss!' said Dizzy out of the corner of his mouth. 'Remember, you are supposed to be a helpless little girl. It is our only chance.'

He was right! If I played a convincing girly-girl, they might take pity on us & let us go & we could get the silver to safety. Then we could alert Pa and the guards in the other stage of their whereabouts.

The team slowed and stopped. I noticed Dizzy did not push the footbrake forward.

'Good evening, y'all,' drawled one of the men. He held a Henry Rifle and wore a small, round, slope-top hat with a visor. I think folk call it a 'kepi'.

Kepi said, 'I am gonna have to ask you not to make any sudden-like moves.' His rifle was pointing at Dizzy.

'Heck, you don't want to bother with us.' Dizzy's voice cracked a little. 'It is only me and my little girl here and some children back from a picnic. You can see their sleeping schoolmarm there in the window. Surely you will let us pass?'

The reins in his left hand were trembling but I felt strangely calm. Maybe it was because I could not see the Road Agents clearly. Or maybe it was because they sounded so polite.

I reckoned I should play the part of a little girly-girl.

'Grandpa?' I said in my high girly voice. 'Are those men going to rob us?'

'Not if you cow operate,' said the other man. He wore a slouch hat & his voice was deeper than Kepi's.

He cocked his piece and said, 'My pard is just gonna have a little peek inside your coach while I cover you. Y'all seem to be riding pretty low, like you are maybe carrying a lot of silver.'

'We ain't got nothing of value,' said Dizzy. 'Just them kiddies, like I said.'

While they were talking, I had started to sneak my

gloved right hand inside the secret pocket of my sacque to get at my Muff Deringer.

'Hands where we can see them, Missy,' said Kepi politely.

I froze. Then I took my (empty) hands out of my sacque.

'Raise 'em high,' said Slouch.

I could not believe this was happening. Did I not look girly enough?

I had to convince them! But how?

I reckoned a girly-girl would whimper.

'Oh, Grandpa,' I quavered. 'They are going to kill us!'

'Cheese it, brat!' growled Slouch Hat. He pointed his big revolver at me.

So much for the Reb Road Agents having a soft spot for little girls!

The one with the Kepi was about three paces from the stagecoach when Dizzy grabbed his black leather whip & yelled, 'Hi-yi!'

Three things happened real quick.

No. 1 – With a report like that of a gun being fired, Dizzy's whip knocked the Henry rifle right out of Kepi's hands.

No. 2 – Our team of horses started moving.

No. 3 – The man wearing the slouch hat shot Dizzy with his big Army revolver.

BANG!

Dizzy did not make a noise. He only slumped against

me. The reins started to slide through his gloved fingers.

Quick as a streak of chalk, I grabbed the reins. 'Hi-yi!' I cried, and gave them a flick. 'G'lang! G'lang, you sons of blanks!'

By the side of the road, Kepi looked up from where he was scrabbling to recover his rifle. He rolled out of the way just in time to avoid getting trampled.

The horses had to strain to get the heavy coach moving. They seemed to be wading through winter molasses.

'Come on, you sons of blanks!' I bellowed again. I was leaning way over to the left on account of Dizzy was slumped against my right side.

We had just passed the Road Agents when something batted my bonnet forward & Dizzy jerked against me & at the same time I heard three more loud reports.

BANG! BANG! BANG!

They had shot Dizzy again!

I flicked the reins & yelled, 'Git!'

I forgot to say 'G'lang!' and 'Hi-yi!' but the horses were moving faster now. I reckon the shots had spooked them as much as my hollering and cussing. We finally crested the hump in the road and were heading downhill. Now the six steeds were running at top speed. It was almost dark and the tall black pine trees either side blotted out the purple sky. I have eyes about as sharp as a telescope but even a telescope cannot see at night. I could hardly make out the road ahead.

I had to trust the horses, like Dizzy had told me.

I kept hold of the ribbons but let them go slack.

Yes, I gave those horses free rein.

The team curved left, following the road, and the curve made Dizzy slump against me even more.

I could hardly breathe & I was in danger of being crushed by his bulk so I gave him a little shove. But I must have pushed too hard for now he was slumped way over to the right, leaning over the side and in danger of tumbling out!

I held the reins in my left hand and grabbed at Dizzy's sleeve with my right.

I caught the cuff of his jacket sleeve just in time!

I knew if his jacket cuff slipped out of my grasp he would tumble over the side of the stage and off the mountain!

I needed help.

'Ray!' I cried. 'Help!'

No answer.

I used all my lungs to holler, 'RAY!'

'Wha?' came his slurred voice from down below. 'Wha's happening?'

'The Reb Road Agents struck! They shot Dizzy. I think he might be dead.'

The horses were going fast now.

Too fast.

I reckon they were spooked.

There was a bend coming up with a three-thousand-foot drop on the right-hand side.

'Help!' I cried. 'Ray! PA!'

(I do not know why I shouted for Pa as he was about an hour ahead of us.)

As we took the bend, the coach listed to the right. I reckon if we had not been carrying a ton of silver we would have been driving on two wheels.

Out of the corner of my right eye, I saw Dizzy twitch. Then his sleeve was jerked from my fingers.

He flew out of the driver's box & went sailing into the thin air above that three-thousand-foot drop.

Then he was gone.

A moment later, Ray's head appeared beside the coach! He was hatless and his red bandana was pulled down around his neck. He was clinging to the slender iron railing around the roof!

'What happened to Dizzy?' I cried.

'Dead weight,' he shouted back. 'Thought it was better to ditch him.'

'He might of still been alive!'

'Whoa!' cried Ray. 'Slow her down!'

He was still hanging off the side of the coach. Even with all those silver bars as ballast I was pretty sure I felt the two left wheels lift off the ground for a moment!

'Get up on top!' I hollered. 'You are throwing the stage off balance. It will fall over and we will be kilt!'

'Stop the coach!' he cried. 'We cannot outrun them.'

He gave himself a heave & was suddenly up in the box beside me.

117

He tried to pull the reins from my hands but I held on tight.

'Don't!' I cried. 'They are spooked but they know this road.'

'Let go, you d-mn blank!' He called me a bad word and I was so astonished that I let him take the reins. But he was not expecting me to let go and he jerked them violently to the right.

Too violently.

I saw the horses thundering straight off the edge of the road towards a three-thousand-foot chasm.

It was my stagecoach-going-over-a-precipice nightmare coming true.

But this was no dream.

This was really happening.

Suddenly we were in the air & my stomach & lungs were all up in my throat & time slowed down & we were falling, falling, falling.

Then everything went darker than the inside of a black bear on a moonless night.

LEDGER SHEET 21

I MUST HAVE PASSED OUT BECAUSE EVERYTHING went black for a time.

When I came to, I found myself still falling through the night.

Yes! I was still falling.

But I did not splat.

This confused me.

Then I had a notion of what was happening.

I was suspended between Glory and the Fiery Place! I had tried to be a Good Methodist but now all my sins came rushing back into my memory, viz: I had killed a man & told lies & played poker & tried whiskey once & a Pousse Lamour cocktail another time & ignored every single one of my foster ma's dying wishes. Also I had pranked the people of Virginia City for over seven months, making them believe I was a boy not a gal.

That might have been the worst sin of all, for they were my friends.

I reckon I was in a place called Limbo.

Methodists do not believe in that place, but Mr. Hazard O'Toole at the Shamrock Saloon across from my office is Catholic. He told me all about it.

He told me that Limbo is where you go to wait while the angels plead your case and the imps of the Fiery Place accuse you.

Gradually, as my eyes adjusted to the darkness, I perceived that I was not in Limbo. I was still in the high Sierras, surrounded by the looming black shapes of whispering pines. Why had I not splatted onto the ground?

Was I dreaming?

My arms were hanging limp. I moved my right hand over to pinch my left.

I pinched hard.

It hurt.

That meant I was not dreaming.

Then I realized that I was kind of tipped forward. I could feel something tugging my underarms & the seams of my coat sleeves straining tight. Someone was holding me up.

Someone . . . or some*thing*!

I knew there were bears in these mountains. Was it a man-eating grizzly bear holding me aloft?

If a prey animal is in trouble, he does one of three things.

No. 1 – He fights.

No. 2 – He runs away.

No. 3 – He freezes, so that he will not be seen or so that his enemy will think he is dead.

I could not fight. And I could not run away. So I decided to use method No. 3 and 'play possum'. Maybe the grizzly bear holding me up thought I was dead. Maybe he was not hungry enough to devour me in my velvet sacque & yellow-straw lighthouse bonnet with its silk flowers & ribbon & ruffles.

I must have been dazed with terror to imagine such a foolish thing. By and by I realized it could not be a grizzly bear holding me so still. Or even a person.

It was one of them whispering pines.

Yes, I was caught by a tree.

My velvet and fur-trimmed sacque must have puffed out as I fell through the air and got caught on a branch.

There was no sound except the wind in the pines and further off the jingling and snorting of horses.

The horses! Had they survived? What about Ray, who had been up on the driver's box with me?

If only I could see!

I reached my arms up over my head and after some groping I clasped on to the branch holding me. I could feel it through the satin-lined velvet fabric of the sacque which was straining under my weight.

It felt brittle and prickly, like an old branch. A dead branch.

Crack!

That was the sound I heard as I found myself tipped forward a little more. My efforts to free myself had caused the branch that was holding me to bounce up and down a little. It was going to break and send me hurtling to the rocky gorge three thousand feet below!

I considered yelling for help but then I reasoned that the only other people for miles around were two Road Agents and one Pinkerton detective, viz: Mr. Ray G. Tempest. The Road Agents might be nearby. And the Pinkerton detective was probably dead.

So instead of yelling, I sent up an arrow prayer to the Lord.

'Dear Lord,' I prayed, 'please forgive me for pranking my friends and help me to be a good girly-girl, if that is your desire. Only save me now in my moment of need! Amen.'

As if in answer to my prayer, some pearly-white rays poked up through the inky-black branches of a pine tree below me. Those rays were like the halo of a saint, all fanned out. A moment later a light shone in my face. It was the moon, rising in the east and shining up through the gulch.

That blessed moonlight showed me that it was indeed the branch of a fir tree holding me.

I looked down.

Hallelujah! I was only about six feet off the ground.

(But I still might have broke my neck if that branch had not caught me.)

The next question was – how to get down?

Crack!

I could use the weakness of the branch.

I flapped my arms to make the branch bob up and down.

CRACK!

My plan worked. I fell the six feet but landed awkwardly on account of I was wearing those button-up boots and not my usual moccasins. The ground was padded with pine needles, which cushioned my fall, but it also sloped gently down so I rolled a few times. The prickly savior branch dug into my back but thankfully it did not pierce the daffodil-yellow frock nor break my skin.

I got up on my hands & knees and straightened my wig & bonnet & pulled the branch out from under my sacque.

Hallelujah! My little 4-shot Muff Deringer was still firmly in the hidden pocket. I took it out & cocked it & crept down towards the sound I had heard earlier, viz: the sound of horses snorting & voices in the pines.

I am used to sneaking in the dark & when I put my mind to it I can go over crispy leaves & crunchy pine needles without making a sound. I crept forward, as silent as a cat on a velvet cushion.

Presently I came to where I could see the flickering yellow light of a fire.

They say a picture is worth a thousand words.

Here is the picture the golden firelight & the silvery moonlight showed me . . .

One papier-mâché torso wearing a pink shawl & a flower-bedecked sunhat on her watermelon head & balanced on the ground as if sitting before the fire with her back to me.

Two Reb Road Agents sitting at the fire facing the dummy & also me & reading letters.

Three wheels scattered in various places around them.

Some pieces of a busted-up old Concord Stage & a tangle of reins & a whippletree & some other tackle lying between me and the Reb Road Agents.

Seven letter-sacks sitting near them.

The six stage-horses standing whole and unharmed, loosely tethered to some pines.

Seventy-eight gleaming bricks of silver piled up beside the fire.

This is what that picture told me, viz:

The stagecoach had crashed but the whippletree had broke loose from the singletree & all the horses had survived. I could see the drop was not as steep as I had feared, though it was still enough to cause the coach to roll over a couple of times and break up, probably on account of the heavy silver bars inside. The Reb Road Agents had obviously come upon the site of the wreck as they pursued us. They had seized all the silver bars and were now relaxing.

I could see no sign of Ray.

I reckoned he was dead.

The decoy stage full of guards and also my pa riding

behind were probably ten miles further along the road. Maybe more.

I was on my own.

I focused all my attention on the Reb Road Agents. The one with the slouch hat was older. He was smoking a pipe & reading a letter. The one with the kepi was younger. He was swigging from a bottle of champagne & reading a letter. I noticed they had an open letter-sack beside them.

I wormed forward to the trunk of the tree closest to their fire.

I was now close enough to hear them talking.

'Hey, darlin',' said Kepi to the dressmaker's dummy. 'Listen to this: *Dear Ma, It is Bonanza here on the Comstock. They struck it rich in the front ledge in Gold Hill the other day. Tell little Pete and Edward they must come and join me. I have got a job working for the Yellow Jacket mine. It is hot and tiring but I get four dollars a day and I have feet. Give Betty my love and tell her she will not have to wait much longer.*' He took a swig of champagne & then he tossed the letter into the flames.

'Hey! I got a good one,' said Slouch. 'It is a love letter from a gal to her betrothed: *Oh Roderick, I count the hours until I see you again.*' He was making his voice all high like a lady's. '*I have not heard from you in three weeks and I fear you have stopped caring for your sweet Elspeth. Are the girls prettier in Frisco? Please write to me, dear one!*'

He also tossed his letter in the fire.

I was outraged. They were burning letters from sons to their mothers & lonely gals to their sweethearts!

Silver could be replaced, but not letters.

I had to stop them!

But how?

LEDGER SHEET 22

I WAS OUTNUMBERED AND OUTGUNNED. THERE WERE
two Reb Road Agents & only one me. They had a big
revolver and at least one rifle. I only had a Muff Deringer.

But I had the advantage of not being dead like they
probably thought I was.

And I had my Indian skills. Using these skills, I
scanned the camp and spotted the Henry rifle leaning
against the trunk of a pine tree not too far from the
fire. Dizzy's double-barreled shotgun was there, too. Ray
must have left it inside the coach when he climbed up to
help me.

I put my little four-shooter back in the inner pocket
of my sacque & made my way carefully back into the
darkness of the pine forest & circled round real stealthy
& slow, so as not to alarm the horses. When I came up
behind the leaning-gun pine, I reached my hand around
kind of groping-like & took first the Henry & then the

double-barreled shotgun. Tucking both guns under my arm, I melted back into the darkness of the forest and returned to my first vantage point.

By now the Rebs were tipping letters out of the leather sacks and filling the empty bags with silver ingots. There were letters scattered everywhere but at least they had stopped burning them.

I was about to step forward & throw down on them, when I remembered I was wearing a velvet sacque and a wig of swinging ringlets beneath a lighthouse bonnet. I would not make a very imposing figure thus attired. At least I could take off the danged wig & silly bonnet.

I took off the danged wig & silly bonnet.

As I was about to toss away those two hated objects, I saw something that made my blood run cold as snowmelt.

There was a bullet hole in the sticking-up part of the bonnet! A hole made by a .44 caliber ball, I reckoned. I remembered how something had knocked my bonnet forward when they had been shooting at us.

'Dang!' I said to myself. 'They were shooting to kill.'

They were pretty drunk by now. I could tell because they were weaving around as they lugged leathern sacks full of silver bricks over to the horses. I reckoned I might as well wait until they finished loading the silver on the horses. Otherwise I would have to do a lot of heavy lifting myself.

The moon was high now and I judged it to be around 10 pm. My stomach was growling but my last few pieces of jerky were in my yellow velvet purse which I had left hanging on the front rail of the stagecoach. I peered at the ruined coach and thought I saw something yellow in the moonlight.

While they were busy loading the last of the silver onto the stage horses, I snuck over to the wrecked body of the stagecoach & got my yellow velvet bag and fished out a piece of jerky. Then I looked inside the coach. I saw Ray's flat-brimmed gray hat lying on top of a letter-sack that was half spilling out its letters. There were also some lengths of whang leather that had bound the mouths of the mail sacks.

I lowered myself down through the open window of the door & I put on Ray's hat. It was a mite too big so I stuffed a few loose letters in the crown to make it fit. But what to do about my puffy sacque with its bell-like outline?

Then I had another idea. I took one of those strips of whang leather & tied it around my waist over the sacque. In the darkness they might take me for a short man in a belted coat. I also tied my yellow velvet purse to the belt of whang leather, but I made sure it was hanging down behind me.

Quiet as a bug on burlap, I climbed out of the ruined stagecoach & lowered myself onto the moon-dappled ground & melted back into the inky shadows of the pines.

Over by the horses, Kepi stretched & yawned. 'Toting those silver ingots has tuckered me out,' he said to his pard. 'Can't we take a little kip?'

'Nope,' said Slouch. 'We gotta put some distance between us and the wreck while the moon is still up. If Chauncy or Jonas find us slacking there will be h-ll to pay.'

'They ain't the boss of us,' said Kepi.

'No, but they promised us a good piece of the pie for our help,' said Slouch.

'H-ll,' said Kepi. 'We got about seventy-five pieces of silver pie right here on these horses. We ought to keep the booty and skedaddle to Frisco. Or we could lay low in Angel's Camp.'

'Better not,' said Slouch. 'They would hunt us down and kill us dead if we betrayed 'em.'

'Aw,' said Kepi. 'I could take 'em easy.'

'You could maybe take Chauncy,' said Slouch. 'But not Jonas. He is as cold-blooded as a rattler.'

'He is most likely dead of a busted neck,' said Kepi.

'Maybe,' said Slouch. 'Maybe not. You willing to take that chance?'

'Nah,' said Kepi, 'I reckon not. Where was we supposed to meet 'em?'

'Grizzly Gulch,' said Slouch. 'Where we stashed the booty. We can make it back to our shebang easy before the moon sets. I reckon it is less than a mile.'

'Better mount up, then,' said Kepi, starting towards their horses.

My heart was pounding in my chest. It was now or never. I could not show any fear or they might throw down on me.

I picked up the double-barreled shotgun & checked it was capped & loaded.

It was.

I took a deep breath & stepped out into the firelight.

'You ain't going nowhere,' I said, making my voice as deep as I could. 'Throw down your sidearms and reach for the sky.'

LEDGER SHEET 23

WHEN I CAME OUT INTO THE FIRELIGHT WITH THE double-barreled shotgun, the two Reb Road Agents stopped and stared at me with Expression No. 4 – Surprise – across both their faces.

'Drop 'em. Now!' I said in my most commanding voice. I held the gun beside my hip, my grip relaxed but not loose.

They looked at me & then they looked at each other & then they started to laugh.

'Lookee there! It is that strange little girl from the stagecoach!' cried Kepi. 'She is dressed up as a midget Marshal, you bet.'

'I reckon if she pulls the trigger the kick will knock her off her feet,' said Slouch.

They were laughing so hard they did not even bother to draw their sidearms.

I pointed the double-barreled shotgun at the branch

above their heads & pulled the trigger. There was a gargantuan explosion that echoed and re-echoed in the mountain night and sent pine needles drifting down into the clearing. The gun had indeed given a powerful kick, but I had been holding it slightly away from my body so it did me no harm at all apart from the ringing in my ears. When the gun smoke dispersed I saw their sidearms on the ground before them and their hands stretched high in the air.

'You,' I said to Kepi. 'Take off your pard's belt and cinch up his hands real good behind his back. But first, back away from your guns.'

They backed away from their guns.

While Kepi was undoing Slouch's belt, I walked over towards them and kicked their revolvers back towards where I had been hiding. Keeping the barrel of the shotgun trained on the two outlaws, I backed up. Then I used my left hand to pick up the biggest revolver. It was Slouch's. One glance told me it was a Remington Army which takes a .44 caliber ball. I stuck it in my whang leather belt.

After Kepi bound Slouch's hands real good, I gestured at Slouch's feet. 'Take off his boots,' I said. 'Then take off yours.'

'No!' whimpered Kepi. 'Not that!'

'Take off your boots,' I insisted, 'or I will blow you out of them.'

With much grunting and glaring, Kepi took off Slouch's boots & then his own.

'Now, take those leather reins and use them to tie him to that tree trunk,' I commanded.

'Listen,' said Slouch, as he backed up to the tree in his stocking feet. 'We got lots of silver here. We are happy to share it with you if you will just let us go.'

'Nope,' I said. 'And stop talking.'

'We were supposed to shoot her dead,' muttered Kepi as he tied his pard to the tree.

'I did my best,' said Slouch.

I only had one shot left in the scattergun so I took that big Remington revolver from my whang leather belt & cocked it & fired another warning shot into the tree trunk a few inches above Slouch's head.

BANG!

'Dang!' yelped Slouch, ducking down.

'Cheese it!' I commanded. 'Now, sit down with your back against the tree. Tie him up good,' I said to Kepi.

Slouch sat at the foot of the tree & Kepi tied him to it real good.

'Now take off your belt,' I said to Kepi.

Kepi took off his belt.

'Use it to bind up your own ankles real good,' I said.

He bound up his ankles. I noticed he had a hole in his sock where his big toe poked through.

'Sit on the other side of the tree from your pard,' I said.

Kepi hopped over to the other side of the tree & sat down awkwardly, with his back to the leather-bound trunk and his belt-bound legs straight out before him. I

134

stuck the revolver back in my belt and put the shotgun on the ground. Then I tied the end of the leather traces to the strip of leather already wound around the tree & I made three circuits of the tree, wrapping them both up real tight.

The fire had died down to a reddish glow so I threw a few more pieces of wood on the embers & stood with my back to it & examined my work. They could both see me if they turned their heads but they could not see one another.

'One word from either of you,' I warned, 'and I will take off your socks and stuff them in your mouths as a gag.'

'You goddam blank!' said Slouch. 'You would not dare.'

I put down the double-barreled shotgun & went over to him & tugged off his smelly socks and stuffed them both in his mouth.

'Try to spit them out and I will shoot you in the foot,' I warned.

Then I went round to do the same to Kepi.

'Please no,' he whimpered. 'I promise I will be quiet.'

But Ma Evangeline taught me never to make a threat unless you are prepared to carry it out. So I took off his threadbare socks and put them in his mouth, too.

I almost felt sorry for them until I remembered the .44 caliber bullet hole in my bonnet.

It was now chilly, even with my velvet, fur-trimmed sacque. I went over to stand by the revived fire. I warmed my hands above it and pondered what to do. They had mentioned a stash of 'booty' at 'Grizzly Gulch'.

Then I remembered Slouch saying the 'shebang' was 'less than a mile'. I reckoned they were talking about their camp. If I set out now with the silver-laden horses, I could get there before the moon set. I might even see another stagecoach or rider on the road and send for the Law. Then they could put Slouch and Kepi in jail to await a trial.

I glanced over at them. They sat barefoot & gagged & back-to-back with a big old pine trunk between them. They could not see each other but they both had their heads turned & were staring at me. With their socks poking out of their open mouths it looked like they were angrily sticking out their tongues at me.

But even as I watched, I saw their expressions change. Their eyes got wider & their eyebrows went up. They were giving me Expression No. 4 – Surprise.

Why were they looking at me like that?

Then I realized. They were not looking at me.

They were looking beyond me.

Someone – or some*thing* – was coming up behind me!

LEDGER SHEET 24

I GRABBED THE SHOTGUN & WHIRLED TO SEE WHAT was coming into the firelight. I was kind of crouched and my scattergun was cocked and ready for action.

Hallelujah!

It was my Pinkerton pa.

Dang!

He was aiming a small pistol at my heart.

I remembered I was wearing my disguise of Ray's hat and a belt around my sacque.

'Don't shoot, Pa!' I put down the shotgun & stretched out my hands. 'It is me! Pinky!'

'Prudence!' cried my pa. He dropped his piece back into the pocket of his overcoat. 'You're alive!' He ran forward & shmooshed me in his pa's bear hug for a long time.

At last he held me out at arm's length. 'I canna believe it!' he said. 'Are ye really all right?'

I nodded. I suddenly felt like crying.

'Praise the Lord,' he said. 'I heard gunshots and rode back as fast as I could. Then I saw firelight, but when I saw ye from behind – wearing that hat – I dinnae recognize ye. Where's yer own wee hat with the daffodils? Why are ye dressed like that?'

I said, 'I am dressed like this so those Reb Road Agents would take me seriously and not try to escape nor kill me.'

'Reb Road Agents?' he cried. 'What Reb Road Agents?'

I pointed to the foot of the pine tree.

The moon had made the tree's thick branches cast an inky black shadow on Slouch and Kepi. They had seen Pa, but he was only just now noticing them.

His face looked white in the moonlight. Now he was the one wearing Expression No. 4 – his mouth & eyes open wide in Surprise.

He looked down at me. 'This was your doing?'

I nodded.

'What did they say?'

'Not much,' I said. 'I gagged them with their own smelly socks.'

My pa gave a crooked smile & shook his head. 'Dang! You are a one. What happened?'

I said, 'We were about five miles out of Friday's Station and it was getting dark when they jumped out of the gloaming and told Dizzy to stop the stage. But Dizzy bullwhipped the one in the kepi and got the team moving again. We almost got away. Then the one in the slouch hat shot Dizzy. I took over the reins. We were going downhill when—'

'Where was Ray all this time?'

'He was inside the coach sleeping on the mailbags. He had drunk a lot of Tooth Elixir. But then he climbed out of the window and pulled poor Dizzy right off the driver's box even though he might have still been alive.'

'By Dizzy, d'ye mean the driver?' asked my pa.

'Yes,' I said. 'Ray climbed up to the box even though we were still going a mile a minute. He told me to stop & surrender to the Reb Road Agents as we would never get away. I was all for driving the team on to Yank's Station but he tried to wrassle the reins from my grip and then it happened, just like in my nightmare. We went off the cliff and down into this gorge.'

'That dam fool,' said Pa. 'Where is he?'

'Dead, most likely.'

Pa shook his head. 'It is a miracle ye're still alive.'

I said, 'Yes. It was a miracle. A branch caught my sacque—'

'Your what?'

'This velvet cape. I reckon it's the only thing that kept me from breaking my neck. Ray was not wearing a sacque,' I added, 'so his neck is probably broke.'

'I never should have suggested this plan,' said Pa. 'Ye could have got kilt. '

I said, 'Never mind, Pa. It would have been a good plan if it had worked.'

'But it did work!' he said. 'Thanks to you. Look at that – you captured them single-handed.'

'Where is the decoy stage full of agents?' I asked. 'Did you bring them back with you?'

'They are probably halfway to Sac City by now,' he said. 'I was hanging back to see where ye were and they got well ahead of me. I don't understand why these rascals did not try to stop them.' He narrowed his eyes at the bound & gagged Reb Road Agents.

I nodded. 'It is almost as if they were expecting us,' I said. Then I thought of something. 'Pa, do you know what a "shebang" is?'

He nodded. 'It's like a rough shelter or hut.'

I said, 'Then I know where they are keeping the rest of the stolen money.'

'Ye do?'

I nodded. 'They were talking about it before I threw down on them,' I said. 'They have stashed some booty at a place called Grizzly Gulch which I think is less than a mile from here.'

He said, 'We had better find it quick.'

I nodded. 'We still have a few hours of moonlight. If we start now with the horses and the silver, we could get there before the moon sets. Once we've found their shebang we can turn in these two and get the reward. Then I can go back to Chicago with you and be a detective,' I added.

Pa looked at me with a strange expression. I could not read it. He picked up the champagne bottle that Kepi had been swigging from and took a suck. Then he held it out to me.

'Here!' he said. 'Dutch courage.'

I said, 'I got my own courage.'

'Then drink a toast to us: Pinkerton and Daughter!'

I hesitated.

'Go on!' he said with a wink. 'Remember? The bubbles mean it ain't spirituous.'

I lifted the heavy bottle to my mouth and took a sip. It was warm & sweet & fizzy. It reminded me of the previous night when we had dined & drunk champagne & then danced the Schottische.

I drank another swallow, then held it out to him.

'To Pinkerton and Daughter!' said my pa, holding the bottle aloft and then taking a drink. 'Now you say it, too.'

I said, 'To Pinkerton and Daughter!' I took another sip, but I swallowed wrong and it fizzed hotly all the way down to my chest and made me cough.

He patted me on the back, laughing.

Suddenly everything felt fine. I was with my pa. We had saved the silver & vanquished the Reb Road Agents & would soon find their stash. Best of all, I was going back to Chicago with Robert Pinkerton as his savior & legally adopted child.

I held out the bottle to Pa. He swigged the last of the champagne & tossed the bottle into the trees.

'Yee-haw!' he cried.

'Yee-haw!' I agreed.

Then he stood up & grabbed me & waltzed me round the campfire among the scattered letters. He was humming the tune of the Schottische we had danced to the night before.

We must have seemed a strange sight to those two Reb Road Agents tied up to their pine tree. A humming Pinkerton Detective aged about 45 dancing with a 12-year-old half-Indian girl in a too-big, flat-brimmed hat & button-up boots & a fur-trimmed velvet sacque belted with a piece of whang leather with a Remington Revolver stuck in the front & a yellow velvet purse dangling from the back.

The almost-full moon was directly above. It seemed to smile down on us. The golden sparks from the fire hurried up to join the wobbling stars.

I felt bubbles of happiness rising up in me, too, like a thousand tiny hot-air balloons. My pa & I were dancing together in a silent glade beneath a million stars.

But as my pa spun me around I caught a flash of something emerging from the shadows into the flickering firelight. It was Kepi. Somehow he had got free.

'Watch out, Pa!' I cried. 'Behind you!'

LEDGER SHEET 25

TOO LATE, **I** REALIZED **I** HAD NOT TIED **K**EPI'S HANDS. That was my mistake. Somehow he must have wormed his way out from under the leather reins wrapping him to the tree & then undone the belt around his ankles. He had also taken his socks out of his mouth.

It only took me an instant to realize this. But in that same moment, my pa whirled around & pulled out his small revolver.

'No!' cried Kepi. 'Chance—'

Bang! Bang! Bang!

Before he could say more, my pa's revolver spat out three .32 caliber balls.

The Reb Road Agent stared down at three little holes & a dark stain spreading on his pale jacket right below the heart. The shots were still echoing in the mountains around us.

'You shot me,' he said, and then repeated, 'you shot me!'

He said it with a half-smile, like he could not believe it had really happened.

He kind of sat down on the ground. Then he fell back onto the carpet of pine needles & stared up at the stars. His kepi had fallen off. He had curly hair.

'Look at them stars,' he said. 'So many. Sparkling like little bitty silver ingots.' Then he spoke no more.

I looked at my pa. 'You killed him, Pa. You killed him dead.'

In the moonlight Pa looked deathly pale. 'He might of hurt you,' he said, staring at the corpse. 'He might have hurt you.'

Over by the pine tree, a movement caught our eyes.

The leather traces binding Slouch to the pine had been loosened by his pard wriggling free. Slouch would have got free, too, but his bare right foot was tangled in one of the reins I had used to tie him. His hands were still bound behind him & the socks were still sticking out of his mouth & his eyes were bugging out, too, as he stared wildly at us.

Pa sucked in a deep breath & picked up the double-barreled shotgun from where it lay & went over to the tree.

Before I could say or do anything, Pa blasted him at point-blank range.

BANG!

Slouch slammed against the tree & then slid down in a sitting position & then slumped forward, as dead as his friend.

'Pa!' I cried. 'Why did you do that? We could have just left him tied up for the Law to collect. Or we could have made him show us where they have their shebang.'

'He was about to get loose,' said Pa. 'Like that one.' He pointed to Kepi with his chin. 'Plus, after a trial they would have hanged him by the neck till dead. It was a mercy I was showing him. Also, they are wanted Dead or Alive. Come on,' he said, tossing the now empty shotgun aside. 'Let us get those silver-laden horses out of here and find their shebang.'

I felt queasy. The champagne, which had been making me happy five minutes before, had turned sour in my gut. The high moon which had been smiling on our dance now seemed cold and distant. In its pale light I saw a gaping black wound in Slouch's chest.

I felt like I might vomit up the jerky I had eaten a while earlier so I turned away.

Pa's stomach was not as strong as mine. Over in the trees, he was being sick. I reckon he had not shot a man in a few years, what with being behind a desk so much.

He wiped his mouth with his C.P. handkerchief & without speaking, he led the silver-laden stagecoach horses up towards the road.

I spotted the Reb Road Agents' mounts further up in the black shadows of some pines. I untied them and chose the smaller one to ride. She was a little bay with a stringy tail. I put Kepi's Henry Rifle in a saddle loop. I had to hike up my daffodil-yellow merino wool dress underneath my belted sacque just so I could get my leg over her back. Thankfully, the velvet sacque covered my legs to just below the knees; it was getting real cold. I was shivery.

Taking the other Reb horse by the reins, I rode after Pa who was trudging the silver-laden stagecoach horses back up the steep mountainside. I glanced back once to see the still form of Kepi lying on his back in the dying firelight. I could not even see poor blasted Slouch. He was lost in the inky shadows.

Up by the road, I found Pa untying his big gray gelding.

He took a crude halter that the now-deceased Reb Road Agents had fixed over the head of the lead pack horse & swung up into the saddle & set off west.

With Pa leading and me following, we had a convoy of nine horses, viz: the six stage horses, the two Reb horses & Pa's gelding. They were strung out in a line, moving between tall black pine trees on the moon-washed wagon road.

We rode in silence. In my head, I kept seeing my pa shoot those two Reb Road Agents. They had tried to kill me, but I still felt bad they were dead.

I thought of Kepi with his bare feet & curly hair & wondering expression on his face as he looked up at the little bitty silver ingot stars.

I thought of Slouch with his eyes bugged out in terror & that black sucking wound in his chest. I wished I had not put a sock in his mouth. Maybe he could have begged Pa to give him a chance, like Kepi had.

I did not even know their real names.

That picture in my head should have turned my stomach sour but I was hungry again. Also, my legs were cold. I wished I had my soft long underwear & my buckskin trowsers & my pink flannel shirt & my blue woolen coat & my nice slouch hat that kept my ears warm. Then I thought of poor dead Kepi & Slouch & Ray & Dizzy. They were all four dead and cold by now. I reckoned I was lucky to be alive and should not be complaining, even in my head. I had been colder than this in my life. I guess living in a boarding house with a feather bed had made me soft.

We had gone barely a mile when the moon showed me a lightning-blasted pine tree on the left-hand side of the road and a meadow beyond & below it.

'Pa,' I said. 'See that tree and that meadow? That might be where they stashed the loot.'

'By God, ye got good eyes,' he said. 'Do ye want to lead the way?'

I nudged my little bay mare forward. I could tell straightaway that she knew the path, so I gave her the reins and let her find the best footing.

'My horse knows the way, Pa,' I called over my shoulder. 'I reckon that is proof we are on the right track.'

'Good thinking,' he said. He sent the silver-bearing stagecoach horses down the track after me & took up the rear.

From time to time the moonlight showed me a path marked by scuffed pine needles and bare earth, but mostly I gave the bay mare free rein to guide us. She led me & Pa & those six heavy-laden horses along the edge of the meadow, close to the trees. All sudden-like, she turned left and passed between two towering pines and we were in another moonlit clearing with a cave like a gaping black mouth in the steep hillside straight ahead.

I smelled an old fire & saw some empty oyster cans & bottles off to one side & a pile of firewood & maybe a latrine pit. Over to the left I heard the gurgling of a brook. I reckoned this was the camp of the Dead Road Agents & that cave was their shebang.

My little bay mare was suddenly pulled up short. The lead horse behind her had stopped. He was snorting & tossing his head & as I had roped his halter to my pommel it made me stop too.

Behind me, the other pack horses started whinnying & snorting & I could hear Pa cussing in Scottish.

I smelled something faintly rank that always makes me think of my Indian ma on account of she used to make hair pomade out of bear fat.

Now I knew why the horses were spooked.

And why they called it Grizzly Gulch.

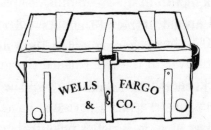

I PULLED THE **H**ENRY RIFLE OUT OF ITS LOOP **&** dismounted & cautiously moved forward into the clearing. I did not see any bears but as I got closer to the cave that rank smell of them got stronger.

'What's wrong with the horses?' called my pa from further back on the trail. 'I almost lost control of them.'

'They are spooked by the smell of bear!' I yelled back.

'Bear?' called Pa from the edge of the clearing. 'There are bears hereabouts?'

'Grizzlies, I'd wager,' I hollered. 'Probably why they call it Grizzly Gulch.'

Pa cursed.

I cocked the Henry & I went cautiously to the cave mouth.

'I can smell bear around here,' I called over my shoulder, 'but I do not think they have been here for a while. That is probably why the stage horses are spooked, but not my

149

mare. She is used to the smell but they are not. I reckon this is their shebang all right,' I added in a carrying voice.

'You mean those danged Reb Road Agents set up camp outside a bear cave?' yelled Pa, still astride his horse.

'By the looks of things, they set up camp *inside* it. But I think it is safe.'

Pa dismounted & tethered the horses & came across the moonlit clearing to join me at the black mouth of the den.

'Anybody in there?' he asked. 'Or anything?'

I sniffed. 'Nope,' I said. 'But bears have been here. Look.' I kicked at a dark pellet near the mouth of the cave. 'See that turd? That is a hibernation plug.'

'What?'

'It is a turd that plugs the bears up all winter,' I explained. 'Like a bung on a barrel. When they come out of hibernation they pop it out of their rear ends. My Indian ma taught me that.'

Pa cussed under his breath. 'Those dang fool idiots.'

'Maybe they were not so foolish,' I said. I had just spotted something inside the cave entrance on the left. Seeping moonlight showed me a box-shaped object. It was one of those iron-reinforced wooden strongboxes favored by Wells Fargo & Co.

'Most people would not look for a Wells Fargo strongbox inside a grizzly bear cave,' I observed.

There was enough light in there to let me see that its lock was smashed to smithereens. I leaned my Henry Rifle against the damp cave wall & knelt down & opened the lid of the strongbox & whistled through my teeth.

'This box is full of gold,' I said. 'That must be the "booty" they were talking about.'

Pa almost knocked me over in his haste to get to the strongbox. 'Sweet Jesus!' he said. Then, 'Help me drag it out of here.'

I helped him drag it out of there & into the moonlit clearing where we could see it was full of gold coins.

'I can't believe it,' said Pa. 'There must be hundreds of twenty-dollar gold pieces in here. They never said, the rascals!'

'Who never said?' I asked.

He looked up at me from his crouched position over the box. The silvery moonlight showed confusion on his otter face, as if he could not remember who I was. Then something shifted and he became Pa again. 'Wells Fargo & Co.,' he said. 'They never said it was gold they lost.' He stood up. 'This will make us rich.'

'No,' said a voice behind us. 'It will make *me* rich.'

We both turned to see a man with an Army pistol in his hand.

The moonlight showed us his bushy black mustache & muttonchop sideburns & long coat & bandana around his neck.

But he was bareheaded, for I was wearing his hat.

Yes, it was Ray G. Tempest, the other Pinkerton Detective. He had not broke his neck but had survived.

Without any more warning, he cocked his Army revolver & fired.

BANG!

Pa slumped to the ground.

'Pa!' I cried.

Then Ray turned his piece on me. Before my head knew what to do, my feet jumped me to one side and then sped me to the nearest shelter: the cave.

BANG!

BANG!

BANG! My hat flew off!

BANG! CRASH!

'Ugh!' I could not help crying out, for I had crashed into the rear of the cave and fallen back. As I lay there on the bear-smelling dirt floor, half stunned, I wondered if I had been shot. I thought not. I felt in my sacque pocket & pulled out my four-shooter. It was a pathetic weapon against a Colt's Army, but it was about all I had.

I cocked it & was about to roll over on my stomach & shoot back when I realized that Ray had stopped firing. He was probably reloading as he had fired five shots.

I decided to play possum & wait for him to come near to see if I was dead. I lay on my back, death-still, with my eyes half closed & my little four-shooter cocked but out of sight down by my side.

This was my plan: as soon as his upside-down face loomed above me, I would jerk up my arm & shoot him!

My foster ma Evangeline had made me promise never to kill a man nor exact revenge, but Ray G. Tempest *had shot and killed my pa*!

My heart was pounding so hard that I could not hear

anything but the blood whooshing in my ears.

But he never came.

I reckoned he'd heard me grunt & saw me fall back on the cave floor & lie still.

I reckoned he thought he had killed me.

I waited and waited.

By and by my heart stopped being so noisy and I heard sounds from outside the cave, viz: the clink of metal and horses snuffling. I reckon he was adding gold coins to the silver ingots in the mail bags on the backs of the six stagecoach horses.

After about 9 minutes of this, I heard the sound of heavy-laden horses being led back out of the clearing towards the main road.

I lay quiet in case it was a trick.

After about six more minutes I uncocked my little pistol & rolled over on my stomach & I wormed my way cautiously forward to the mouth of the dark cave.

The moon was on its way down and was almost touching the tops of the pines. But it was still high enough to show me that Ray & the horses were gone. The only thing left in the moon-washed clearing apart from the empty strongbox was my pa, lying hatless & awful still. I ran to him & looked down.

His white shirt was soaked with blood. I tore it open and found the bullet hole about half an inch below where his ribs ended.

I knelt down & I rested my head against his bare chest. The skin was still warm & I could hear his faintly

153

beating heart. In the moonlight his face was pale as milk.

'Pa?' I said. 'Pa, are you conscious?'

'He took my hat,' said Pa in a faint voice. 'Ray took my new beaver-felt brown hat that you bought me.'

'Probably because I have his,' I said.

'I am gut shot,' said Pa in a whisper. 'I am a goner.'

'Don't say that!' I cried. 'I will go and get you help.'

'No,' he said, lifting his head a little. 'Don't go. I don't want to die alone.'

'All right then, Pa,' I said. 'I will stay with you.'

He let his head sink back onto the ground & closed his eyes.

'Please do not die,' I said. 'Everybody dies on me. I could not bear it if you did, too.'

He did not reply.

Lying there in the soft dirt of the clearing with his eyes closed and his face relaxed, he looked almost as young as Kepi.

My vision got blurry. I blinked & it got clearer. Suddenly something made me look to my left.

I saw two dark bushes at the edge of the clearing by the dark pines.

In the eerie moonlight they almost looked like bears.

Then one of them moved.

They *were* bears.

LEDGER SHEET 27

TWO GRIZZLY BEARS WERE SHAMBLING ACROSS THE moonlit clearing.

They were heading for me and my dying pa.

When I saw them, my hair lifted up like a porcupine's quills & my heart started pounding like a war drum & all the juices in my body were screaming 'RUN!'

As everybody knows, the surest way of getting a bear to chase you is to skedaddle. Nobody can outrun a bear, especially when wearing girly-girl button-up boots. Also, I could not abandon my dying pa to their hungry jaws.

I took a deep breath & mustered up my courage & stood up slowly.

When the bears saw me rise, they stopped & stood up, too. That scared the bejeezus out of me. I had never been this close to a bear that was not a tame bear.

My Indian ma once told me that if I should ever find

myself face to face with a bear, not to run nor look him in the eye, but to sing him a special Lakota bear song. This tells the bear three things:

No. 1 – Where you are.
No. 2 – That you are not afraid.
No. 3 – That you are not a threat.

I used to know the Bear Song, but I am not as good at remembering things I hear as I am at remembering things I see. Also, I had not sung the Bear Song in a long time. It had flown plumb out of my head.

So I sang the only song I could think of.

It was the song whose lyrics had once helped me find a poor fugitive girl named Martha.

It was the song that played day and night in Virginia City.

You might say it was the state anthem of Nevada Territory.

'De Camptown ladies sing dis song,' I began. My voice kind of cracked so I cleared my throat. *'Doo-dah! doo-dah!'*

At that, both bears slumped back down onto all fours. The smaller one tested the air with his nose. The bigger one turned his head a little, like maybe he wanted to hear better.

'P.K.?' came my pa's feeble voice from the ground. 'Why are you singing?'

I did not want him to worry, so I told a lie. 'I thought a song might cheer you.'

I sang a little louder. *'De Camptown race-track five miles long, Oh, doo-dah day!'*

'So kind . . .' murmured my pa. But I did not pay him any mind. I was thinking about how to vanquish those grizzlies.

My pa and I both had pistols, but their .32 caliber balls would have no more effect than a mosquito bite against a couple of grizzlies. (My friend Stonewall killed a grizzly in December and he said it took thirteen .44 caliber rifle balls to bring him down. And that was not even a full-grown bear.)

'I come down dah wid my hat caved in, Doo-dah! doo-dah!'

I had Kepi's big Remington New Model Army Six-shooter stuck in my belt. But it only had a single .44 caliber ball as he had not reloaded.

'I go back home wid a pocket full of tin,' I sang. *'Oh, doo-dah day!'*

The Henry Rifle I had taken from the Reb Road Agents also takes .44 caliber balls. But it was about ten paces behind me, in the cave.

'Gwine to run all night! Gwine to run all day!' I sang. (But I was thinking, 'No, no, no. I must not run!')

The bears started to move towards me again.

There was only one thing to do. I pulled out the Remington & cocked it & fired its last remaining ball into the air.

BANG!

'P.K.?' came my pa's feeble voice. 'Why are you shooting?'

'To attract help,' I lied.

But my real reason for firing was to frighten off the bears.

And it worked! The bears had vamoosed.

My knees were so shaky that I had to sit down for a spell.

Sitting by Pa, I could see his face looked deathly white in the moonlight. I feared he was dying.

'Do you want me to pray with you, Pa?' I asked.

'Yes!' he whimpered. 'Pray that God will forgive me my sins.'

'Heavenly Father,' I prayed. 'Please forgive my pa for all his sins. And please may he not die. Amen.'

'Will you forgive me too?' he said in his feeble voice.

'I ain't got nothing to forgive you for.'

He kind of groaned.

I said, 'Can you tolerate me dragging you back into that cave?'

'I reckon.' His voice was barely a whisper.

I got hold of his ankles and dragged him towards the dark mouth of the cave, going as slow as I dared so I would not hurt him.

My reasoning was this: if we were in a cave those bears could not perform a 'flanking manoeuver' & come up on us from behind.

Pa groaned again, so I finished off the song to distract him from the pain.

'I'll bet my money on de bob-tail nag, Somebody bet on de bay.'

Once I had got Pa safely inside the cave, I grabbed the Henry Rifle that was leaning against the opening. That made me feel better until the moonlight showed me the little brass follower underneath the barrel. It was right up near the stock of the rifle, which meant there was only 1 bullet left in the magazine.

Dang those Reb Road Agents! They had not reloaded. Everybody knows you should reload once you have fired.

My pa was trying to say something so I brought my ear to his mouth.

'Whiskey,' he murmured. 'Is there any whiskey for the pain?'

'I will look, Pa,' I said.

I leaned the rifle back against the wall of the cave.

Before I searched for whiskey, I needed to find more cartridges for the Henry or balls for the Remington. And before I searched for more ammunition, I needed to make a fire. Fire would light the cave. Also, bears do not like fires. It might keep them at bay when they returned.

For I was sure they would return.

I went and got some firewood from the stack near the cave.

Using a Lucifer match from my medicine bag, I quickly kindled a fire just outside the mouth of the cave.

When the fire was going good, I breathed a sigh of relief. It would make a useful barrier between us and the bears.

Also, it lit up the inside of the cave. Its flickering light showed me two rolled-up blankets in a low, dark niche of the cave. There were also some other things, viz: two greasy decks of cards, a cribbage board, a Ledger Book, a box of Lucifers, two pencils & a small Bible.

Joy! There was a box of .44 caliber balls for a Remington revolver!

Despair! There was no powder. Too late, I remembered Slouch had worn a powder horn on his belt. Now all his big Remington pistol was good for was clubbing those bears.

Nor did I find any cartridges for the Henry Rifle.

However, in another niche I found 1 frying pan & 1 coffee pot & 2 tin mugs. There was water in the coffee pot but no ground coffee nor any other provisions to fry in the frying pan.

'P.K.?' asked Pa. 'Did you find anything to drink?'

'No whiskey, Pa,' I said. 'But I did find a little water.'

'Yes, please,' he murmured.

I poured water from the coffee pot into one of those tin mugs & knelt by Pa & helped him drink. Then I eased his head down on one of the rolled-up blankets and covered him with the other. He winced and kind of groaned.

'Does it hurt, Pa?'

'Yeah. It hurts real bad,' he said in a voice so faint I could barely hear him. Then he said, 'P.K.?'

'Yes, Pa?'

His lips moved. I brought my ear real close. He was

saying something about his murdering pard, Tempest. Then he said something that might have been 'Blizzard's a coming.'

'Don't worry, Pa,' I said. 'There ain't no blizzard coming and you will see the sun once more.'

But he shook his head no & the firelight showed me tears dribbling from the corners of his wide-open eyes.

Then I quoted Malachi chapter 4 verse 3 over him, viz: *The sun of righteousness will arise with healing in his wings*, and after that I said a prayer of my own devising. His eyes were now closed and he slept.

I took the Ledger book out from under the cribbage board. When I opened it, I found it was a Wells Fargo & Co. Ledger Book, with only a few pages full of legitimate numbers. The Dead Reb Road Agents had filled the next few pages with scoring for their cribbage games. I saw for the first time that their names were Johnny and Jimmy.

Most of the other pages were blank, so I took that as a Sign from God that I should write an account of how I came to be here.

I sat down Indian fashion & started writing this account.

That was about four hours ago. I have been using the Squiggly Worm shorthand that I learned last November in Carson City. I have used up two and a half pencils and am now on the last page of the book.

The moon sank behind the trees a couple of hours ago and all I have is the light of this little fire, but I am almost out of wood & although the bears have stopped growling I can still smell them so I know they are lurking nearby.

Like I said before: all I have for protection against them is this small fire and—

I just had to shoot the last bullet from my Henry Rifle in the air to frighten off those bears.

They will probably get me at dawn but it does not matter.

Nothing matters any more.

Pa is dead.

LEDGER SHEET 28

WELL, YOU HAVE PROBABLY GUESSED THAT THOSE bears did not eat me after all. You can tell by the fact that I am writing this bit in plain English – not squiggly worm-writing – and also because I am writing it in a new Ledger Book. A lot happened which I will try to recount here, even though it is painful to do so.

After Pa died, I did something I cannot remember doing in my whole life.

I cried.

I was crying for my pa.

But once I started crying, I could not stop. I cried for Ma Evangeline & Pa Emmet, for my dead Indian ma & for Dizzy the stagecoach driver.

I even cried for those two Reb Road Agents, especially the curly-haired one who had looked up at the stars.

I confess I also cried for myself as I would soon be eaten by bears. Dawn was lightening the sky.

By and by all that crying tuckered me out. I curled up on the dirt floor of the cave near the body of my poor dead pa. While I was down there I realized that part of the ground was too flat & hard.

I pushed myself up on one elbow & squinted down with swollen eyes. I thought I saw wood. I brushed at the earth.

Then I brushed a tad more.

There *was* wood under there.

A crate was buried with a little dirt sprinkled over it.

It was treasure.

But not gold.

Something better.

Inside the crate was a bag of coffee, a bag of sugar, a wooden spoon & another tin coffee pot. When I opened the lid I saw a big lump of fresh honeycomb. There was also a half-full bottle of whiskey.

I swallowed hard.

If I had found that box of honey & coffee & whiskey earlier, could I have saved my pa's life?

I dipped my finger in the liquid honey around the comb & licked it off.

That honey was about the best thing I have ever tasted.

It was like the honey Jonathan ate while fighting the Philistines near Michmash in 1 Samuel chapter 14. I dipped in my finger again & sucked off the honey & 'mine eyes were enlightened'.

Suddenly, I realized why the bears had been a-prowling and a-growling all night long.

They were not hungry for me – a poor, skinny, 12-year-old, half-Sioux Misfit – they had a hankering for that honey!

Bears have real good noses. They must have got a whiff of it even though it was closed up in a tin coffee pot & boxed up in a crate & sprinkled with earth.

That is why the Dead Reb Road Agents buried the honey and not the gold. Bears will do almost anything to get at honey, but they are not bothered about gold.

I tested my theory by tossing that sticky lump of honeycomb as far out into the clearing as I could. Sure enough, I saw those two bears come out of the trees and lumber after it. I licked the rest of the honey off my throwing hand while I watched them circle it for a spell, with gruntings & growlings & roarings. Then one of them finally grabbed it in his jaws and vamoosed towards Carson City with the other one in hot pursuit.

I was safe for the moment.

But my discovery had been too late for Pa.

I looked down at his body.

I reckoned it was my duty to bury him, lest the bear who did not get the honeycomb return for a consolation snack of carrion.

There was a spade over by the oyster cans & empty bottles, near the pit those Dead Reb Road Agents used as a latrine.

I went to the latrine & while I was there I used it. Then I got the shovel & came back & dug a hole. In the forest around me, woodpeckers had started tapping & some chickadees were conversing & the early morning sunbeams were slanting through pine boughs. It was a frosty morning but digging warmed me up so much that I took off my velvet sacque. When I finished I got cold so I put it on again.

I went back to the cave and looked down at Pa's body.

'I am sorry I let you down, Pa,' I said. 'I will try to be a good detective. If you are looking down from heaven, I will make you proud of me.'

I drug his stiff & spiritless corpse out of the cave until it was lying next to the grave. I was about to roll him into his last resting place when it occurred to me that he might have some personal effects on his body. Such objects might help me remember him when I was older. I patted him down.

In the right-hand pocket of his trowsers, I found his Smith & Wesson No. 2 & also his wife's handkerchief with C.P. embroidered on the corner.

In the left-hand pocket of his trowsers were some paper dollars, some Lucifers, a pouch of Lucy Hinton & his Lion-faced Meerschaum pipe. I took out the pipe and looked at it. The lion's chalky face, which had looked fierce before, now appeared stricken by grief.

I thought, 'I will have to take all these things to Chicago and give them to his grown-up sons who are my half-brothers.'

Then I found the Letters.

That was when I realized I had made the biggest mistake of my life.

LEDGER SHEET 29

WHAT IF A FEW SHEETS OF PAPER COULD CHANGE the way you see the world? What if a Letter made your brain do a handspring, so that topsy became turvy and everything looked wrong?

I had been patting my dead pa's coat to see if there were any hidden pockets when something pricked my finger. It was a straight pin in the seam on the left front of the coat. Not just one pin, but six of them.

As I removed the 6 pins, the seam opened. An envelope fell out. It was folded lengthwise. It contained 3 things . . .

No. 1 – A newspaper clipping.
No. 2 – A telegram.
No. 3 – A page torn from a notebook.

I looked at the newspaper clipping first. As I scanned it, I saw the names Pinkerton and Lincoln. It was an article about how my uncle Allan had thwarted an assassination attempt on Lincoln 2½ years ago. I remembered my Ma Evangeline reading me that very article. We wrote to Allan Pinkerton at that time, but never got a reply.

Next I turned my attention to the telegram.

It read as follows:

From J.C. Harris, Chicago, to Chauncy Pridhaume, c/o Occidental Hotel, San Francisco.

Dear Chauncy, You asked for facts about Robert Pinkerton of the Detective Agency here in Chicago. Have not been able to find many. The following are general knowledge: Robert started agency, not Allan. Robert resents his brother's political ambitions. Angry when Allan accepted IOUs from Gen McClellan in return for spying out Reb positions and numbers. Robert still supervises some rail and stage protection operations, but is mainly concerned with Agency accounts. Works behind a desk. Wife named Bella (short for Isabella), four children, all boys. Robert suffers poor health after taking bad chill during efforts to help slaves escape on the 'Underground Railway'. Smokes Lucy Hinton, is teetotal, speaks with noticeable brogue.

Finally I studied the page torn from the notebook. The notes were as follows:

Born 1815 in Glasgow, supported Chartist movement, involved in riots, warrant for arrest, hastily married Isabella AKA Bella, fled Scotland for America, survived shipwreck off Newfoundland and made way to Chicago. Worked as canal digger then est. Pinkerton & Co. in '43; partnered w/ bro in '50 to form Det. Agency; resents younger bro's fame & fortune; disapproves of his spying for McClellan as only being paid in IOUs.

I did not understand what I was reading.

Why would my pa have a telegram addressed to a man named Chauncy Pridhaume?

Why would he have a page of notes about himself?

Had he caught someone trying to personate him and had he kept these documents as evidence?

I felt the seams on the other side of the coat in case there might be an answer there.

There was.

I found no pins, but as I worked over the seams with my forefinger and thumb something crinkled in the lining of the right-hand side.

I used my Indian ma's flint knife to cut some big uneven stitches and take it out.

It was another envelope, also folded twice lengthwise. In purple ink & what appeared to be a feminine hand, it was addressed to a certain Jonas Blezzard, Esq.

There was no address.

A single sheet of stationery lay within. On the top it read, *From the escritoire of Mrs. V.F. von Vingschplint,*

Occidental Hotel, Corner of Montgomery & Bush Streets, San Francisco

Dearest — You have asked me to jot down a few facts about the background of the person we were discussing at cards last night. Very well. Your three 'trump cards' are these. Firstly, 'he' is really a 'she', a fact known to only one or two people. Secondly, she herself does not know what the initials P and K signify. Thirdly, she is worth a deal of money. She has three feet of the Chollar mine which people are clamoring to buy. I heard of a man who paid ten thousand for one foot! Other facts? She is twelve years old, born in the autumn of '50 if I am not mistaken. She claims her father was Robert Pinkerton, older brother of the celebrated detective, and she longs to go to Chicago and work with him. They say her mother was a Sioux Indian. This must be true, for her sallow complexion, black hair and cold eyes betray savage blood. The mother was obviously wild and wayward, even for a heathen. Although the daughter is stoical of expression I believe she has inherited much of this savagery, so beware! Other facts? She drinks black coffee and is partial to layer cake. She carries two talismanic objects in a greasy leather neck pouch: a flint knife and a small brass button with the words Pinkerton Railroad Detective on it. She has an extraordinary visual memory, yet she often forgets faces. If you—

I turned the page over but there was nothing on the

back. If there had been more pages, they were missing.

My stomach felt like a cold rock.

I looked at the dead man lying by the shallow grave I had dug.

He was not my father. He had never been my father. He was a man *personating* my father.

I felt numb, like I did the time Doc Pinkerton dosed me with laudanum so he could remove a bullet from my arm.

In the forest around me, woodpeckers were still tapping & the chickadees were still conversing & the early morning sunbeams were still slanting green-gold through pine boughs.

But the whole world had changed. I had been looking at it wrong. I had been looking at the world as if 'through a glass, darkly'.

I thought, 'Of all the detectives in the whole wide world, I must be the worst.'

The man lying at my feet was not my pa; he was a clever impostor.

Or maybe not so clever, as he was now dead.

My real pa – that is, the real Robert Pinkerton – was still in Chicago.

You would have thought that discovering my pa was bogus might have dashed my spirits. But instead it lifted them, on account of it made me mad. Real mad.

I looked down at the man who had pretended to be my pa.

I had all the clews right there in front of my eyes:

No. 1 – He was too young to be my pa. I knew the
    famous detective Allan Pinkerton was born in 1818
    and so he was 45 yrs old which meant his older
    brother had to be at least 46 but the man lying at
    my feet was probably 36 at most. How had I not
    seen it?

No. 2 – I remembered how his Scottish accent had come
    and gone. Sometimes he said 'ye' and othertimes
    'you'. Sometimes 'wee' and other times 'little'. It
    especially went when he was excited or not paying
    attention.

No. 3 – He had claimed to be 'teetotal' but had drunk
    champagne and asked for whiskey in his final
    hours.

No. 4 – Kepi had called him something like 'Chance'
    and I had not thought that strange.

No. 5 – He had a handkerchief with the initials C.P. on
    it. It was not a woman's handkerchief, but a man's.
    The initials were his.

He was Chauncy Pridhaume.

What had fooled me was that he knew facts only my
pa could have known. And that he had pretended not
to recognize me at first, which made *me* try to convince
him, not the other way around.

That made me even madder. I looked at the grave I
had dug him. Then I yelled, 'Come back, Bears! You can
come eat this one. He is a piece of tasty carrion!'

My teeth were chattering & I was shivering hard.

My bogus pa was still wearing that warm woolen greatcoat.

I bent down & I yanked it off his cold, stiff body.

I rolled back the cuffs of the sleeves & pinned up the hem with the straight pins. Then I put it on over my velvet sacque & buttoned it up.

Immediately I felt warmer.

I would gladly have changed out of my yellow dress and put on some of his other clothes, but his trowsers & jacket were too big and his shirt was stiff with blood.

I had been planning to leave his body lying there, but I remembered how he had asked me to forgive him with tears trickling down his face so I pushed his body into the hole I had dug & shoveled some of the earth back over the corpse & tramped it down.

'Ashes to ashes, dust to dust,' I said. 'Amen.'

Up on the main road the early morning sun clearly showed me the hoof prints of nine horses, six of them deeper, as if carrying a heavy load. Ray G. Tempest and the booty-laden horses were heading west.

As I followed those clear tracks, I thought about those documents, especially the letter.

Who was Mrs. V.F. von Vingschplint? Why was she writing to a Jonas Blezzard? What did she have to do with my bogus pa & Mr. Ray G. Tempest?

Walking always helps me think and after a mile or so I remembered my bogus pa's dying words, 'Blizzard's a coming.'

Suddenly I realized it wasn't 'blizzard'. It was 'Blezzard'.

But it was an easy mistake to make on account of Blezzard sounds like blizzard and a blizzard is a kind of storm or tempest. Tempest!

Also, the Reb Road Agents had spoken of someone named Jonas, who was meaner than a rattlesnake.

I stopped in my tracks. In the pine woods the woodpeckers stopped pecking, like they had realized it, too.

How had I been so stupid?

Just as Chauncy Pridhaume had taken the name Robert Pinkerton, Jonas Blezzard must have taken the name Ray G. Tempest.

It was a *pseudonym*!

I guess my bogus pa had been struck by a spasm of conscience, for with his dying breath he had tried to tell me that Ray G. Tempest was really Jonas Blezzard.

But who were those two men? Why had they plotted to deceive me? Were the Reb Road Agents involved in the scheme? And how were they all linked to Mrs. V.F. von Vingschplint?

I had to know.

LEDGER SHEET 30

I WAS FOLLOWING THE TRACKS OF MURDERING **R**AY G. Tempest, AKA Jonas Blezzard, when I saw that something had happened.

A passel of wheel ruts & footprints & hoof prints on the muddy road told me that Ray & his nine horses had overtaken a big flatbed wagon pulled by two oxen. After some milling about, the horses had all gone down off the left-hand side of the road into the pine trees & the wagon had carried on with just two oxen but much deeper wheel ruts.

I deduced that Ray had either threatened or bribed the driver to help him transfer the gold and silver to that wagon. Then he had set the incriminating horses free, to fend for themselves. Then the two of them had carried on west.

Ray had a good head start on me: at least four hours. But I reckoned I knew where he was headed.

I reckoned he was going to meet Mrs. V.F. von Vingschplint in San Francisco!

A bend in the road brought me to Yank's Station where the only person in sight was a woman pumping water outside the stage house. I asked her if she had seen a man with a beaver-felt brown hat riding in an ox-cart just after dawn.

She said yes, there had been a man riding with 'Dung' O'Dowd. She told me Dung plied a flatbed ox-wagon from Placerville to Friday's Station. His habit was to fill that wagon with whiskey and head east, dropping whiskey off at all the stations. Then at Friday's he would turn around and fill his wagon with manure so it was full when he got back to Placerville. She said she noticed the man because Dung usually traveled on his own.

I reckoned Ray had hidden the leather mailbags full of gold and silver in the manure where nobody would care to look for them!

I said, 'Placerville is on the road to Sacramento, ain't it?'

'You bet.'

'When is the next stage?'

'Next stage to Sacto should be coming through in half an hour.'

'Is there a telegraph office here at Yank's Station?' I said.

'Course there is,' she replied. 'Three doors down. Little one-room shack beside the stables at the base of one of them telegraph poles.'

I went three doors down and found a raw-plank, one-room building beside the stables at the base of one of them telegraph poles. The telegraph operator was snoozing with a slouch hat over his face and his feet up on a desk. On this desk was the machine for sending messages & a sheaf of forms & a tin can with pencils & a green blotter & a little bell with a dinger.

I brought my gloved hand down on the dinger.

Ding!

'What?' The man's chair rocked back and almost tipped him out.

'How much to send a telegram to Virginia City?' I asked.

He pushed the hat back on his head. 'Penny a word.'

I decided to save the $20 gold piece in my medicine pouch for the train and/or ferry to San Francisco. I fished around in my bogus pa's greatcoat and pulled out 2 paper dollars & showed them to him.

'Two pennies a word if you are payin' in greenbacks,' he said, and spat into a corner of the room.

He pushed a form forward. 'Write the person's address and fill it out,' he said.

I paused for a moment to ponder. Whom should I wire for help?

My first thought was Mr. V.V. Bletchley, but I wanted to solve the mystery and recover the treasure myself.

My second thought was Jace, but a telegram might take a day or even two to reach Jace down in Steamboat Springs.

I finally decided to ask Ping, even though he had claimed to be quit of me.

I said, 'Do you know of a good and cheap hotel in Frisco?'

The telegraph operator opened a drawer in his desk & handed me a cherry-red slip of paper. It read as follows:

WHAT CHEER HOUSE

San Francisco, Sacramento Street,
Between Montgomery and Sansome
B.B. WOODWARD, Proprietor

This favorite and well-established House
is now conducted on the Enterprise at New York Prices –
Guests paying for only what they order.

FIRST CLASS LODGING, 50 cts PER NIGHT
and less Rates by the week

☞ An extensive Library, Museum and Reading Room
FREE TO ALL THE GUESTS

☞ The **OMNIBUS** will take Guests and Baggage
to the House Free of Charge
☞ Look to the name of the Omnibus to avoid imposition

Also, the **CENTRAL RAILROAD CARS** now connect with the
Inland Steamers arriving at San Francisco, passing through
Sansome Street, and crossing Sacramento Street, within half a
block of the What Cheer House. Fare 5 cents.

BEWARE!! of a place adjoining the What Cheer House
called the "Original House". Said house is not
in any way connected with this hotel.

'May I keep this?' I said.

He nodded & yawned. 'Sure,' he said. 'I got a whole passel of 'em.'

I folded the cherry-red slip of paper and put it in the pocket of my pa's greatcoat. Then I wrote my telegram.

From: P.K. Pinkerton, Yank's Station

To: Ping at the Pingerton (sic) Detective Agency,
South B Street, Virginia City

Need help. Rbt Pinkerton bogus. Real name Chauncy
Pridhaume? Shot & killed by bogus Pinkerton Det.
Ray G. Tempest AKA Jonas Blezzard? Tempest left
me for dead, took treasure. Come to Frisco. What
Cheer House. Bring money & my woolen trowsers.
You said you were quit of me, but reward will bring
you, as money all you care about. Yrs, P.K.

As I watched the telegraph operator tap out the message on the contraption before him, I imagined it whizzing along the wires to Virginia City in only moments.

My stomach growled. I was ravenous, for I had only tasted a little honey that morning. 'I will be back in a quarter of an hour to see if there is a reply,' I said.

He nodded & leaned back & put his feet on the desk & tipped his hat over his eyes.

I went to the stage house.

It was empty as the stage had not yet arrived.

I sat at the end of a long table & an old man brought me a bowl of stew. It was about the worst stew I had ever tasted but I forced myself to eat it because I did not know how long it would be until my next meal.

I was wiping my bowl with a piece of stale bread when a young man came running in.

'They's struck again!' he cried. 'Them danged Reb Road Agents!'

I froze in the act of wiping my bowl with the piece of stale bread.

'What?' The old man who had served me stew looked up from laying out spoons & cups on the table next to me.

'They found Dizzy a few miles out of Friday's Station,' cried the youth. 'He had a ball in his chest and a busted-up leg. He said it was them Reb Road Agents. He was babbling about a stage full of silver and bull-whippings and two men and a little girl and being thrown off the stage into a gorge. He lost consciousness and they do not expect him to live.'

'Two men and *a little girl*?' said the man who served the stew.

'Yup. She was in cahoots with them Reb Road Agents!'

I was tempted to sprint for the door but I knew that would give me away.

'I got some WANTED notices here,' said the youth.

'Dang!' I thought. 'I should have wired Mr. V.V. Bletchley. Now I am a fugitive on a WANTED notice.'

Then I thought, 'I wonder how much I am worth?'

And finally, 'I wonder if they want me "dead or alive"?'

LEDGER SHEET 31

I NEEDED TO SEE THE **WANTED** NOTICE TO FIND out what it said about me so I could make myself look different.

'I have posted one of these outside your front door,' said the young messenger, 'and I will leave you this one. Make sure you tell all the stage drivers and passengers. I'm off to Strawberry to tell them, too!'

I heard the crinkle of paper as he passed over one of the WANTED notices to the old man. Then I heard the door of the stage house slam. Then I heard the sound of a horse's hooves galloping west.

I put the last piece of bread in my mouth but it was as dry as a pine knot and I felt the lump of it go all the way down and sit like a pebble in my stomach.

'What did Toby want?' asked the old woman who had been drawing water earlier. She had appeared from a back room. She wore a stained apron & was drying her hands on a towel.

'Them Reb Road Agents struck again,' said the old man. 'But this time they had helpers – two men and a little girl.'

I heard the WANTED notice crinkle as he showed it to her.

'A little girl?' said the old lady. 'Oh, pshaw!'

'Says it right here,' said the man, 'so it must be true. Prudence Pinkerton, aged 12.' I winced at the mention of my girly name.

'Fur-trimmed purple cape?' said the woman. 'Yellow dress? Lighthouse bonnet?'

I breathed a small sigh of relief. I was wearing Ray's flat-topped gray hat and my bogus pa's greatcoat buttoned over my dress and sacque. Yes, I was wearing girly-girl boots, but they were black and in that long coat only the toes were visible so they could be mistaken for a boy's shoes.

The lady's voice went higher. 'It says she is half Sioux Injun and of a sallow complexion.'

Dang! That was bad. There was nothing I could do about my skin. I stood up & mumbled my thanks & turned for the door.

'Hey, you!' cried the old man.

I froze.

'That will be four bits,' he said.

Fifty cents was a lot of money for rancid stew and stale bread and a cup of water, but I did not object. I fished in the pocket of the greatcoat and found 2 quarters & put them on the table & went out as casually as I dared.

On the outside wall of the stage house were half a dozen notices. I saw the newest handwritten one at once. It read as follows:

WANTED
for Robbery & possibly Murder!

MR. RAY G. TEMPEST, aged around 30.
Tall and dark with mustache, sideburns & a bad tooth.
Last seen wearing gray flat-topped hat.

MR. ROBERT PINKERTON, aged around 35. Medium height, brown hair, mustache, speaks in a Scottish accent. Last seen wearing a brown greatcoat & brown beaver-felt hat.

MISS PRUDENCE PINKERTON, his daughter, aged 12, last seen wearing a fur-trimmed purple cape, a yellow dress & a lighthouse bonnet. She is half-Sioux Indian with dark hair & eyes & of a Sallow complexion.

THEY ARE ALL ARMED AND DANGEROUS.
Reward: $100 each for their capture.

I felt queasy. Now all the stage drivers & passengers & pedestrians & riders traveling this road would be on the lookout for me.

The sleeves of my greatcoat were folded back and the pinned-up hem nearly touched the ground. This was not normal attire for a child. All a person had to do was imagine a 12-yr-old half-Sioux girl in a man's greatcoat and flat-topped gray hat, and they would have a mental picture of me.

I had to get out of there.

I had to get to Frisco to solve the mystery and prove my innocence.

But how? This was the only road in or out of the mountains. Standing there in the sunshine outside the stage stop, I looked around to get my bearings. Rising up behind the stables and a few other buildings stood thick ranks of pine trees, all dense and dark. That gave me an idea of how to get to Frisco unseen.

But first I had to find out if Ping had replied to my telegraphed plea for help.

I sauntered towards the telegraph building, all careless-like. As I neared the shack, my footsteps slowed down.

My telegraphic message to Ping had named all three people on the WANTED poster, viz: Robert Pinkerton, Ray G. Tempest & me, P.K. Pinkerton.

Had the telegraph operator seen the poster yet? Or heard about the robbery?

I went to the office & peeked into the doorway, ready to skedaddle.

'Your reply just came through,' said the man, with only a cursory glance. He finished tapping something on his telegraph machine & held up a slip of paper with his free hand.

'Here it is,' he said. He did not even look at me.

I breathed a sigh of relief.

He had not heard the news.

Or, if he had, he had not put two and two together, as they say.

I stepped forward and took the paper from him & read these words:

From: Hong Ping, proprietor Pingerton Detective Agency

To: P.K. Pinkerton, Yank's Station

It is not true that I only care about money. I care about other things than money. But I think you only care about yourself. So I will NOT help you. We are no longer pards. You can go to the Fiery Place. Yrs, Ping

This surprised me in three ways:

No. 1 – I did not know Ping's other name was Hong.

No. 2 – I did not realize that Ping cared about other things than money.

No. 3 – I had not thought Ping would hate me enough to want me to go to H-ll.

Then I got a 4th surprise.

I heard the sound of a gun being cocked & looked up to see the telegraph man on his feet. He had a Colt's Navy in his hand & a glint in his eye. 'Miss Prudence Pinkerton, I presume?'

The revolver was pointed at my heart.

'You didn't think they would tell me first?' he said.

Inwardly I was cursing my stupidity, but I said nothing.

'I have just been telegraphing every stage station on both sides of the border that you are here,' he added, 'so you may as well sit down to wait for the Law.'

LEDGER SHEET 32

'I said sit!'

The telegraph operator at Yank's Station was aiming a cocked Colt's Navy Revolver at me and his tone was firm.

But I did not sit down to 'wait for the Law' as he suggested.

Instead, I feinted to the left, dodged to the right, grabbed the rickety straight-backed chair on my side of the desk & swung at the Telegraph Operator with what I hoped was a blood-curdling Lakota war cry, 'Aiiieeee!'

Normally you should not attack someone who is pointing a loaded firearm at you.

But I was riled.

I was riled at Ping.

I was riled at my dead & bogus pa.

I was riled at Mr. Ray G. Tempest.

I would search out the Truth and have my Revenge.

And I was d-mned if anybody was going to get in my way.

THUMP! I knocked the gun out of his hand.

CLONK! It hit the raw-plank wall and rebounded back onto the floor my side of the desk.

CRASH! I smashed his telegraph machine with the chair.

The gun was still spinning on the floor at my feet. I threw down the broken chair and had the revolver in my hand before he could react.

'God d-mn,' he said. 'You busted my machine.'

'Tear out the rest of those wires,' I commanded. 'And use them to tie your feet to the chair.'

He opened his mouth to protest.

'Do it!' Using both hands, I cocked the pistol & raised it & pointed it at his heart.

He tore out the wires & tied his ankles to the chair legs with trembling fingers.

'Take off your belt,' I commanded.

'Stick your arms through the back slats of the chair,' I added.

And finally, 'Wedge them in real good.'

When he had wedged his arms in real good, I went around behind him. Once I was out of his sight, I quickly uncocked the Colt's Navy & stuck it in a pocket of my bogus pa's greatcoat & used his own belt to tie his already wedged arms to the back of the chair. Then I came round to the front of the desk again & pulled the revolver out of my pocket.

'Close your eyes and count to one hundred,' I commanded.

Outside I heard the sound of a cavalry bugle sounding charge.

'What is that noise?' I said, re-cocking the Navy. 'Is it the cavalry come to rescue you?'

'No,' he said, his eyes still closed. 'That is the 10 o'clock stage on its way to Virginia City. Major Micky is the driver. He always blows his trumpet when he is about to arrive or depart.'

'Will they stop for lunch?'

'They will stop for coffee, and stew if any passengers want it. Shall I carry on or start again?'

'Carry on what?'

'Counting to one hundred.'

'Start again,' I said. 'And keep your eyes shut. I am going to stand right here. I will shoot you if you open your eyes before you reach one hundred.'

But as soon as he started counting again, I backed outside & dropped the revolver into a rain-barrel so he would not find it in a hurry.

I glanced around to make sure nobody had seen me. Then I ran for the pine woods. Once again I heard the blare of the bugle & also the jingle of harness & clop of hooves & knew the Virginia-bound Stage was pulling up in front of Yank's Station. Soon they would all know about the half-Indian fugitive, viz: ME!

I went into the silent & dappled pine forest & circled west, going where the pine needles were thickest in case there were any trackers on my trail. I found a hiding place behind some big pine trees near the top of a rise in the road near where any Sacramento-bound coach would have to slow down on account of the steep grade.

My plan was to jump onto the back of a stagecoach while it was going slow, and then slip inside the rear boot which is a big pouch of waterproof leather where they carry parcels & mail. I reckoned I was small enough to fit in. Unless I wanted to foot it one hundred miles or steal a horse, it was the only way I could get to Sacramento now that I was a WANTED desperado with a price on my head.

The pine forest was still chilly in the shadows, but it was real quiet with no noise apart from the echoing knocks of woodpeckers deep in the forest and the occasional squitter of chickadees. I put up the collar of my bogus pa's coat and took stock of my position.

From my skin out, I was dressed in bloomers & chemise & 1 petticoat, and over that a gaudy yellow & green dress, and over that a purple velvet sacque trimmed with white ermine & cinched by a whang leather belt with a yellow velvet reticule tied to it, and over all that my bogus pa's greatcoat, with the cuffs folded back & the hem pinned up so it did not drag on the ground. I had two guns that both took .32 caliber rimfire cartridges. In the pockets of my bogus pa's greatcoat was his Smith & Wesson No. 2, a few coins, some greenbacks, a lion-headed meerschaum pipe, tobacco, matches, a ledger book & a couple of pencils. In the medicine bag around my neck were my Muff Deringer, 5 spare rimfire cartridges, 3 Lucifers, my Indian ma's flint knife, a silk butterfly, a $20 gold coin & my genuine pa's Detective Button.

Finally, I had my black button-up boots & a flat-crowned gray hat that had belonged to that murdering varmint Ray G. Tempest.

It was a useful hat, but it had been described in the WANTED poster. That meant people might be on the lookout for a hat like that. Without a hat, my short hair would make me look like a boy. So I spun the hat up into a pine tree and watched it stick in some of the high branches above me.

Then I sat still to wait for a lift to Sacto.

I must have dozed for I woke with a start to the sound of whip cracks coming from the east and a rough voice yelling, 'Come on, you beauties!'

Up the hill came six fine horses pulling a Concord Stage.

They were heading in the right direction, but I was dismayed to see not only a driver & conductor but about half a dozen people sitting on top. Some of them were facing out and two were facing back! Also, the mail boot at the rear was crammed full to bursting.

A few moments later I heard another stagecoach. This one was coming from the west. It was the original Decoy Stage that had set out 24 hours before, with Icy riding shotgun but a new driver and a team of horses I did not recognize. They must have heard the telegraphed news that Dizzy was hurt & the silver stage wrecked.

I reckoned they were heading back to investigate the scene of the crime.

I caught a glimpse of Icy on his conductor's seat as the stage raced downhill. His hat & little blue goggles hid his eyes but the rest of his face was 'set like flint'.

I thought, 'As soon as they find the wreck and/or those horses they will come back this way. They will be looking for me!'

I was about to have a bad case of the Mulligrubs when I heard another whip crack.

Hallelujah!

This stagecoach was going my way and it was not as crowded as the previous one.

The conductor was dozing in the noontime sunshine and so were the two skull-capped, pigtailed Chinamen sitting on top among the luggage. I gathered myself and as it rumbled past I jumped onto the back like a tick onto a deer. There was a gap in the fastening of the leather 'boot' and I wormed my way through just as the team topped the rise & we started to speed down the next hill.

The inside of the mail boot smelled strongly of leather & faintly of ink. It was dark & warm. I spent the next half hour burrowing behind all the letter-sacks & canvas bags of printed matter. Some of the canvas bags were a bit spiky where corners of books & magazines were poking out, but I had four layers of clothes including my bogus pa's woolen greatcoat to protect me. I took a strange pleasure in being squished tight between the weight of the mailbags and the leather at the back of the stagecoach. I felt like a mole in its burrow: snug and safe.

It must have been one of them new Concord coaches, for the thoroughbrace made it rock like a cradle. I reckoned I had found the best place to ride in a stagecoach, viz: the hidden depths of the mail boot!

I settled back & closed my eyes & offered up a prayer to the Good Lord.

'Lord,' I said, 'if you help me get to Frisco so I catch Mr. Ray G. Tempest and find out why he and Chauncy Pridhaume involved me in this crime, I promise I will not kill the lying varmint myself but will hand him over to the Law so that he can be hanged by the neck until dead. Amen.'

LEDGER SHEET 33

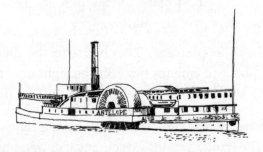

RIDING IN THE BACK OF THAT STAGECOACH, I FELL
into a deep & dreamless sleep. Sometimes I half woke up
when we reached a station & they opened the mail boot,
but it was always to put something in. Nobody saw me
burrowed in my nest. I slept through Placerville which
used to be called Hangtown. I slept through Diamond
Springs & Mud Springs & Buckeye Flat & Shingle
Springs & Durock's & Mormon Tavern & Folsom where
there is a big prison full of desperados. I slept for about
7 or 8 hours and when I was woken by the letter-sacks
being lifted up & out, it was like a resurrection. I
suddenly felt damp & shivery & exposed, like a butterfly
whose chrysalis has been peeled off too soon.

I blinked up into the face of a big, black-skinned man
who had been hefting out the mailbags.

Behind his head I saw the pale purple sky of dusk.

He was making Expression No. 4 – Surprise.

I said, 'I am half Indian so they made me ride in the mail boot.' Before he could question this statement, I said, 'Is this the right place to catch a steamer to Frisco?'

'Yeh,' he said.

'Do any of the steamboats travel by night?'

'Not usually,' he said slowly. 'But the *Antelope,* she be delayed by boiler problems. They had to fix the machinery. She just about to embark now. She be right over there.'

I tried to move but my legs were full of pins and needles.

'Will you help me get out?' I asked. 'My legs are full of pins and needles.'

He helped me get out.

'Thank you, sir,' I said. 'May the Lord bless you for your kindness.'

As I hurried in the direction he pointed, a sudden Thought came to me. If the steamship to Frisco had been delayed, maybe I was not too late to catch that murdering Ray G. Tempest. He might be on board with his dung-smelling booty!

I was bareheaded but double-coated & still wearing button-up boots. I ran tippy-tappy across the levee dodging people & pack animals & piles of suitcases, etc.

I saw a line of people shuffling onto a big steamboat: the *Antelope.*

In the dusky half-light it looked like a white hotel with a big smokestack rising up out of it & a big wheel on the side. I could not even see the river, though I could smell it.

As I went across the wooden wharf, I saw a sign:

PASSAGE TO SAN FRANCISCO
$2.00 Cabin
50 cts Steerage

'Excuse me, sir,' I asked a man in the line. 'Where do you buy tickets?'

'Get away, Injun!' He raised his cane to strike me. 'I know your type: beggars and pickpockets!'

I backed away, but a woman pointed. 'Over there,' she said. 'But this steamer is full and the ticket office closed for the day.'

The woman was dressed all in black. She had three children with her: two hatless little boys and a girl in a tattered bonnet. I reckoned she was a widow so I thanked her but stayed close. I shuffled along behind them in the evening gloom & hung my own hatless head like her twin boys. I hoped the ticket man would think I was with them, and he did, for he let me pass. Hallelujah! I sent up a silent thank you to the Lord.

I followed the widow woman & her family into the 'steerage' section. It was like a wide wooden corridor with wooden chairs all ranked in rows.

There were no empty chairs left, so the woman sat on the hard floor by a wall and gathered her children around her. The little girl started to cry.

'Shush, Eunice,' said the woman. 'Crying never did nobody no good.'

I sat nearby.

I hoped she would not notice but she did.

'Did you follow me?' she said in a low voice. 'What do you want?' Her face, half hidden by a black poke bonnet, was pale.

'Please, ma'am,' I said. 'My name is P.K. Pinkerton. I am a private eye in disguise.'

'You do not look like a private eye in disguise. You look like a desperate half-Indian pickpocket. I am in half a mind to summon a steward.'

'Please ma'am,' I said. 'Do not give me away—'

I was interrupted by a terrible grinding that started low but got louder & louder & then ended in a shriek. I had heard of boilers exploding on steamboats and sending scalding bodies flying a mile high into the air. But nobody else seemed to mind so I guessed it was normal.

'Go along now,' said the widow lady. 'You cannot stay here with me. I used the last of my money to buy this ticket and I cannot fend for another child.'

'Please,' I said above the noise of the throbbing engines. 'You do not have to fend for me. Just let me stay here with you until we get to Frisco. Then I will leave you alone forever. But I need you to pretend I am your kid, if anyone should come by.'

I could see she was wavering.

Or maybe shivering.

I stood up & unbelted my greatcoat. Without removing it, I took my arms out of the sleeves & shrugged off the velvet sacque from underneath & put my arms back in the coat sleeves & stepped out of the sacque which was now on the floor. I picked it up & held it out to her.

'Here,' I said. 'You can keep this purple velvet silk-lined, ermine-trimmed cape as proof of my good will.'

She made Expression No. 4 (Surprise) and then Expression No. 1 (a Genuine Smile).

She took off her own thin shawl & wrapped it thrice around the narrow shoulders of her little girl & put on my velvet sacque.

Then she began to weep.

'Oh,' she said, stroking it. 'I never felt nothing so beautiful and warm. Children, feel the fur!'

Eunice and her twin brothers all snuggled up to their ma & stroked the velvet cloth & white ermine trim of the sacque. Without exchanging a word or glance, the twin boys burrowed under the sacque, one on each side, so that the mother looked like a big purple hen sheltering chicks beneath her wings.

Eunice curled up on her ma's lap & fell asleep sucking her thumb.

'Come sit here,' said the woman to me, as the steamboat started to move.

I sat down on the floor with my back against the wooden wall. I could feel the whole vessel throbbing.

Out of the corner of my eye, I saw the ticket-taker hurrying in our direction.

What if he asked me for my ticket and found I did not have one? Would he toss me into the river?

'Lean your head on my shoulder,' urged the widow lady. 'Pretend you are asleep.'

I leaned my head against the widow lady's shoulder & pretended to be asleep. In the golden light of oil-lamps would he notice my skin did not match her other children's? His footsteps went past so I guessed he had not noticed.

Soon they dimmed the oil-lamps and most everybody slept, including the widow lady.

But I had just woken from my 8 hours good sleep in the depths of the stagecoach so I was now wide awake. I reckoned it was time to see if my enemy was aboard.

I crept up and down steerage and sniffed the keyhole of each cabin. Mr. Ray G. Tempest and his dung-smelling gold & silver sacks were not there.

I went downstairs to the engine room which was like the Fiery Place with its heat & noise & its diabolical pounding pistons & half-naked men all glistening with sweat as they shoveled wood into a gaping mouth of fire. Mr. Ray G. Tempest was not there.

I went outside into cool damp night air but found only a narrow walkway ending in the starboard paddle-wheel on one side and the port paddle-wheel on the other. The turning wheels slapped the black water into pale foam that glowed for a moment & then melted into darkness behind us. The sight of it and the swishy noise almost entranced me but I was brought to my senses by a shower of sparks falling around me. I looked up and saw a towering smokestack.

While I was looking up, I saw another deck up there. I followed the pointing finger up stairs to the HURRICANE DECK at the top of the steamboat.

Mr. Ray G. Tempest was not up there.

I saw a lone man, smoking a pipe in the moonlight.

The man was leaning on a rail, looking out at sedge & tule reeds poking up from black sheets of standing water.

I went over and leaned on the rail beside him.

'Howdy,' he said.

'Howdy,' I replied.

He was smoking St. James Blend, the same tobacco my photographer friend Isaiah Coffin smokes. The smell of it made me pang for Virginia City. But I had Burned My Bridges and would not be returning there any time soon.

The man with the pipe introduced himself as Mr. Alfred Doten. He told me the *Antelope* was the best steamer of them all.

'She is a hundred and fifty feet long,' he informed me. 'And she carries up to three hundred passengers. There is a special reinforced room right in her middle,' he added. 'It is called the Gold Room.'

I said, 'Gold Room?'

He nodded. 'It has got an extra strong floor so the gold does not fall through and sink the boat.'

'Do you reckon it is strong enough to hold an ox-cart full of dung-smelling gold and silver?'

'You bet!'

I was about to ask him to show me where it was. Then I had a thought.

'How long would it take a stagecoach to get from Friday's Station to Sac City?'

He puffed his pipe for a moment. 'About eight hours, I reckon.'

'And what about an ox-cart?'

'Day or two,' he puffed.

I thought, Dang! Ray was in a slow-but-steady ox-cart while I had been flying along on a stagecoach that changed teams of horses every 15 miles. Even though he had a four-hour start, I probably overtook him somewhere on the road while I was curled up asleep in the mail boot!

At first my spirits sank. Then I had another idea.

I turned to Mr. Alfred Doten. 'Have you heard of the Occidental Hotel?'

'Why, surely,' he replied. 'It is one of those fancy new hotels on Montgomery Street.'

I pulled out the cherry-red slip in my pocket and showed it to him.

'Is it near the What Cheer House?'

'It surely is,' he said. 'Only a block or two away.'

Hallelujah! I said to myself. If Mrs. V.F. von Vingschplint is still at the Occidental Hotel then I can find out what role she played in all this & solve the mystery & clear my name.

LEDGER SHEET 34

DAWN BROKE AS SAN FRANCISCO CAME INTO VIEW
across a sheet of pearly water. The rising sun lit up its
forest of ship masts & made the city beyond look fresh
& roseate.

My dear departed foster pa, the Rev. Emmet Jones –
may he rest in peace – once told me that San Francisco
was the Devil's Playground. As if to prove my pa
wrong, the church bells of Frisco started pealing in a
joyous fashion the moment I stepped off the steamboat
Antelope and onto the wooden jetty. It was as if the town
was saying 'This ain't the Devil's Playground; this is a
God-fearing place!'

Then I remembered it was Sunday and the bells were
merely announcing early morning church services. I saw
that the 'Broadway Wharf' was full of people & baggage
& traps & drays & omnibuses. Beyond the wharf lay a
hilly town with scattered buildings & houses & even a

windmill or two up on the highest points. The sky was blue and the air was mild and the sun had a kind of sparkle to it.

I saw a 2-horse omnibus waiting on the wharf. It had an advertisement for the What Cheer House on it! Because I was the only person not waiting for baggage to be unloaded, I got the best place: right at the front where I could see the driver & horses & the city. It only cost 5 cts for a ticket. I got a book of 6 tickets for a quarter, thus saving 5 cts.

Soon the omnibus was filled up with people. The conductor pulled a cord which made a *ding-ding*.

He said, 'Hold on!' so I held on to a green-painted metal bar at the front. The driver flicked the horses' reins & we were off. We clopped south over boards at first & then onto a wooden street called 'Davis' between brick warehouses. By and by we turned west on a wide street called 'Washington' which had two-story buildings made of stone, and when the conductor dinged the bell and told us 'Montgomery!' I got off.

This was the biggest street yet, with fancy white buildings & street-level shop signs in gold paint on wood & awnings as colorful as the people who strolled on the sidewalks below them.

I found the Occidental Hotel with no problems as it was about a block long and four stories tall with each window like a little Greek temple and also some statues of naked ladies above the entrance. I saw some high-tone men & women coming out.

The women had big hats & little parasols. The men had silver-headed walking sticks & shiny black stovepipe hats. But then I saw a man in a plug hat going in. He did not look as high-tone as the others and this gave me courage. I took a deep breath and followed him in. I found myself in a luxurious lobby with chandeliers & ferns in brass pots & big leather chairs to sit in. The man in the plug hat was striding purposefully across a Turkey carpet towards a big mahogany counter with a man in a Magenta-colored uniform standing behind. I hurried to catch up and then listened hard, to hear how it was done.

'Is Mr. Potts residing here?' asked Plug Hat.

'Yes, sir,' said Mr. Uniform. 'He is in room three-oh-five.'

After Plug Hat left I stepped up to the desk & stood on tiptoe to make myself look as tall as possible.

I said in a high-tone English accent, 'Excuse me, sir, can you tell me is Mrs. V.F. von Vingschplint residing here?'

Mr. Magenta Uniform wrinkled his nose to make Expression No. 3 – Disgust – and said, 'What business is it of yours, boy?'

I said, 'I have an important message for her.'

He said, 'You may give it to me.'

I said, 'I have been instructed to place it in her hands only.'

He came out from behind the tall counter & looked me up and down, taking in my short black hair & muddy complexion & oversized greatcoat which almost reached the ground & thus hid most of my girly-girl button-up boots from his view.

'A likely story!' he said. 'As if a savage like you would have anything to do with Mrs. von Vingschplint.' He grasped my arm so hard it hurt and started to haul me through the lobby towards the glass & brass double doors.

I was trying to think what to do when my sharp nose caught an unmistakable scent. It was the 'pipe of a thousand smells'!

Digging the heels of my button-up boots into the Turkey carpet of the Occidental Hotel, I looked around for its owner.

Sure enough, I saw two clean-shaven men, one slightly plump with a hangdog expression, the other good-looking with fox-brown hair and a slim figure.

I recognized them both and cried out, 'Mr. Clemens! I mean, Mr. Twain! Please help me! Tell this man I am not bogus!'

The man with fox-brown hair stopped & turned & peered over at me with bloodshot eyes.

'Why, P.K.!' he slurred. 'Imagine seeing you here in Frisco. Ain't it fine? And ain't this hotel the bulliest thing? It is like heaven on the half-shell.'

'Help me!' I repeated. 'I am on a detective job and they do not believe me.'

Magenta Uniform said, 'Do you know this boy, Mr. Twain?'

'Sure,' drawled Sam Clemens AKA Mark Twain. 'He is a famous personage in Virginia City. He is a miniature Pinkerton Detective.'

I was thankful he had left Virginia before the news about my being a gal got out.

The man gave Mr. Mark Twain Expression No. 5 – Suspicion. And with good reason; the newspaper reporter was a known prankster and brazen liar.

'You on the trail of a desperado, P.K.?' Mark Twain winked at me.

I nodded, and tugged my arm free of the clerk's grasp. 'I have to find a Mrs. V.F. von Vingschplint and I think she is staying here. It is a matter of life or death!'

Mark Twain turned to Magenta Uniform. 'Please assist this young Pinkerton Detective,' he slurred.

The clerk heaved a deep sigh. 'Very well, sir,' he said. 'If you are certain you can vouch for this person.'

'I am certain,' said Mr. Twain. 'Is Mr. Shplingvint residing here?' It was clear from his bloodshot eyes and languorous drawl and whiskey breath that he had not yet been to bed.

'*Mrs.* von *Vingschplint* is in room two-oh-two,' said Magenta Uniform. 'But she is not here at present. She departed a few minutes ago, on her way to *church*.'

'Which church?' I said.

'Why, the Unitarian Church of course,' he replied. 'Mr. Starr King is preaching this morning. He is small in stature but big of heart and all the ladies swoon for him.'

'Dang my buttons!' exclaimed Mark Twain. 'Is it Sunday? I promised John D. Winters I would escort his wife to church. I said I would meet her here at ten to eleven.'

'Here she comes now,' said his friend, Mr. Clement T. Rice. 'Perhaps I should nip upstairs and attend to my toilette.'

'No!' cried Sam. 'Last Sunday you drenched yourself with so much cologne and bergamot that you smelled like the owner of a drug store and barber shop combined. Why hello, Miz Winters,' he drawled as a lady in gray swept up. 'We have been waiting for you.'

Mrs. John D. Winters was wearing a gray silk gown with puffy sleeves and a lighthouse bonnet with little sprigs of gray-green sage-brush on it. I had seen her once or twice last November when I was working on a case in Carson City. Her husband was one of the legislators who had hammered out new laws for Nevada Territory. (He was a hot-tempered man who had also hammered another legislator with a piece of firewood.)

Mark Twain gestured towards us. 'You remember Clement T. Rice AKA The Unreliable? And this here is our young friend Pinky,' he added. 'AKA P.K. Pinkerton, Private Eye.'

Mrs. John D. Winters greeted The Unreliable with a smile but only looked down her nose at me. I allow I must have looked like a half-Sioux street-urchin in that oversized coat and with no hat.

'Let us all waltz down to the Unitarian church,' said

Mark Twain. 'I understand the Reverend Starr King is packing them to the rafters.'

Mrs. Winters smiled & nodded graciously & took his arm.

The four of us exited the hotel & soon found ourselves among a passel of finely dressed men and women all heading west on Sutter Street. At Stockton Street everybody turned south & so did we. On the other side of a grassy plaza stood a squat & spiky stone church with a round window of colored glass.

Mrs. John D. Winters had taken Mr. Mark Twain's arm so Mr. Clement T. Rice was walking beside me.

'Do you happen to know what Mrs. V.F. von Vingschplint looks like?' I asked him, as we joined a log jam of people shuffling into the church.

Mr. Clement T. Rice AKA The Unreliable nodded, 'I have seen her in the hotel a couple of times. She is young and shapely.'

That surprised me as the name *Mrs. V.F. von Vingschplint* brought to mind the image of a stout German lady of at least 50 yrs.

'She will be near the front if I am not mistaken,' said Mr. Clement T. Rice. Then he lowered his voice. 'They say she is climbing the Social Ladder, and that she has buried three or four husbands. She gets richer with every marriage.'

I nodded. I had met such women before. One of them was my mortal enemy: Mrs. Violetta de Baskerville. She had also made a career of marrying and then burying. I had only narrowly succeeded in preventing my mentor, Poker Face Jace, from falling into her deadly web of deceit. In fact, my little silver-plated Muff Deringer had once been hers. I patted the medicine bag hanging from my neck to make sure it was still there. It was.

It was not quite 11 o'clock. The fine May morning was already hot, but inside the church it was cool & airy & full of deep organ music. I noticed the front pews were reserved for the most fashionably dressed. The usher took one look at my hatless head and oversized coat and shooed us towards the back.

Mr. Mark Twain found us a pew in the middle. We had to squish in real good. I made sure I was on the end of the row with an exit in sight. (I always like to have an exit in sight as I do not like feeling trapped.) By the time the last surge of the organ died away, I reckon there were about a thousand people packed into that church.

A shapely lady in a lighthouse bonnet went up & stood by the pulpit & faced the front.

I turned to Mr. Clement T. Rice, who was sitting next to me. 'Is that her?' I asked. 'Is that Mrs. V.F. von Vingschplint?'

'No,' he said. 'That is a famous opera singer. She is going to sing a Religious Song.'

Sure enough, the lady started to trill and warble in some foreign language.

I had never heard such singing in a church before & when she finished, I half expected everyone to stamp and applaud as they did at Topliffe's Theatre in

Virginia, but of course this was Church and not a Music Hall.

Then a man of about 35 rose up from behind the pulpit & read from the Bible in a voice that seemed too big for his slight frame. He was clean-shaven with flat, dark hair that covered his ears & almost reached his collar.

The Unreliable nudged me. 'That is Starr King. There in the pulpit.'

I said, 'That little nondescript man with flat hair?'

'Yup,' said the Unreliable. 'Despite his youth, he is one of the most famous preachers in the world.'

This made me eager to hear him speak, but as the lady singer launched into a second hymn, Mr. Rice bent down & whispered in my ear.

'Do you see the lady in the front pew with the violet-colored skyscraper bonnet?'

I nodded.

'*That* is Mrs. V.F. von Vingschplint!'

'Are you sure?'

'I am positive. She always wears that color.'

Heart thumping, I slipped out of the pew & started down the side aisle. The opera singer was still trilling and the organ was still groaning.

Out of the corner of my eye I saw a black-clad usher scowl & shake his head at me, but he was way over yonder on the other side of the church so I reckoned I could make it. The music drowned out my tippy-tappy boots as I clamped my arms to my sides and broke into a fast walk. (How I longed for my butter-soft moccasins!)

I was almost at the front when the opera singer ceased her song & sat down.

Mr. Starr King stood up, rising in his pulpit. 'Today's lesson,' he said, 'will be taken from Psalm one hundred ten and verse three, *Your troops will be willing on your day of battle*. Please be seated.'

He was interrupted by shouting from the back of the church. Many people looked to see what was causing the commotion, including Mrs. von Vingschplint. She turned her skyscraper-bonneted head to glance back.

At last I saw her lovely face.

My stomach did a somersault.

Mrs. V.F. von Vingschplint was not *like* Mrs. Violetta de Baskerville. She *was* Violetta de Baskerville.

LEDGER SHEET 35

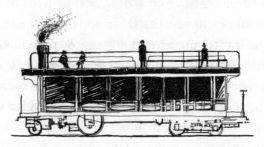

I HAD JUST SPOTTED MY MORTAL ENEMY, **M**RS. Violetta de Baskerville from Carson City.

My head was spinning with questions & my heart was full of exclamation points!!!

But I did not have time to ponder the implications for I suddenly realized what the commotion was at the back of the church.

It was a man with a rose-pink stovepipe hat and droopy gray mustache. He was flanked by two uniformed policemen.

The gray-mustached man was pointing at me with a silver-tipped walking stick.

'Seize that kid in the brown greatcoat!' cried the man. 'He is wanted for theft and possibly murder!'

Everyone turned to look at me, including Mrs. Violetta de Baskerville.

My lightning-quick reflexes made me flip up the collar

of my greatcoat & pull my head into it like a turtle in his shell before she could identify me.

Men were shouting & women were screaming & hands were reaching out to grab me.

I did not hesitate.

I took the only way out I could. I ran forward at a crouch & leaped up onto the stage & nipped between the open-mouthed hymn singer & wide-eyed Rev. Starr King & found a door near the organ at the back. It led into a little back room that Methodists would have called a 'vestry'. (I do not know what Unitarians called their little back rooms.)

I looked around the small dim space for some means of escape.

Then I spotted it: a door in a corner.

I ran to it & opened it & saw a sunlit churchyard promising Freedom!

But just as I was starting through that door, I was pulled up sharp by a fist grasping the turned-up collar of my greatcoat.

'Got you!' cried a man's voice.

I did not wait to see if it was the man in the rose-pink stovepipe hat or one of the policemen or the Reverend Starr King himself.

I writhed out of my greatcoat like that 'certain young man' in Mark chapter 14 and verse 52, who left his garment in the hands of the soldiers at Gethsemane.

Bareheaded, and clad only in that danged daffodil-yellow dress and my girly-girl button-up boots, I burst into the brilliant Sunday morning. I whizzed across the green grass of the churchyard & I lifted up my yellow skirts & vaulted a low, wrought-iron fence. Out on the street now, I ran like a boy. My arms were pumping and my knees almost touching my chin as I pelted through the streets of San Francisco. Without even stopping to get my bearings, I swerved south & raced along the sidewalk, then veered west down a shaded alley between two lofty brick buildings.

I modified my run to a fast walk so as not to attract attention.

About a block on, I passed a girl who had removed her pink poke bonnet to fiddle with the ribbon. I am sorry to confess I snatched it from her fumbling fingers. I needed to cover up my short & boyish hair, which was a dead giveaway.

(The glimpse I got of her startled face and round gray eyes has now been imprinted on my memory like an ambrotype.)

'Sorry!' I called as I tied the ribbon under my chin & burst into a fresh sprint. Now that I was bonnetted, I tried running like a girl, with my arms clamped to my sides & my hands bent at the wrists with fingers splayed out & palms facing the ground. The green flounces sewn to my waistband were flapping like half a dozen dog tongues.

Tip-tap, tip-tap, tip-tap! went my button-up boots on the sidewalk.

By and by I found myself on a wide & crowded street

214

that cut across the normal grid of city blocks. I reckoned it was one of the main thoroughfares of San Francisco.

Once again, I forced myself to walk, not run; I did not want to turn heads and thus draw attention to myself. Straight ahead, I saw the rear end of an omnibus just moving off. There were people inside & also up on top.

I did a fast walk to catch up & was now glad of my tippy-tap boots for they went with my girly outfit. I hopped up onto the back of the omnibus just as it was gathering speed.

A man in a uniform was selling tickets. I had pulled out my medicine bag & was fishing in it for my book of tickets, when the ticket-taker pushed me through the door.

'Better get inside, Missy,' he said, patting my pink poke bonnet. 'Your folks will be wondering where you got to.'

Gratefully, I plunged into the crowded carriage & squished past people in their Sunday Best. The omnibus seemed longer than normal ones and there were stairs to the roof in the middle. When I reached the far end I was surprised to find another carriage hooked to mine!

I took a big step over to the next car & pushed through the throng & went up the stairs of the second omnibus & found more people sitting on the roof. I was astonished to see big puffs of white steam rising up from the black smoke stack.

I was not riding an omnibus.

I was riding a steam-powered railroad car disguised as an omnibus!

As a cloud of steam dispersed, I looked back to see if I was still being pursued.

From my lofty vantage point atop the train, I saw a group of four men standing a few blocks back by the alley from which I had emerged only moments before. They were gesturing & looking around. I was glad of the stolen bonnet, for it hid my face. I could see the man with the rose-pink stovepipe hat & the 2 uniformed policemen. Then I spotted someone else, viz: a white-faced man in black with little round blue goggles.

My heart jumped like a jackass rabbit. It was Icy Blue, dauntless conductor for the Overland stage!

As I sat down in the last free seat up there on the top deck of the street train, I thought I saw him turn his little blue goggles in my direction.

Had he spotted me?

I prayed not!

The seats on that street train did not face forward. They faced sideways so you could watch buildings slide by & see right into the upstairs windows. I sat there facing the buildings and not daring to move. By and by the buildings got smaller & sparser & there were more sand dunes and trees. As we went up hill and down, I pondered my revelation and my predicament.

My revelation was this: Mrs. V.F. von Vingschplint was my mortal enemy, Violetta de Baskerville.

My predicament was this: I was a fugitive in black

button-up boots, a daffodil-yellow dress & pink poke bonnet. Most of my money & my bogus pa's revolver & his Meerschaum pipe & my ledger book & pencil stubs had been in the pockets of my abandoned greatcoat. I feared I would never get them back. Thank goodness I had the medicine bag which I always wear around my neck. I patted myself below the neck and felt the reassuring bulge. It contained my Muff Deringer, 5 spare rimfire cartridges, 3 Lucifers, my original ma's flint knife, a silk butterfly, a $20 gold coin & my real pa's Detective Button.

'You going to see the emeu?' said the man sitting next to me.

'Emeu?' I said.

'Why, yes!' he said. 'It is an exotic bird. It looks like a chicken but is as big as a man.'

He recited, *'Oh, say, have you seen at The Willows so green, so charming and rurally true, A singular bird, with a manner absurd, which they call the Australian Emeu?'*

'No,' I said. 'I have never seen this Australian Emeu nor even heard of one until today.'

When the steam train disguised as an omnibus reached the end of the line about 10 minutes later, everybody piled off and headed for a gate by a white picket fence with a big sign above it that read,

The Willows Amusement Park

Although I was intrigued by the prospect of a Giant Australian Chicken, I decided to stay on the street train for its return journey. I needed to get back to the Occidental Hotel & search room 202 for evidence to prove Violetta had plotted against me.

But then I saw a sight that gave me the fantods.

It was an albino man dressed all in black and wearing little round blue goggles. He was riding a big roan gelding up the street.

Had Mr. Icy Blue spotted me atop the street train? Or was he just acting on instinct?

Either way, I had to get away from him!

LEDGER SHEET 36

Mr. Isaac 'Icy' Blue was about to spot me, so I crept off the train and plunged into the crowd of people entering The Willows. I do not like seething masses of mankind but I let myself be carried along with the shuffling & laughing throng. I had to find somewhere to hide out until he had gone.

At a ticket booth beside the gate, they were asking a quarter a person for admittance to the grounds and theater. I had to use the emergency coin in my medicine bag to make 25 cts for the entry fee. I thought they might baulk at the sight of a $20 gold eagle but the ticket man accepted it without comment and made change for me at once, partly in coins, partly in dollar bills.

I put the change back in my medicine bag and slipped it back into the neck of my yellow dress. I was surely glad I carried it around my neck. Otherwise I would be 'broke'.

As soon as I got through the gate I looked for a hiding place. I saw several weeping willow trees near a big white house. I ran past a sign telling me that the Troupe from Gilberts Melodeon was Performing 2 Shows Daily. I parted the curtain of green fronds of the second nearest willow & sought refuge in its cool depths. By and by I peeped out to see if Icy Blue was still on my tail.

I could not see Icy, but I could see that The Willows Amusement Park was aptly named. It had lots of weeping willow trees giving welcome shade on this hot Sunday noontime. I counted six pathways & two duck ponds & various grassy expanses all laid out with stalls and cages. I saw colorful throngs of people dressed in their Sunday best, including ladies in hoopskirts & parasols with children in boots & bonnets.

Over by the white house, a little boy of about 8 years old was walking up and down the line, calling out in a piping voice, 'Get 'em here! All your favorite entertainers. Lotta Crabtree! Minnehaha! Martin the Wizard! Little Jennie Worrell, with or without her sisters! The California Pet! Dressed as a boy or dressed as a girl!'

This last statement caught my ear. A girl dressed as a boy sounded even more interesting than a Giant Chicken.

I waited about 10 minutes, and when I was sure Icy Blue had not entered The Willows Amusement Park, I parted the draping green willow branches & ventured across the grass to where the boy stood with various photographic cards hung around his neck.

'Help you, Miss?' he said.

'Is that the California Pet, a girl dressed as a boy?' I asked, pointing to one of the photographic cards on his board.

'Yup, that is the California Pet,' he said. 'That one shows her blacked up as a minstrel singer,' he added.

I examined the two cards showing the 'California Pet'. I could not believe it: here in Frisco a girl could wear trowsers & get paid to do it! Then I saw a card of an Indian girl. She wore a tight buckskin top & puffy embroidered skirt with leggings & moccasins & she had long wavy black hair with an eagle feather in it. On the border underneath, someone had written *Minnehaha*.

I pulled out two quarters they had given me as change and bought a photographic card of the California Pet dressed as a young man and also a photographic card of Minnehaha.

'Where can I see this California Pet?' I asked the boy. 'Is she performing with Gilbert's Melodeon in that white house?'

'She was here last week but she has gone to Sac City,' he said. 'But you can see Minnehaha. She is right over there on the other side of the pond. Look for her Medicine Show wagon.'

I looked where he was pointing & saw something colorful showing between the willows on the other side of a duck pond. It was a small yellow and blue platform like the outdoor stage of a music hall. It had red curtains. Behind it I could see a wagon and a dun horse tethered nearby. I put my 2 photographic cards in my neck pouch and started towards Minnehaha's show. I kept a sharp lookout in case Mr. Icy Blue had come in by another entrance, but I saw only ladies rolling tenpins on a smooth grassy pitch & men popping pistols at a shooting gallery & children riding Flying Horses round & round a carousel.

At last I found myself standing on green grass in front of a small stage with a wooden frame & the words *Minnehaha's Famous Indian Medicine Show* above & red velvet curtains either side. On the stage was the girl from the photographic card wearing exactly the same outfit of tight buckskin top & puffy embroidered skirt & an eagle feather in her glossy, wavy hair. Minnehaha had a gun belt slung around her hips with cartridge holders and holsters containing a pair of Smith & Wesson's No. 2 with ivory grips. And she kept reaching into a leather shoulder bag and then making a throwing motion with her arm.

She was throwing knives!

She was facing a big wheel like a giant target with a spread-eagled man strapped to it. The wheel was revolving & the crowd was cheering as she threw those knives at him. Some of them were striking only inches from his head & limbs!

I was impressed. So was the crowd. They clapped & cheered.

When the Indian girl had thrown all her knives, she turned the disc so the spread-eagled man was right side up & she unstrapped him & helped him down &

she curtsied to him & he laughed & wiped his forehead with his handkerchief & bowed to the applauding crowd. Minnehaha presented him with a hawk feather for bravery & a signed photographic card of herself as everybody cheered again.

For her next act, she got people to throw tin cans up into the air & she shot holes in them with her pistols & never missed once.

I was entranced & watched until the end of her show. When she had taken her 'curtain calls' she jumped down off the stage & passed through the crowd with an empty quiver instead of a hat. I saw people dropping coins in. When she got to me she winked.

Danged if I did not put in a whole greenback, willy-nilly!

I wandered off in a kind of daze.

My ears were still ringing from the gunshots & my mind was spinning with the revelation that here in California, gals could wear buckskin and/or trowsers in public! I looked up at the blue sky, which was softer than the hard desert sky of Virginia City. The sun warmed me all over, neither too hot nor too cold. I could smell flowers & grass & I even saw a butterfly flutter by.

I thought, 'Maybe Frisco is the place for me.'

Then I thought, 'If I lived here, I could dress like a boy. Or an Indian. Or both!'

And finally, 'I could set up a detective agency here, now that I have burned my bridges back in Virginia City.'

That reminded me of my mission. I needed to make my way back to the Occidental Hotel and search Violetta's room for evidence that would get me off the hook.

I had almost reached the western exit of The Willows when I saw a cage full of monkeys and next to it what appeared to be a giant chicken in his own cage! He had long grayish brown feathers & a black neck & orange eyes. There were some women & children tossing him pieces of bread pulled from a fine white loaf.

I pushed forward to have a better look.

I looked at the Emeu and the Emeu looked at me. He seemed to be smiling.

I thought, 'You are a Misfit like me. But you seem to like it here, too. Maybe Frisco is the place for Misfits.'

Then I got that prickly feeling I get when someone is spying on me. I looked past the giant emeu chicken through the bars of the cage & the pale-green willow branches, and I saw two figures. One of them was in black and one in a blue uniform. The one in black wore a pair of round blue goggles beneath a black bowler hat.

It was Icy Blue, and he had found a policeman.

They were heading my way with purpose & intent!

LEDGER SHEET 37

I LEFT THE EMEU'S CAGE AND WENT RACING BACK the way I had come. I whizzed down crowded paths, across bowling greens & through the fronds of willow branches. As I rounded the carousel of flying horses, I slipped in those danged girly boots and twisted my ankle.

My limpy run would not get me away. I must hide!

Then I saw a wagon such as peddlers use to sell notions and potions. On the side it said *Minnehaha's Medicine Show*. There were wooden steps going up the back and before I knew it I was up those four wooden steps & through a kind of curtain.

Imagine my surprise when I saw Minnehaha herself, sitting in front of a table with a mirror. She was smearing white cream on her face. She whirled round on her seat & gave me Expression No. 4 – Surprise.

I was breathing hard. 'Please can you hide me?' I

asked her in gasping Lakota. 'Some men want to arrest me for something I did not do.'

'What are you doing in my wagon, at all?' she asked in English. She did not appear to understand Lakota.

'Please can you hide me?' I asked her in gasping English. 'Some men want to arrest me for something I did not do.'

Close up, I could see she was taking off face paint with the white cream. She was a bogus Indian!

'Why are they after you?' she asked. Her eyes were wide which meant she was surprised not angry.

'They think I killed a stagecoach driver and that I stole some silver ingots and gold coins.' I pulled off my pink poke bonnet and laid it over my heart. 'But I am innocent.'

'Bejeezus!' she cried. 'You have short hair. Are you a boy or a girl?' Her eyes were wide.

'I am a girl,' I confessed, surprised at how easy it was to tell her. 'Only I hate dressing like one.'

The sound of men's voices reached us. They were outside!

She chewed her lower lip for a moment and her eyes darted here and there, looking for a place where I might hide.

From outside came the sound of footsteps on the wooden stairs and a man's voice. 'Minnehaha? You in there?'

'Yes?' she replied. 'Why?'

'I got a representative of the Overland Stage Company

and a policeman with me. They are looking for a Wanted Person. They would like to question you. May I send 'em in?'

Minnehaha lifted the flounce of the table at which she was sitting & looked at me & pointed underneath.

I did not wait to be asked twice. I jumped under & scrouched down like a mouse in the pantry.

'Enter!' Minnehaha said.

I felt the wagon rock and heard it creak as they came aboard.

'My name is Isaac Blue,' growled a familiar voice. 'I am looking for a dangerous fugitive.' I heard the rustle of paper. 'You seen this girl?' he asked. Then he added. 'Or maybe it is a boy. Folk are not decided.'

'*Miss Prudence Pinkerton,*' said Minnehaha. I could tell from her halting speech that she was reading it. '*Aged 12. Half Sioux Indian. Wearing a fur-trimmed purple cape, a yellow dress & a lighthouse bonnet.*'

'She changed her lighthouse bonnet for a narrow pink one,' he added. 'And she prob'ly ditched the cape.'

'They are offering *one hundred dollars*?' cried Minnehaha.

'Actually,' growled Icy Blue, 'it is two hundred. They have just doubled the reward money.'

I held my breath. All Minnehaha had to do was jump up & pull back the flounce. My crouching form would be exposed & she would be $200 richer. There was nothing preventing her, not even loyalty among Lakota, for she was a bogus Indian.

'Well,' she said at last. 'I do remember a girl in a green and yellow dress and a pink poke bonnet was watching my twelve o'clock show. She put a greenback in my quiver. And just now, on my way in here, I thought I saw that same girl running past.'

'When was that?' said another male voice. It was probably the policeman's.

'Two or three minutes ago,' said Minnehaha. 'Maybe less. She was heading towards the main exit.'

Blue swore in language unfit for publication & I felt the wagon rock as they hurried back down the steps.

'If you hurry,' cried Minnehaha, 'you might catch her!'

A moment later she whispered, 'You can come out now. The coast is clear.'

I came out from beneath the table.

'Thank you for not giving me away,' I said in a low tone. 'I will make it up to you when I find the real robbers and get the reward.'

'That would be bully,' she said, and added, 'We tomboys have to stick together.'

I said, 'Tomboys? What is a tomboy?'

She said. 'Why, someone like you and me! Girls who like to dress like boys and play with guns and knives and such like.'

I said, 'There is a word for us?'

'Why, sure! That word is Tomboy.' She draped her bare white arm around my shoulders; I could feel it firm & cool & round through the merino-wool fabric of my dress. 'Did you think you were alone in the world?'

I nodded. 'I feel a bit like that Emeu in his cage. Like a giant plucked chicken. I used to dress a bit like you. Then my bogus pa burned my buckskins and flannel shirt. I surely do miss them.'

She stood up & went over to a box & opened it & pulled out a pair of buckskin trowsers with beads on them and fringe, too.

'I have outgrown these trowsers,' she said. 'I bet they will fit you. And these moccasins, too. Take them!'

I felt prickly-eyed all of a sudden and there was a bunch in my throat. 'Thank you,' I said. It seemed the least thing made me want to blub these days.

Minnehaha's face showed Expression No. 1 – a Genuine Smile. 'As I am feeling generous,' she said, 'you may borrow one of my wigs until you are safe. This one has hair like yours would be if you let it grow. It came from a real Cheyenne squaw, they say.'

The hair of the wig was beautiful: straight & black, long & shiny.

'Let me pay you for the clothes,' I said. 'I do not like to owe people.' I pulled my medicine bag out from the neck of my daffodil-yellow dress and took out the coins & greenbacks.

'There,' I put the money on her dressing table. 'Eighteen dollars and twenty-five cents. It ain't much but it is all I have left.'

She gathered up the money and pressed it back into my hand. 'I will not take all the spondulicks you have left. But if you get a reward, you can share it with me like you said.' She winked at me. Her eyes were sparkly green and she had freckles on her nose. She rolled up the wig and moccasins in the trowsers to make a kind of parcel. Then she tied it all with a piece of twine.

Once again I had to swallow a lump in my throat.

'What is your real name?' I asked.

'Bridget,' said she. 'Bridget O'Malley. But you can call me Minnie.' She held out her hand & I shook it. Her hand was small, but her grip as firm as a man's. 'I take it you are Prudence?'

'Never call me Prudence,' I said. 'That is a bogus name. My name is P.K. Pinkerton, Private Eye. You can call me Pinky if P.K. seems too strange.'

'You are a private eye?' Her eyes glittered. 'That sounds exciting.'

'Yup,' I said. 'It is exciting, all right. Dangerous, too.'

She said, 'Well, P.K., I was just going to drive into the city to attend Mass. May I take you anywhere? Where are you staying?'

I said, 'I have heard the What Cheer House is only fifty cents a night.'

She laughed. 'The What Cheer House is for men only. And they pack lots of them in each room.'

'Oh,' I said. That part had not been on my cherry-red slip of paper.

She said, 'You got any family or friends here in Frisco?'

'My newspaper friend Mark Twain is here,' I said. 'But he is more an acquaintance than a friend and I don't reckon it would be proper for me to stay with a bachelor, anyways.'

'Anybody else? Any lady friends?'

At first I thought of Mrs. John D. Winters, but then I remembered how she had looked down her nose at me.

Then it came to me. Of course I had gal friends! They had even written to invite me to stay with them any time I was in Frisco.

'Yes!' I said. 'I know a ten-year-old Negro girl named Martha. She was my first client. After she witnessed the murder of a Soiled Dove, the man who done it tried to kill her. She came to me for protection.'

'Did you protect her?' Minnehaha's green eyes were round.

I nodded. 'After I vanquished the killer, Martha left Virginia City for Frisco with a pretty seamstress named Zoe Brown. They invited me to stay with them any time I was in Frisco.'

'Well, there you are, then! Do you know where they live?'

I nodded. '88 Sansome Street was the return address on the letter they sent me.'

'I know that street,' said Minnie. 'It should be easy to find them – if they are still there.'

LEDGER SHEET 38

'**WHAT BROUGHT YOU TO SAN FRANCISCO?**' **MINNIE** O'Malley asked me a short time later.

I was standing behind her in the moving wagon & looking over her shoulder as she drove north up Valencia Street.

I told her my story and concluded with these words, 'I have got to find evidence proving that those two bogus detectives were using me. Otherwise I will be WANTED till the end of time.'

'And you are hoping to find it at the Occidental Hotel?'

'Yes. My mortal enemy Violetta de Baskerville is involved and she resides there.'

'Crouch down!' she hissed. 'I think I see some policemen up ahead.'

I retreated into the dim & rocking interior of the Medicine Wagon.

'All clear,' she said presently, 'but you better lay low.

You can use my bed.'

She had a kind of padded shelf along one side of the cluttered space of her wagon. I stretched out on it.

I must have dozed off for I was suddenly awoken by the juddering noise of iron-rimmed wheels on a corduroy road.

'Whoa!' said Minnehaha, and put her head into the wagon. 'We have arrived.'

'Already?' I said.

She grinned. 'I am guessing you had forty winks!'

I sat up & stretched & yawned. Then I tucked my bundle of new clothes under my left arm & went down the back steps of the wagon & stood blinking in the bright sun. I judged it was about 2 and a half o'clock. When my eyes adjusted, I saw a wood plank street lined with the backs of some nice buildings and the fronts of some crowded-together buildings.

Minnie had stopped the cart outside one of the crowded-together buildings. I saw a chalk number 88 scrawled on the wall beside a door.

'Will you wait a moment to see if they are in?' I asked.

'Surely,' said she.

I knocked on the door and then took a step back.

It was a warm day. I could smell a kind of swampy smell coming up from beneath the wooden road & fresh-baked bread. I could hear hammering & sawing somewhere & also tinkly piano music from a saloon. I could see the same hill that had loomed behind the Occidental Hotel.

'Are we near the Occidental Hotel?' I asked.

She nodded and tipped her head. 'Montgomery is the next street along. And the Broadway Wharf where the inland steamers dock is only a few blocks the other way,' she said.

I knocked again. Louder this time.

No reply.

I called out. 'Martha? Miz Zoe?' (That was what Martha called Mrs. Zoe Brown.)

Then I heard a feminine voice from on high.

'What do you want?'

I looked up to see the pretty head of Mrs. Zoe Brown sticking out of a raised sash window of an upper floor.

I said, 'I want you, Miz Zoe. It is me: P.K. Pinkerton.' I lifted up my pink poke bonnet to show my short dark hair. 'I am in disguise.'

'P.K.?' The head retreated & presently I heard feet on stairs & a moment later the door flew open.

'Oh, P.K.!' She rushed forward & hugged me to her frilly bosom. 'It is wonderful to see you!'

Miz Zoe Brown is a quadroon, which means she has a dash of Negro blood. This makes her skin the color of caramel. She is shapely with big brown eyes & long eyelashes & a smell of honeysuckle.

I squirmed out of her embrace. 'Miz Zoe,' I said, 'I am in trouble and need a place to lay low. Can you shelter me for a day or two?'

'Why, of course!' she cried. 'Martha and I have been hoping for a visit!'

I turned & waved to Minnehaha. She gave me a

thumbs-up. 'Don't be a stranger!' she cried. 'You know where to find me.' Then she flicked the reins & carried on down Sansome Street.

'Oh, P.K.,' said Zoe, again. 'Martha will be overjoyed.'

'She ain't here?'

'No,' said Zoe. 'She works as a chambermaid.'

'Even on the Sabbath?'

Mrs. Zoe Brown nodded. 'Even on the Sabbath. It is harder than I thought it would be to make ends meet.' She gave a sigh & a smile & then looked me up and down. 'That is some disguise. I cannot wait to hear why you are here in Frisco dressed like that.'

She led the way up dark & narrow stairs and said over her shoulder, 'Martha will be home soon. I am just making a pot of tea. Do you like tea? Martha is partial to China tea with a slice of lemon and I have got a taste for it, too.'

I said, 'I have never tried China tea with a slice of lemon.'

'Please excuse the disarray,' said Miz Zoe as she went into a large room. The sun shining through red calico curtains gave it a roseate glow. She pulled open the curtains and a strong flood of afternoon light showed a wrought-iron table with one of those newfangled sewing machines like the one Mrs. Wasserman had used to alter my dress.

'That is my Singer sewing machine,' said Zoe. 'I had to sell Sassy to buy it. All the ladies here in Frisco want machine-sewn seams on their dresses,' she explained.

'Now, how about that cup of tea? We do not have a kitchen but I have a little camp stove and there is a baker downstairs who gives us day-old rolls for a fraction of the price. I have got cinnamon rolls today.'

'You had to sell Sassy?' I asked. (Sassy and Sissy were the names of the two white horses that had pulled Zoe and Martha over the Sierra Nevada.)

Miz Zoe nodded. 'Sissy, too. And the lacquered buggy. Since I wrote to you our fortunes have dipped a mite. This city is a lot like Virginia, only bigger. And the weather is perverse.'

I did not reply, for there was a full-length mirror leaning against one wall & I had just caught a glimpse of myself in it.

I said, 'I look like an Indian brave who has just massacred a little white girl and dressed in her frock for a hideous jest!'

Miz Zoe giggled. 'Well, let us just say that color and style don't flatter you much. Whatever possessed you to wear such a thing?'

I was about to tell her everything when I heard footsteps on the stairs. Was it Martha?

No. These steps were heavy & menacing. Zoe must have thought so, too, for she ran to the door & bolted it with a wooden bolt. Then she stepped back a few paces & put her hand over the base of her throat like some women do when they are upset or scared.

The footsteps on the stairs got closer & closer & closer.

They stopped right outside.

For a moment there was silence.

Then the latch slowly moved but the bolt was down and the door stayed shut.

A sudden heavy pounding on the door made my heart leap up into my throat.

'Dang it! You come out now!' a man's voice shouted. (Only he did not say 'dang'.) 'I know you are in there!'

My heart was beating like a rabbit's. Somehow my pursuers had found me.

I looked at Zoe. 'Is there any way out of here?' I said in a low tone.

Her pretty eyes were round with fear. 'No,' she said. 'There is no way out. I will have to open the door.'

I stared at my erstwhile friend in dismay.

I thought I had found a person I could trust in this strange city. But Mrs. Zoe Brown was about to hand me over to my pursuers!

I LOOKED AROUND DESPERATELY FOR A PLACE TO
hide.

Could I crouch unseen behind that mirror leaning
against the wall? No, it was not big enough.

There was a pair of camp cots but you could easily see
the wood plank floor beneath them.

There were three wooden chairs & a stool & a sugar
crate with a calico tablecloth over it & that expensive
sewing machine in the center of the room.

Then I spotted Zoe's old traveling trunk near the
dimmest corner of the room. On it were two hairbrushes
& a comb & some folded towels & a pitcher & basin. It
was her Toilette Trunk. Quick as a streak of chalk I
nipped behind it, nearly kicking over a half-full chamber
pot as I did so!

My Indian ma once told me about the Bush Trick: if
you crouch behind a bush and imagine real hard that you

are that bush, you become invisible to your pursuers. I tried the Toilette Trunk Trick. I crouched behind that toilette trunk and imagined I was part of it. But I knew that being dressed like a giant daffodil in a pink poke bonnet would not help my ruse.

My eyes were squinched shut but I heard Miz Zoe lift the latch and open the door.

A man's voice said, 'You been hiding from me, Miss Zoe?'

'Of course not,' stammered Miz Zoe. 'I always keep the bolt down against intruders.'

'You got visitors? I told you I would not tolerate no gentlemen callers.'

'I have not entertained a single gentleman caller since I arrived in this city,' said Zoe.

'What about me?' he said.

'You are my landlord.'

That was when I realized the man was after her, not me.

I opened my eyes and peeped over the edge of the trunk.

'Who is that in the corner?' asked the fat & bald man standing in the doorway.

'It is just my friend Pinky from Virginia City. Come out, Pinky,' she added. 'This is my landlord, Mr. Nasby. He will not hurt you.'

I stood up. Mr. Nasby was a fat man with a cigar stub in his mouth. He was not wearing a hat nor coat nor jacket and I could see sweat stains on the armpits of his shirt. His head was as bald & shiny as a billiard ball.

Mr. Nasby pushed past Zoe & came over to me & looked me up and down. He licked his lips. They were kind of blubbery.

'Your name Pinky?' he said. 'It should be Buttercup, you dressed all in yellow like that.' He turned back to Zoe. 'You still have not paid me the last six weeks' rent: fifteen dollars.'

'I can pay you tomorrow,' said Zoe, her hand covering the base of her throat.

'You will pay me today, one way or the other.' He gave her Expression No. 2 – a Fake Smile.

I stepped forward & said, 'I got fifteen dollars.' I pulled out my medicine pouch & fished around in it. My fingers froze as they touched my four-shot Deringer. For a moment I was sorely tempted to pull it out & draw down on him & tell him to vamoose, but that would accomplish nothing so I resisted that wicked impulse. I dug deeper and brought out fifteen paper dollars.

'I don't much like them greenbacks.' Mr. Nasby wrinkled the side of his nose to make Expression No. 3 – Disgust. He looked me up & down in a way that made my skin prickle like when my pet tarantula Mouse perambulates on my arm.

Then he said, 'But I will make an exception for you.'

He took the fifteen 'greenbacks' & licked his fingers & carefully counted them.

Then he took them over to the window and held each one up against the light.

Finally he stuffed them in his trowser pocket & wiped his nose with his forefinger.

He did not thank me but turned to look at Zoe with heavy-lidded eyes. He said, 'Next time, make sure your rent is on time or I will have to take my payment in other ways.'

When he had gone, Zoe kind of slumped down on one of the wooden chairs. She was a bit trembly.

'Oh, P.K.,' she said. 'I feel so bad that you had to pay our rent.'

I tipped the remaining coins in my medicine bag out into my hand. There were 3 silver dollars and 25 cts. 'Here,' I said. 'Take it. It is not much, but it is enough for food and coffee.'

'Oh, P.K.!' she cried. 'Only give me a dollar.' She handed back the quarter & two of the silver dollars & kissed the coin in her hand. 'This is enough for a feast. We will celebrate. You wait here. I will be right back.'

But Martha was back first. I thought it was an old woman coming to visit, by the sound of her slow stumping up the stairs but then she appeared in the doorway. Dressed in a long black shift with a white pinafore, collar and cuffs, she looked tired & thin. But there was no mistaking her.

She recognized me, too, and her dark face lit up with Expression No. 1 – a Genuine Smile. 'P.K.!' she cried. 'You have come to see us at last!'

She ran to me & then stopped. I reckon she remembered I do not like to be touched. Instead of hugging me, she looked me up & down. 'What on earth is you wearing?'

'I know,' I said ruefully. 'I got some buckskin trowsers in there.' I pointed at the parcel Minnehaha had given me. 'But I need to get a shirt to wear with them. I don't suppose you have any spare shirts around here?'

'We sometimes mend men's shirts,' said she. 'But today we only got dresses.'

'Oh,' I said. And then, 'Is that your uniform?'

She nodded. 'I am a chambermaid at the finest hotel in Frisco.'

I said, 'The Occidental Hotel?'

'No,' she said. 'The Lick House Hotel.'

When she said that, I thought of a giant leaning down out of the sky and licking a house. (My mind is peculiar like that sometimes.)

Martha had a drawstring calico bag and she put it on the table. 'I got some fruit and cold bacon. A rich lady left them on her breakfast tray. She hardly touched them at all. Where is Miz Zoe?'

'She has gone shopping,' I said. 'I paid your rent and gave her a dollar for food.'

'Oh, P.K.,' she cried, and this time she did throw her skinny arms around me. 'You always been so good to us.'

I stood still & endured her embrace & after a spell she let me go. She went smiling to the little camp stove & commenced to brewing the pot of tea. She poured me some and dropped in a slice of lemon. It looked like a little yellow wagon wheel floating on top of a brackish pond. She also gave me a cinnamon roll on a saucer.

'Ain't you having one?' I said.

'I ain't hungry,' said Martha brightly. 'This lemon tea is enough for me.' I looked carefully at her face. I was almost certain it was Expression No. 2 – a Fake Smile.

Then I noticed there was only one roll left on the plate.

Some detective I am. I had not even realized they were so poor they could only afford one day-old cinnamon roll apiece!

'Shall we split this one?' I said.

'No need!' cried Mrs. Zoe Brown, coming through the door with a brown paper bag. 'I got fresh ones! And a whole chocolate layer cake because I know it is your favorite, Pinky. And a nice plump lemon for you, Martha! It is her passion,' she said to me.

'Did P.K. really pay our rent?' Martha asked Zoe.

'Yes, indeed,' said Zoe. She was cutting the chocolate layer cake. 'So we are safe for another month or two. Anyways, I expect Mrs. Prendergast will pay me soon for that fine ball gown I made her.' Zoe pointed to a pale blue ball gown hanging on the flour-sack-covered wall of the room.

Martha shook her head. 'She should have paid you by now. What if she wears it and then returns it for alterations like she did last time?'

'Hush, Martha,' said Zoe. 'We do not want to burden P.K. with our troubles.'

As I sipped my lemon tea, I realized I would have to come clean with Miz Zoe and Martha and tell them I was a gal. Would they be mad when they discovered I had been pranking them? Would they tell me to skedaddle?

I did not know how to begin, so I tried to make Small Talk.

'This lemon tea is mighty fine,' I said. 'My friend Stonewall likes lemons. Have you met him?'

'No,' said Martha. 'I don't believe I have.'

But Miz Zoe flushed prettily. 'Is he a friend of your handsome gambler friend, Mr. Jason Francis Montgomery?' she asked.

'Yes, that is the one,' I said. 'He calls himself Stonewall on account of he idolizes General Stonewall Jackson. Jace does not gamble so much these days,' I added. 'He and Stonewall bought themselves a little ranch in Steamboat Springs. They raise mustang horses and have some beef cattle, too.'

'It sounds lovely,' said Mrs. Zoe Brown. She gave a sigh & a smile.

The talk of mustang ponies made me think of Cheeya, my own mustang. I felt my throat go tight. Would I ever see my beloved pony again?

Miz Zoe handed me a plate of chocolate layer cake and a fork. 'You said you were in trouble and needed a place to lay low?'

I said, 'Yes. I am in trouble and need a place to lay low. I was lured into a scheme to help stagecoach robbers and now I am on the run. I have got to get proof of my innocence before the authorities get me.'

'Will you tell us all about it?' said Martha. 'Maybe we can help.'

'I will tell you everything,' I said, 'but first I have a confession to make. It might make you angry at me.'

'Confession?' Martha cried. 'Like folk do after they commit a crime?'

I nodded.

Miz Zoe said, 'You are a dear friend and nothing you can say will change that.'

I could not face them, so I stared at the piece of cake on my lap. I took a deep breath and said, 'Here is my confession: I am not a boy; I am a girl.'

There was an awful moment of silence.

Then Miz Zoe and Martha burst out laughing.

LEDGER SHEET 40

'WHY ARE YOU LAUGHING AT ME?' I ASKED ZOE AND Martha. I felt my cheeks go hot. Dang my changing body!

'We figured out you was a gal months ago,' said Zoe.

'Around Christmas time,' added Martha.

'You did?'

Martha nodded. 'We were talking about you one day,' she said. 'I was saying how nice you looked in that pink dress you had last year and how you were awful purty for a boy, what with your big eyes and long eyelashes and smooth skin—'

'And we just looked at each other and said together: "P.K. is a girl!"' finished Zoe.

I felt a flood of relief. My eyes suddenly filled up with tears. Dang my body!

To hide my embarrassment I ate a forkful of chocolate cake. I was hungry and it was good. It revived my spirits.

Between bites of cake & sips of lemon tea, I told them everything.

I told them about the arrival in Virginia City of my Pinkerton pa & how he did not seem to know me at first but then realized I was his daughter. I told them how he dressed me like a girly-girl, and taught me how to eat & dance & make Small Talk. I told them about his plan to catch some Reb Road Agents by putting a fortune in silver on a decoy stage and then using me in my lighthouse bonnet to put them off the scent of the real silver. I told how the plan 'backfired' when the Rebs held us up anyway & how Dizzy almost saved us but then my pa's evil pard yanked Dizzy off the coach & how we crashed but I was saved by my sacque catching on a tree branch. I told them how I managed to find those Reb Road Agents & tie them up & recover the silver & then my pa arrived & shot them both dead.

'Oh!' cried Zoe & Martha together, and clapped their hands over their mouths.

I told them how my pa & I found the Reb Road Agents' cave in Grizzly Gulch & about the Wells Fargo Strongbox full of gold & how the evil Ray G. Tempest ambushed us & shot my pa & loaded the silver & gold on the six stagecoach horses & left us for dead.

'Oh, P.K.' Zoe's big brown eyes were brimming with tears. 'You have *got* to find another line of business.'

'Ray G. Tempest?' said Martha. 'Is that a real name? It sounds like a raging tempest.'

I nodded. 'It was a sort of *nom de plume*. You guessed

it straight away but I never did. Anyway, I stayed with my gut-shot pa all night, fending off two grizzlies, and then he died at dawn.'

'Oh, P.K.!' they both cried.

'That ain't the worst of it.'

'What could be worse than that?' Zoe exclaimed.

'When I was fixing to bury him, I found some damning documents sewn into the seam of his greatcoat. One of them was a letter to a man named Mr. Jonas Blezzard from a lady staying in the Occidental Hotel. The other was a telegram to a Mr. Chauncy Pridhaume about how he could pretend to be Robert Pinkerton, my pa.'

Once again they clapped their hands over their mouths.

Then Zoe took her hands away and tilted her head to one side. 'Do you mean that the man who died was not your pa after all?'

'That is exactly what I mean. He was a bogus detective and a bogus pa.'

'But why?' cried Martha. 'Why would they play such a trick on you?'

I said. 'I think it has to do with the author of one of the letters – the lady in the Occidental Hotel. She is my mortal enemy, Mrs. Violetta de Baskerville.'

Martha frowned. 'Why mortal?' she asked. 'What does that mean?'

I said, 'It means she is prepared to kill if necessary. She is a Black Widow. That means she marries men for their money and then kills them. I am sure she is behind this.'

'Why is she *your* enemy?' asked Zoe.

'Because I stopped her from marrying my friend, Poker Face Jace.'

'Oh!' Zoe put her hand to the base of her throat.

I said, 'If only I still had those documents. Then I could prove my innocence and get the bulge on her.'

Martha said, 'What do you mean by doc-you-mints?'

I said. 'I mean letters and telegrams and suchlike. The ones I found in my bogus pa's greatcoat.'

'What happened to them?' asked Zoe.

I said, 'I put them in the pockets of my bogus pa's greatcoat along with a full account of my misadventures in a ledger book. I was wearing that coat but someone snatched it from me at the Unitarian Church this morning. Now I have no proof. If only I could sneak into Violetta's room at the Occidental Hotel and see if there are any more incriminating letters. She is in room two-oh-two but I don't know how to get in there.' I trailed off and rested my elbows on my knees and my chin in my hands.

For a moment we were all quiet. Then Martha jumped up and clapped her hands.

'I got an idea!' she cried. 'An idea of how you can get the bulge on that nasty Violetta!'

LEDGER SHEET 41

'**What is your idea?**' **I asked Martha.** '**Do you** know how can I get into Violetta's hotel room?'

Martha nodded. 'All the maids at all them big hotels on Montgomery Street have uniforms like mine. And we can go anywhere in the hotel and don't nobody get suspicious.'

I sat up straight. 'Martha, that is a bully idea! Would you really be willing to sneak into Violetta's room at the Occidental Hotel and look for evidence?'

'Oh lawd, no!' she squealed. 'Not me! I thought *you* could dress up in *my* outfit and sneak in. I had to help out a friend who works at the Occidental Hotel one time,' she added, 'so I knows my way around a little. What room did you say that Violetta lady is in?'

'Room two-oh-two,' I said.

'Then it is easy,' said Martha. 'All you have to do is go into the side entrance of the Occidental Hotel – it is on

Bush Street – then go in the second door on the right – or is it left? Anyways, it is a white door. In there you will find lots of folded towels. Get two of them clean towels and go up some narrow stairs to the second floor and ask any chambermaid passing by if she could open the door to room two-oh-two as the lady has requested fresh towels and you have left your pass key downstairs. They will let you in. If someone is in the room, then just say "Excuse Me" and leave the towels and go.'

I said, 'What if the people in the hotel lobby recognize me from this morning when I was dressed in my pa's greatcoat?'

'You probably will not see those people from the lobby,' said Martha. She tipped her head on one side. 'Also, when I wear my uniform folk look right through me. It is like I ain't even there. Like I am a piece of furniture.' She stood up. 'If you wear this I reckon they won't see you neither.'

'Will I have to put on black face?'

'Lawd, no! We got all colors of skin. There is even a half-Indian maid like you.'

I nodded and looked at the uniform she was wearing. 'Will it fit me?'

'I think so,' said Zoe. 'I made it with room for Martha to grow.'

'But what about the cap?' I said. 'It ain't much more than a handkerchief and it will not cover my short hair. I don't have a girl's wig anymore— Wait! Yes, I do!' I went to my buckskin bundle & undid the twine & showed them the beautiful buckskin trowsers & the beaded moccasins & the wig of straight black hair.

'Why, this is just like your own hair,' said Martha, taking the wig. 'Only long.'

Zoe said, 'I can pin this hair up and then we can put on Martha's handkerchief cap.'

Martha was taking off the white pinafore that went over her black dress. 'I feel sure this uniform will help you get the bulge on Mrs. Violetta de Baskerville!'

I nodded. 'Only she ain't called Mrs. de Baskerville anymore. Now she is going by the name of Mrs. V.F. von Vingschplint.'

Martha stopped unpinning her white handkerchief cap. 'What did you say her new name was?'

'Mrs. V.F. von Vingschplint,' said I. 'Why do you ask?'

Martha frowned. 'I ain't sure.' Then her face lit up. 'I know!' she cried. 'She is getting married tomorrow afternoon and they is having a big dance at my hotel around 4 o'clock. I know because it is all happening at "short notice" and they have to clear out the dining room to make it a ballroom. Everybody is talking about it,' she added. 'They say the Cream of San Francisco society will be there.'

I said, 'That figures. She is always marrying and burying. What is the name of the man she is to wed?'

Martha shrugged. 'Ain't nobody talking about him. They are all talking about her and about what she will wear.'

'Well, I ain't wearing this thing ever again,' I said as I

took off the daffodil-yellow frock. 'You can have it!'

Miz Zoe added hot water from the kettle to the cold water in the pitcher on the Toilette Trunk and I washed myself while Martha changed into a dress of the same red calico they had used for their curtains and tablecloth.

Martha loaned me a pair of clean bloomers and a chemise and then helped me put on her black shift. It had a white collar & also white cuffs at the end of long black sleeves. It was a little tight around my bosom even though I do not have much there yet, but the pinafore covered up what little I got. Miz Zoe put my new wig on me & coiled up the straight black hair & pinned that little white handkerchief cap on top.

'Black and white suits you better than daffodil yellow,' said Miz Zoe with a nod.

Martha clapped her hands. 'You look fine dressed as Prudence the chambermaid.'

'Never call me Prudence,' I said. 'I am almost one hundred percent certain that is not my Christian name.'

When I spoke those words, I suddenly got a queasy feeling in the pit of my stomach and a kind of niggle at the back of my head, like I should be putting two and two together somehow. But I could not think what the 2 + 2 might equal.

It was niggling me as I went out of Martha and Zoe's apartment and onto wooden-plank Sansome Street.

It was niggling me as I turned south along wide Montgomery Street in the late afternoon sunshine, past stock-brokers with their walking sticks & women in their bonnets with the slanting sun lighting up their parasols.

It niggled me as I went into the side entrance of the Occidental Hotel & picked up two fluffy towels from a room with a white door & went up the service stairs to the second floor & asked a passing chambermaid if she could open 202 as the lady had requested fresh towels and I had left my pass key downstairs.

But when I entered the spacious hotel room and smelled Jace's cigar, I suddenly put two and two together and knew why I felt queasy.

I remembered a line from the letter in my bogus pa's pocket, viz: *She herself does not know what the initials P and K signify.*

How had Violetta found out about my not knowing the P and the K?

It could only be from the one person apart from me who was privy to that fact: Poker Face Jace.

He had betrayed me.

That was the awful 2 + 2 it had taken me so long to put together.

LEDGER SHEET 42

Mr. Jason Francis Montgomery smokes a high-tone Cuban cigar called Mascara, which means 'mask' in Spanish.

I guess all this time he had been wearing a 'mask' of deception.

I thought, 'I saved Jace from Violetta's love snares last winter, but here is evidence of his presence in her hotel room.'

Then I thought, 'She has got him under her spell again and recruited him into her army of lovers.'

And finally, 'I bet he is the one she is about to marry.'

I almost got a bad case of the Mulligrubs as I stood there in that west-facing bedroom lit all gold in the light of late afternoon. But instead of going into a bad trance, I felt I might be sick instead, so I looked around for the jug & basin. I saw them sitting on a chest of drawers and started towards them.

Then I heard an inner door open behind me.

Someone was here in Violetta's suite!

I kept walking towards the chest of drawers but turned my head just a little. I had an impression of a tall man dressed all in black.

Jace!

I knew it was him by his smell & by the way he moved & by the way the whole room held its breath.

I hoped my black & white outfit would make me no more noticeable than a chair or a spittoon. I hoped he would see a chambermaid who had come in to replace some towels. When I reached the chest of drawers I put the towels beside the jug & bowl. Then I turned & started for the door with my head down, willing him not to recognize me.

'P.K.?' he said in a low voice. 'Is that you?'

I stopped. I could feel my cheeks burning.

Then I took a breath and turned to face him. 'Yes,' I said. 'It is me.'

His eyes got wider. 'Dang!' he said. 'I almost did not recognize you.' He trailed off & took his cigar from the ashtray & sucked on it. 'What are you doing here?'

'I came to get the bulge on Mrs. Violetta de Baskerville AKA Mrs. von Vingschplint,' I said. 'And also on you, and on whoever else is in cahoots with her.'

'You think I am in cahoots with her?' said Jace. He blew smoke down. 'Why, I have not laid eyes on her for nearly half a year!'

'You are a lying, two-faced varmint,' I said. I tried

to make my voice calm but I could hear it was shaky. 'You were the only other person on this earth who knew about my initials. You told Violetta so she could use that information against me. That is how a trickster convinced me he was my long-lost pa.'

'D-mn!' said Jace. He turned away and then turned back. 'It ain't like that, P.K.,' he said, but he was rubbing the back of his neck with his free hand. He himself had taught me that was a sign that someone was probably lying!

'It ain't like what?' I said. 'You swore you had not told anybody. Now I know you are a lying varmint. You being here in her room proves it!'

I went to the door & opened it.

'Dang it, P.K.,' he said. 'Don't go. Let me explain.'

'No,' I said. 'I never want to see you again.'

My eyes were blurring up & I felt sick again so I went out fast & closed the door behind me hard. I ran to the service stairs & down & along a dark corridor & out into the streets of San Francisco all lit with sunshine like watered-down honey.

I headed towards the setting sun and walked up hill and down.

I was in a perverse state of mind.

I was having a kind of Civil War in my head.

Part of me was thinking, 'Jace would not betray me. He has always been a friend to me.'

But another part said, 'He was there in her hotel room. He is her lover!'

257

By and by I found myself at the fort they call *The Presidio*.

The sun had set & lit up a few clouds & I saw the vast sparkling bay & what I now know is the blue Pacific Ocean through a gap in the dusky hills.

Somewhere in the Presidio, a lone trumpet was playing Taps, which is sad and beautiful at the same time.

That tune always makes me think of death.

I closed my eyes and said, 'Dear Lord, why is it that everybody I care about either dies or betrays me? Will I ever find a place I can call home?'

LEDGER SHEET 43

WHEN I GOT BACK TO MARTHA AND ZOE'S, I FOUND they had company.

'Look who's here!' cried Martha, as I stepped through the door into their one-room abode. 'Look who done come to help you.'

The dim lamplight showed me a Chinese boy in a worsted suit and a youth with blond hair & glinting wire-rimmed spectacles. It was Ping & Affable Fitzsimmons.

'P.K.?' said Affie. 'Is that you?'

'Yes,' I said. 'I am disguised as a chambermaid. I was trying to get the bulge on a suspect.' I turned to Ping. 'What are you doing here?' I asked him. 'I thought you had renounced me.'

Ping shrugged & scowled at the floor. 'Just when I finish sending reply to your telegram, another telegram comes in. Says you are wanted for robbery. I think maybe you need help so I go to office to get ready. Find Affie waiting there.'

Affie nodded. 'I went to your office to warn you that I was uneasy about your father's claim to be Scottish,' he said. 'There was something not quite right about his accent. When Ping told me you had telegraphed to say your father was a fake and that you were pursuing his double-crossing partner to Frisco, I offered to accompany Ping in order to help you,' he added.

I said, 'You came all the way to Frisco just to help me?'

'My parents are building a house here and have rented a suite at a hotel until it is ready,' said Affie. 'I convinced them to let me return a few days early. They were happy to let me travel on my own as Ping was going with me,' he added.

'We catch noon stage out of Virginia,' said Ping. 'Very bumpy. Very fast. Arrive Sac City around midnight. Get few hours' sleep. Catch morning ferry. Arrive Frisco three o'clock today. Go to What Cheer House, but they no know you.'

'It is a hotel just for men,' I said. 'How did you find me?'

'I remember you get letter from Zoe last Christmas. But don't remember address.'

'Jolly good luck you were in the directory,' said Affie to Miz Zoe. 'And that you still reside here.'

'You did good detective work,' I said to them.

Ping said, 'We also got info on Chauncy Pridhaume

260

and Jonas Blezzard. They are Confidence Tricksters.'

I said, 'What is a "Confidence Trickster"?'

Affie said, 'That is what they call people who play a "Confidence Game". This is their modus operandi. First they find a rich Mark. Then they dangle some bait. They get *you* to come to *them*. That is how they gain your trust.'

I was confused. 'Who is Mark?' I asked.

'The "mark",' explained Affie, 'is what they call the victim, that is to say the person they want to trick. When the mark trusts them, they isolate him or her from friends and family.'

Ping nodded. 'Like vaqueros separate calf from herd for branding.'

'Once you are abandoned by friends and family,' said Affie, 'these Confidence Tricksters become your new friends. They get you to trust them and loan them money and leave them property in wills. It was easy for Pridhaume and Blezzard to separate you from your friends, and partner,' he glanced at Ping. 'All they had to do was show that you had been deceiving everybody.'

'I warn't deceiving,' I said. 'I was just dressing in trowsers and a flannel shirt.'

'You pretend to be boy,' said Ping. 'That is big lie. That is like Chauncy Pridhaume personating your pa.'

'I was not trying to be someone else,' I protested. 'I was just trying to be me.'

But I knew Ping was right. I was not much better than the man who had personated my pa.

'To thine own self be true,' quoted Affie. Then he scratched his head. 'What I cannot understand,' he said, 'is why they directed their deception at *you*. Ping tells me you have some valuable shares in a mine that might possibly be worth thirty thousand dollars. That is a good deal of money, but there are richer people in this region. *Much* richer.'

'It is not just about money,' I said. 'It is about revenge.'

'Why?' said Ping. 'What man could hate you so much?'

'Not man,' I said. 'Woman.'

Ping's eyes went wide. 'Violetta!' he said. 'You stop her marry Jace last winter in Carson City. You send her back to Frisco with tail between legs.'

'Yes,' I said. 'My mortal enemy, Mrs. Violetta de Baskerville. I reckon she wanted to take everything from me. My friends, my money, my livelihood and even my life.' I looked at the floor. 'The worst thing is that she convinced my mentor to betray me.'

'Your mentor?' said Affie.

I nodded. 'A gambler and rancher, name of Poker Face Jace.'

'No,' cried Miz Zoe. 'That cannot be!'

'It is true,' I said. 'Jace told Violetta a certain fact about me that was the key to their success in tricking me.'

Ping stared, too. 'You think Jace is in cahoots with them?'

I nodded and kept my eyes on the raw-plank floor. 'He is the only one apart from me who knew the secret of the

262

P and the K. I reckon he decided to go back to Violetta.'

'Oh, P.K.,' cried Zoe. 'I cannot believe he would knowingly harm you. He has been so good to you.'

'I know,' I said. 'But I found him in her hotel room a few hours ago. I reckon he is the one she is going to wed.'

'Oh,' said Zoe. She had just stood up to boil more water, but now she sat down real sudden.

'I say!' cried Affie. 'We have a suite at the Lick House Hotel and there was a notice pushed under our door saying that there is to be a big wedding ball in the dining room tomorrow afternoon.'

'That's it!' cried Martha. 'That's the one!'

'All the residents of the hotel are invited,' added Affie.

'Who is the groom-to-be?' I asked.

'I didn't examine the details,' said Affie. 'Let's all go back to my hotel and find out.' He looked at me with twinkling spectacles. 'For that is not all I have to show you.'

LEDGER SHEET 44

PING & AFFIE & MARTHA & MIZ ZOE & I SET OFF
through the warm San Francisco night towards the Lick
House Hotel.

As we walked, I looked at Ping & Affie. 'How did the
two of you find out so much about those Confidence
Tricksters?'

Affie gave me a Genuine Smile. 'Teamwork! Ping and
I did some research and found damning evidence against
them. It is not hard when you have access to a hundred
newspapers, magazines and telegrams.'

'Where do you have access to a hundred newspapers,
magazines and telegrams?' I asked him as we crossed
Montgomery Street.

'Right here!' he said pointing to the gas-lit entryway
of the Lick House Hotel. 'All the best hotels have reading
rooms with books, magazines and newspapers. This
one even has a desk where you can send and receive

telegrams. That's where Ping found the article about two Confidence Tricksters named Chauncy Pridhaume and Jonas Hurricane.'

'Jonas *Hurricane*?' I said. 'Not Blezzard?'

'Probably another pseudonym,' said Affie, and added, 'A storm by any other name . . .' He looked at me. 'Would you like to see the Reading Room here?'

'I would rather see the notice about tomorrow's wedding ball,' I said. 'I want to know who that Black Widow has caught in her net.'

'Then I'll take you to our suite. It's only one floor up.'

As Affie led the way through a lobby even more high-tone than the lobby of the Occidental Hotel, Ping fell into step beside me.

I glanced over at him. 'I am sorry I pulled the wool over your eyes for so long,' I said. 'It is just that I hate dressing like a girly-girl. And I did not rightly know how to tell you.'

Ping did not look at me. He said, 'I am not very good detective if I cannot tell difference between girl and boy.'

'You *are* a good detective,' I said. 'Also a danged good bookkeeper. And a good pard,' I added.

He grunted. But I saw his eyes flick towards me and then quickly away.

Upstairs, Affie used a key to open a door & we all followed him in to a room softly lit by gaslight.

'I'll be right back,' said Affie, and disappeared through another door.

Ping & Zoe & Martha & I looked around the room

while we waited for him. It had Turkey carpets and wooden bookcases and a four-poster bed just for Affie. There were books and specimen cases on just about every surface.

On one of the tables was a tray with a small gauze pyramid stretched over bent strips of cane. I had once seen someone put a similar net dome over a platter of food at a church picnic in Virginia City. It was for keeping the bugs off. But this one held bugs in. It contained my butterfly branch!

'Look!' I said. 'My butterfly branch.'

'Affie brought it,' said Ping. 'We took turns holding it on the stagecoach.'

'Look!' said Martha. 'One of them has hatched. It is all crumply.'

I looked closer. 'It is drying its wings,' I said. 'I cannot tell what species it is yet.'

Then I spotted something else in a glass case on a polished mahogany table.

'Mouse!' I cried. I stepped forward & sure enough, there was my pet tarantula in his little glass case. No: two tarantulas. Looking closer I saw that one tarantula was the husk of the new one!

'Clever Mouse,' I said. 'You cast off your old skin.'

Ping scowled down at my tarantula and its husk. 'Both look the same,' he observed. 'What good is shed your husk if you are the same inside?'

'Eureka!' cried Affie, coming back in with a piece of cream cardboard in his hand. 'Here is the notice. Mrs.

V.F. von Vingschplint is marrying Jonas Blezzard!'

'Jonas Blezzard,' said Ping. 'AKA Ray G. Tempest.'

'Of course!' I cried. 'The man who killed my bogus pa is the one in cahoots with her. But how did he get here so fast? He was traveling in an ox-cart.'

'Maybe he got a faster carriage,' suggested Affie.

'Maybe he is not yet here, but sends telegram,' offered Ping.

'When did you hear about the wedding?' I asked Martha.

'Late yesterday afternoon,' she said.

'Do you know what this means?' cried Zoe.

I nodded. 'That it all makes sense.'

'Also,' said Zoe. 'It means Jace did not betray you.'

'No,' I said. 'He betrayed me all right. He just ain't the one marrying her.'

'We have to tell the police about Violetta and Blezzard!' cried Affie. To me he said, 'You have got to testify against them in a court of law.'

'I cannot testify against nobody,' I said. 'I am a half-Indian and WANTED by the Law. No jury will listen to me nor will any judge accept my testimony.'

'But that ain't fair!' said Martha. She was standing by the single crumpled butterfly in its gauze prison. It was night & it was sleeping. But in the morning when light streamed through the east-facing window all his fellows would emerge & dry their wings & the net would soon be full of trapped creatures.

'Eureka!' I cried. 'I have just had an idea of how

to trap Mr. Jonas Blezzard like a butterfly in a net.' I looked around at them all and said, 'Will you help me implement a bold and dangerous plan? It involves us putting on a music-hall type show.'

'You bet!' cried Martha. 'Especially if it means I get to disguise myself or dance a jig.'

'Yes,' said Zoe. 'Especially if you need costumes.'

'Yes,' said Ping. 'I have been practising magic tricks.'

I looked at Affie. 'You would have the biggest part to play,' I said.

He grinned & saluted & I reckoned my plan might just work, for by chance he quoted the same verse I had heard in church earlier that morning, viz: *'We are your troops and we will be willing on the day of your battle.'*

LEDGER SHEET 45

THE NEXT MORNING I WOKE TO THE SMELL OF coffee and doughnuts.

'Have you finished it?' I heard Martha whisper.

'Just this very moment,' said Zoe, and then I heard her give a big yawn.

I sat up to find I was on one of the camp cots, covered in a soft blanket. I had stayed up late talking to Miz Zoe and Martha about woman things. Then Zoe had let me take her cot as she had an 'All Night Job'.

'Look what Miz Zoe done made you last night,' said Martha. She held up a beautiful quilted jacket. It looked like a soldier's padded jacket – if the soldier had been a gal.

'Martha helped,' said Zoe. 'We did it together.'

I blinked at them. 'What is it?'

Zoe said, 'It is a Zouave jacket, named after a famous infantry regiment from New York. Such jackets are all the fashion for ladies this season.'

I said, 'That was your All Night Job?'

Zoe nodded.

'I got some sleep,' said Martha, 'but Zoe was up all night.'

I pushed away the cover & got up off the camp cot. My legs were stiff from all the hill walking I had done the day before. I splashed some water on my cheeks from the basin & dried my face using one of the towels on Miz Zoe's Toilette Trunk, then went over to where Martha stood holding my new jacket. It was made from different scraps of cloth. Most Zouave shirts have curlicues but this one had zigzags.

I said, 'I like this a lot. I am partial to zigzags.'

'The zigzags were Martha's idea,' said Zoe. She was over at the camp stove, brewing a pot of coffee.

I took it in my hands and felt it. 'How did you make it so soft?'

'We used old scraps,' Zoe said. 'But they are clean,' she added hastily.

Martha said, 'We have a special way of sewing seams so they do not rub. Put it on.'

I put my new Zouave Jacket on over the fresh cotton chemise and bloomers. Then I put on the things Minnehaha had given me the day before: the fringed buckskin trowsers & beaded moccasins. Oh, how good they felt! Finally I put on the wig. The shiny black hair was not pinned up but flowing down.

'Oh, Pinky!' said Martha.

And Zoe said, 'How does it feel?'

'It feels bully,' I said. I swallowed hard. 'How do I look?'

'See for yourself,' said Zoe. She said it with a kind of hush in her voice as she turned me to face the mirror leaning against the wall.

I could not believe my eyes.

I saw a girl with fringed buckskin trowsers and a zigzag Zouave jacket & long, silky black hair. She had slightly slanting black eyes & toffee-colored skin & symmetrical features.

She was beautiful.

I said, 'She is beautiful.'

Zoe said. 'No, *you* are beautiful.'

Martha said, 'You look like a buckskin butterfly.'

When she said that, I remembered something. A few months ago in Eagle Valley, I had dreamed of a beautiful half-Indian girl. And now there she stood reflected in the full-length mirror. Almost.

'I need a sombrero hat and some firearms,' I murmured.

'What?' said Zoe.

'Nothing,' I said. And then, 'Do you think I will attract much attention walking down Montgomery or Market Street dressed like this?'

'I should say so!' laughed Zoe.

'You will attract forty kinds of attention!' Martha giggled.

'Then do you have something I could wear that will help me not attract attention?' I asked.

Martha nodded. 'I can adjust one of Miz Zoe's old frocks,' she said. 'They are still a mite big for me but one of them might fit you.'

'Red calico?' I asked.

'How did you guess?' asked Miz Zoe with a yawning smile.

I said, 'I have got to go to The Willows and see if Minnehaha will help us in our plan to trap Jonas Blezzard. Will you come with me?'

Martha sighed. 'I would love to go and watch them jig-dancers,' she said. 'Miz Zoe and I saw Little Jennie Worrell at the Melodeon one time. But I got to go in to work this morning on account of us getting ready for the big wedding dance.'

'And I have got to catch forty winks before this afternoon,' said Miz Zoe.

After a breakfast of black coffee and chocolate layer cake, I put on the disguise of a red calico dress and a straw bonnet & went outside to find it foggy and cool. I caught the Mission Railroad Cars to The Willows. I stayed downstairs in a corner where nobody would notice me.

It was still early on a Monday morning and I found The Willows open but almost deserted and no shows starting until noon. It was foggy there, too, and I was glad of it, for it offered a kind of protection. I breathed a sigh of relief when I found Minnie relaxing in her

Medicine Show Wagon. She was reading the paper and smoking a pipe. A pipe!

I told her my plan and asked if she could help.

She said she was meeting an important Event Manager that evening for dinner but as it was very quiet on Mondays, I could use her equipment. She said her knife-throwing trick was easy & that she would show me how to do it.

She took me outside to her portable stage and showed me how to do it.

'Can you pack up this stage and move it?' I asked.

'Sure. I do it every time I move on,' she said.

'Can you let me borrow the actual stage for the afternoon?'

'Sure,' she said, 'Where shall I bring it?'

'Lick House Hotel,' I said. 'About 2 pm, if you can. I will be waiting.'

The fog was just burning off when I got back to Montgomery Street and the Lick House Hotel. The lobby and dining room were a hive of activity and nobody stopped me or even looked at me when I went inside and up to Affie's room.

Ping and Affie and I discussed the final arrangements over lunch in Affie's suite and at 2 pm we were downstairs as Minnie pulled up with her medicine wagon full of stage equipment. Affie had recruited some hotel staff to help us.

When I went back to Sansome Street to change my attire, I found a lady coming downstairs carrying a pale blue ball gown.

'That was Mrs. Prendergast,' said Zoe when I came in. 'She just paid me for this job and two others! We are now flush, not bust. Here are the sixteen dollars I owe you, Pinky. How are the arrangements going for our music hall?' she added.

'Everything is all set up,' I said. 'Let us go and mete out some justice!'

LEDGER SHEET 46

IN THE LICK HOUSE HOTEL, A DINING ROOM THE size of a cathedral had been transformed into a ballroom the size of a cathedral. According to Affie, the room was modeled on the banquet hall of a famous French palace.

Violetta and Blezzard were holding their wedding reception here on account of this hotel was even grander than the Occidental and quickly becoming all the fashion because of this splendid ballroom, the finest in the state of California. The room was made of cream-colored marble with gold trim & columns & the biggest mirrors I had ever seen that doubled and tripled the other walls so that it seemed there were about ten more cathedral-sized rooms giving off of this one.

If you looked up, the ceiling was so high it made you dizzy. There were little arched alcoves on the walls up high, with circular windows at their backs and rails at their front. That was where the musicians went. There were three fiddles and a cello up in one of those alcoves and they were already playing waltzes & polkas.

All around the sides of the dining room stood linen-covered tables laden with sugared fruits & candied nuts & blancmanges & suchlike. Turkey carpets had been rolled up to reveal a wooden parquet floor specially built for dancing.

On the north side of the ballroom, set between two fancy paintings of pine-clad mountains, and hiding a door leading to the kitchens, stood Minnehaha's stage. She and Affie had directed hotel staff and they had set it up real good.

It looked like a miniature music hall, with a stage, curtains and side bits. You could get to the back of the stage by a nondescript door leading to a corridor used by waiters to take away dirty dishes & suchlike. Miz Zoe was in a room back there with my 'troops', viz: Martha, Ping and Affie.

Without Affie I never could have done it, but he had spoken to the hotel owner and said it was a wedding present from his pa, Sir Fitzhugh Fitzsimmons, who was not only a famous naturalist and jungle explorer, but also distantly related to Queen Victoria.

It was not yet 4 o'clock but people had started arriving & were already dancing. The men wore black & white. The women sported puffy silks & satins & foulards & suchlike. Their ball gowns matched the colors of the sugared fruits & candied nuts.

I was peeping out from between the closed curtains

of the stage to see if my mortal enemies had arrived yet.

I was hiding as I did not want to let Violetta or her evil husband know I was in Frisco and 'on to them'. But by and by I got impatient and ventured out onto the dance floor.

I was wearing my wig with the long black hair and a hawk feather for bravery in it & my zigzag Zouave jacket & my fringed deerskin trowsers & butter-soft moccasins.

I was not prepared for people's reactions when they saw me in my Indian gal get-up. Some of the women uttered little cries and fanned their fans, whereas several of the men swore under their breath and raised their eyebrows.

Suddenly Jace stood before me, tall & slim & dressed in black, smelling of musky pomade and Mascara cigars.

'P.K.?' he said. 'Is that you? D-mn me! Ain't you a vision?'

I did not reply but walked around him & carried on through the twirly, swirly couples. He was not marrying Violetta, but he had betrayed my secret to her. It was his fault I had been made the target of a cruel Confidence Game designed to ruin and kill me.

Then the musicians struck up a different song & the couples stopped dancing & turned to the main doorway of the ballroom & began to applaud.

Dang! The bride and groom had arrived! All might be lost if they spotted me.

Quick as a whip crack, I skedaddled back to the curtained stage. I slipped between the red velvet curtains to find Affie and Zoe just setting up the man-sized, knife-catching wheel target.

'Blezzard's a comin!' I cried. 'Violetta and her new husband are here!'

'Good!' said Affie. He draped a dust sheet over the target.

Zoe went to the doorway at the back of the stage and called out softly, 'Martha, are you ready?'

Martha emerged from the door leading to the kitchens and mounted the two steps to the back of the stage. She was wearing my daffodil-yellow frock! But it looked bully on her.

'Martha, you look bully,' I said.

'I know!' she replied. 'I am frightened and happy all mixed together.'

'Stage fright,' said Affie. 'Every good performer experiences it.' He glanced up at the little orchestra in their lofty alcove halfway up the wall & gave them a little wave. Immediately they stopped their waltz & began to play a jaunty Irish Jig.

Miz Zoe pulled the curtain from one side (and stayed hidden behind it) & I pulled the curtain from the other (being careful to stay hidden, too). We each had a tiny crack to spy on the audience.

The crowd said 'Oh!' as Martha danced out onto the stage. She danced a capering little jig. Her yellow skirt spun & the green flounces flounced & her feet twinkled & her teeth beamed. I was so astonished that I stood there with my mouth hanging open, you bet!

Martha finished her jig and the room erupted in thundering applause.

Affie stepped forward. Did I mention he was wearing his jungle explorer outfit of palm-leaf sunhat & beige linen knickerbockers?

'Welcome to the Lick House Music Hall,' he said in his English accent, 'a wedding present from my father, the famous naturalist and jungle explorer, Sir Fitzhugh Fitzsimmons, in honor of the newlywed couple Mr. and Mrs. Blezzard.' Affie gestured towards Martha. 'Please express your appreciation for Miss Martha May and her energetic jig.'

Everybody expressed his or her appreciation.

I saw Violetta and her groom exchange smiles.

'And now,' cried Affie in a carrying voice, 'straight from the Spice Courts of China, I bring you Ping the Wizard and his "magic rings"!'

'Ping?' I said to myself. 'The Wizard?'

The musicians started playing oriental-type music as Ping came up the steps onto the stage. He was dressed in jade-green silk pajamas and a skullcap. He had three silvery metal hoops about the size of big dinner plates. He could put them together in a chain and then pull them apart unbroken! He bowed! He smiled! I was amazed and so were the people.

The crowd said, 'Ooh!' and 'Ah!'

Once again I saw Violetta and Jonas Blezzard look at each other. They had each raised an eyebrow. I think that was Quizzical or maybe Ironikle but I could not be sure as my Christian ma had not taught me those Expressions.

'Ladies and Gentlemen,' cried Affie. 'Express your appreciation for Ping the Wizard and his "magic rings"!'

Ping bowed and everyone clapped.

'Before our finale,' said Affie, 'I would like to pose some conundrums.'

There was a happy murmur. San Franciscans obviously liked conundrums.

'How is matrimony like a game of cards?' Affie gestured towards Violetta and Blezzard and then answered his own question: 'The woman has a heart, the man takes it with his diamonds, and then her hand is his!'

Everyone laughed and some people clapped.

Through my spyhole I noticed that Violetta & Blezzard were not among those clapping.

'What four letters of the alphabet would frighten a thief?' Affie pointed at Blezzard. 'O I C U!'

The crowd groaned and there was a smattering of applause.

Violetta and her groom were no longer smiling.

'And now for our grand finale!' cried Affie. He glanced to where I was waiting behind one of the curtains. I nodded.

'Before we start, I require a volunteer!' cried Affable. 'A man of exceptional bravery and fortitude. I need a fearless hero to show his wife he will always protect her.'

From my spyhole I saw several men raise their hands. Mr. Jonas Blezzard was not one of them. He was still too busy giving Affie Expression No. 5 – Anger and/or Suspicion.

'You sir!' cried Affie, pointing at Blezzard. 'Yes, you! Ladies and Gentlemen, the happy groom has volunteered to put himself in the hands of a lovely savage! Please applaud Mr. Jonas Blezzard!'

To the universal sound of clapping, Mr. Jonas Blezzard AKA Ray G. Tempest slowly made his way forward. He wore an expression which I could not read.

'And now the lovely savage,' cried Affie, 'all the way from the Black Hills of Dakota: Kimimila!'

I stared at him for a moment in surprise. He had used the Lakota word for 'butterfly'! He had given me a new Indian name!

I took a breath, stepped out onto the stage and faced the dancers.

Everybody gasped.

Then I heard a nearby woman clap her hands and say, 'Ain't she pretty!'

Another lady said, 'I wish *I* could wear trowsers!'

A man said, 'Look at that bully pistol belt!'

I looked at Violetta. I could tell she recognized me, for her long-lashed eyes were as round as blue poker chips and her mouth resembled a red O. Then her pretty face went from Expression No. 4 – Surprise, to Expression No. 5 – Anger.

But my other mortal enemy did not seem to recognize me. The face of Ray G. Tempest AKA Jonas Blezzard showed a strange commixture of a Genuine Smile &

Surprise. He was only two feet away but he did not recognize me!

Behind us, Affie removed the dust sheet from Minnehaha's wheel with a flourish.

People gasped at the sight of the giant target with its rings of blue & red & its yellow disc in the middle & also those leather straps. Some knew what it was and began whispering to their partners. Others were asking what it could be.

Nobody asked for the dance to resume.

Blezzard AKA Tempest turned and saw it and his face went white. Then he looked at me and I saw understanding dawn.

'Thank you for volunteering, brave sir!' cried Affie. 'Please step up upon the target!'

LEDGER SHEET 47

EVERYBODY WAS CLAPPING & CHEERING.

Earlier that day, Affie had told me there was nothing a man feared as much as being shamed in public. It appeared he was correct, for my mortal enemy was slowly putting his feet on the little wooden footrests on the target. His face was white as chalk and made his bushy mustache and sideburns looked extra black.

'Now sir,' said Affie, 'if you will just allow me to strap your arms and legs to this giant target . . .'

I watched with bated breath as Mr. Ray G. Tempest, AKA Jonas Blezzard, allowed himself to be strapped to the giant target.

At last I had my mortal enemy where I wanted him, viz: spread-eagled on a giant target like a butterfly on a corkboard.

Strapped to the giant target, Blezzard cursed me under his breath.

I *could* tell you what he said, but decency forbids.

Affie turned to the crowd and said, 'Please give our bold volunteer an enthusiastic round of applause.'

When the applause died down I stepped forward.

'Mr. Jonas Blezzard,' I said in a loud voice. 'Chinese, Negroes and half-Indians like me cannot give testimony in a court of law. That is why me and my pards have called this informal hearing. *You* are the accused!'

The ball-goers laughed.

'Please tell us how you murdered your pard and stole half a million dollars' worth of gold and silver!'

The ball-goers gasped.

Then I picked up the first knife and poised it for a throw.

Once again, the ball-goers gasped.

I must confess I was nervous, too, for I had never done this before.

I had expected Jonas Blezzard to now be paralyzed with terror, so I was surprised when he gave me a smile. It was a No. 2 smile – stiff and bogus – but still a smile!

I practised my Snake Eyes glare on the man who had thrown poor unconscious Dizzy off the stagecoach and who had kilt my bogus pa.

I said, 'You set out to trick me, didn't you? You and your pards weren't just after the Wells Fargo gold. You were after me and my feet. That is to say, my shares of the Chollar mine.'

He said, 'I do not know what you are babbling about. Is this another conundrum?'

I pulled back my arm and 'threw' a knife like Minnie had taught me, pushing with my foot at the same time. Sure enough, the quivering knife appeared close to his shoulder.

For a third time, everybody in the ballroom gasped.

Mr. Jonas Blezzard did not even flinch. He said to the people, 'Do not listen to this heathen savage. She is spouting nonsense.'

'Spin the wheel,' I commanded, and Affie spun the wheel.

To the slowly turning man I said. 'You threw poor harmless Dizzy off the coach and he might never wake up.'

I 'threw' another knife and it struck beneath his upside-down armpit.

The crowd gasped. This time there was a spatter of applause.

The still-turning Mr. Jonas Blezzard sneered. 'Your music hall tricks hold no fear for me. I know them all. I used to be an actor.'

I said, 'You stole a wagonload of silver and gold. Tell us where you have hid the loot and it will go easier for you.'

I 'threw' another knife & it struck between his legs near his crutch.

He only laughed. He said, 'Those are not real knives you are throwing. It is just a Trick. It is a Frost on the Public.'

I ground my teeth. Dang it, he was right. My knife-throwing *was* a 'frost on the public'. I was not throwing real knives but only pretending to throw them while bogus knives popped out at the flick of a lever operated by my foot.

I could not throw a real knife lest I kill him in front of a hundred witnesses. But I had an Ace up my sleeve.

I turned to Affie. 'Jungle Explorer,' I said. 'Do you have the tarantula?'

Affie nodded and went behind the spinning wheel and emerged a moment later with a big hairy spider on his palm.

Women screamed and men cursed.

Affie reached out with his free hand & stopped the wheel from spinning so that Jonas was upright again. The actor-turned-murderer looked like Leonardo da Vinci's Vitruvius Man whom Ma Evangeline had once shown me in an art book.

Affie brought the tarantula close to Jonas's face.

'Confess!' I cried. 'Confess your odious crime! You are a confidence trickster. You prey on the gullible and the innocent.'

At first Jonas looked scared, but as Affie brought the tarantula closer his eyes narrowed into expression No. 5 – Suspicion.

'Wait a minute,' he said. 'That is just the husk of a critter.'

(He was correct: it was not Mouse but his husk.)

'I know that trick, too!' cried Jonas. 'Now let me go or I will call the authorities.'

286

'The authorities are already here!' I said, for I had spotted the gray-mustached man in the rose-pink stovepipe hat with his two uniformed policemen. They were standing nearby & had not tried to arrest me, so I reckoned they wanted to hear the truth as much as all these people. I said, 'Where have you hidden the silver and gold?'

'This is preposterous!' said Jonas in his carrying actor's voice. 'I have done nothing wrong!'

I heard angry mutterings among the Cream of San Francisco Society. I was losing their sympathy.

But I had another 'Ace' up my sleeve.

I turned to Affie. 'Jungle Explorer,' I said. 'Do you have the fritillaries?'

'What do you mean, "fritillaries"?' asked Mr. Jonas Blezzard in a higher voice than normal.

'She means "butterflies",' said Affie, and from behind the target he produced a tray covered by a net dome and full of fluttering fritillaries. All my butterflies had hatched and they were crowding the inside of the net, ready to burst forth in flight!

'Yes!' I cried. 'Hundreds of butterflies with their "wee feelers and flapping wings"! Now tell us where you stashed the spondulicks or I will set them upon you!'

'I . . . I don't know what you are talking about!'

I turned to Affie. 'Release the fritillaries!'

'No!' cried Jonas Blezzard. 'Please, no!'

Some people were laughing now and I glanced over to see that Violetta's face was as pale as alkali powder.

She had not known that her new husband was afraid of butterflies.

As Affie lifted the gauzy dome, a dozen butterflies fluttered out onto the stage.

They were all the same.

They were pale golden-brown with black dots and zigzags.

They were Buckskin Fritillaries, the only kind of butterfly my foster pa had never been able to catch!

When they saw Jonas on the target, I reckon they thought it was a big flower for they fluttered straight towards him in a zigzag fashion.

'Oh!' cried the crowd and clapped their hands.

'Aiee!' screamed Jonas Blezzard and writhed on his wheel.

As the butterflies zigzagged closer and closer, he squinched his eyes closed.

'Not the butterflies!' he moaned. 'Not the butterflies!'

But then the butterflies must have caught sight of those high-up windows with the late sunlight slanting through, for they started to flutter up into the lofty atmosphere above the ballroom.

What would happen when Jonas opened his eyes and realized he was not in danger?

Thinking quickly, I fished out my medicine bag & opened it & brought out the little silk butterfly I had pulled off the stage-dummy's straw sunhat back in Virginia City.

People were still laughing as I held it up before the

face of my writhing enemy. He opened one eye & saw my silk butterfly looming.

'I confess,' screamed Mr. Jonas Blezzard AKA Ray G. Tempest, squinching his eyes shut again. 'Yes! I did it! Me and my friend Chance hatched a plot to rob the Nevada Stage. But we did not act alone. We had a partner. Violetta was in on it with us!'

'No!' cried Violetta, her previously ashen face now flushed & pink. 'It ain't true.' She glanced around her, but the Cream of San Francisco Society had stopped laughing. They were now backing away from her as if she had a catching disease.

'It *is* true!' cried the man who had styled himself as 'Raging' Tempest. He was writhing on his wheel. 'You will find the gold and silver in her bedroom over at the Occidental Hotel. I just had it delivered in a couple of fine leather traveling chests as my wedding present to her.'

'You traitor!' screeched Violetta in an unladylike voice. 'You vile creeping thing. You coward!'

She pulled a double-barreled Deringer out from between her bosoms & cocked it & aimed at him & fired.

Bang!

Then she turned her little piece on me.

LEDGER SHEET 48

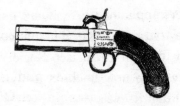

BANG!

Just as the second shot rang out, a black-clad arm knocked Violetta's wrist from below, causing her ball to fly up into the rarefied air of that big ballroom.

If you should ever dine in the Lick House Hotel, look up at the fancy ceiling square they call a 'coffer' between two other coffers with chandeliers in them. If you have eyes as sharp as mine, or a pair of Opera Glasses, you might perceive a tiny hole in the gilded wood. That hole was meant for me, but Poker Face Jace saved my life.

'Jacey!' cried Violetta when she saw who had thwarted her shot. Then she swooned into his arms.

I reckoned she was play-acting, for I know that nothing short of being sawed in half would make that lady faint.

Jace caught Violetta in his arms. Then he took the empty Deringer pistol from her limp hand and slipped it in his pocket.

'You all right, P.K.?' he asked me.

'Yes, sir,' I replied, and then looked away. He was probably going to be Violetta's next husband, but at least he had not wanted me dead. That was some consolation.

From beside the big target, Affie cried, 'Mr. Jonas Blezzard is all right, too! The bullet only creased his shoulder.'

The ball-goers applauded.

(Later, Affie told me it was their clapping that gave him a Brilliant Idea.)

Affie stepped forward. 'Ladies and gentlemen, we hope you have enjoyed our presentation. Of course it was all "staged". Nobody was ever in any *real* danger.' He turned & helped Mr. Jonas Blezzard off the wheel & I saw him say something under his breath.

Jonas Blezzard was white as chalk, but he bowed and so did Affie. Martha & Ping came out and they bowed, too.

I did not realize what they were doing. Affie slid me a sideways glance.

'Bow!' he hissed.

I bowed, too, just as the curtains closed.

Beyond the curtains, loud applause rose up and was lost in the cavernous ceiling.

I wondered if Violetta had been apprehended. But before I could go to the curtain and peep out, a man with a black beard like a big bib appeared through that tee-pee door at the back of the stage.

He went to Affie & shook his hand.

'That was inspired, young man! You have turned a disaster into a triumph. I cannot thank you enough. This is Detective Rose. He is the best detective in this city.'

Behind him emerged the man in the rose-pink stovepipe hat and droopy gray mustache who had chased me from the Rev. Starr King's Unitarian Church.

Two uniformed policemen came through the low door after him.

Detective Rose looked down at me. 'You have played a dangerous hand, Miss Pinkerton,' he said, 'but it appears you got four aces.' He nodded to his policemen and they each gripped an arm of Mr. Jonas Blezzard. Detective Rose turned to the man with the bib-like beard, 'Mr. Lick,' he said, 'is there a private chamber where I might interview this man?'

'My office,' said the owner and proprietor of the Lick House Hotel.

As the band struck up again, we all repaired to a back room of the hotel to get the final pieces of the puzzle.

MR. LICK'S OFFICE WAS NOT PLUSH LIKE THE OTHER rooms in the Lick House Hotel, but simple. It had leather chairs & a workbench at the back with woodworking tools & sawdust on the floor.

Two policemen helped Mr. Ray G. Tempest AKA Jonas Blezzard into one of the leather chairs. Detective Rose let me come in, and also Martha, Zoe, Affie & Ping. The five of us stood with our backs to the workbench.

Two more policemen came in, along with Mr. Isaac 'Icy' Blue. They held some familiar-looking leather mailbags.

A distinct smell of horse manure pervaded the room.

'The stolen silver ingots and gold coins,' I cried. 'You found them!'

'Where were they?' asked Detective Rose.

'In two big traveling trunks,' said one of the policemen. 'Just like he said.'

'There were tags on the trunks,' said the other. 'It appears the two of them had tickets on a cruise to the Sandwich Islands departing this very evening.'

No wonder everything had been done in such a rush. They were going to take that gold and silver with them, you bet!

'I will get you for this!' gasped Blezzard. He was looking at me.

'If you confess now,' said Detective Rose to Blezzard, 'It will go easier for you. You might not swing.'

'Swing?' said Blezzard, his face blanching. 'Do you mean at the end of a rope?'

I fished in my medicine bag for my silk butterfly but Mr. Jonas Blezzard was already co-operating.

The double threat of death by hanging and butterflies made him Spill the Beans, as they say.

Right there in that sawdust-scented workroom he told us how he had come up with the plan.

'It all started with that half-Injun,' he said, glaring at me. 'She riled Violetta, who became intent on revenge.'

'Start from the beginning,' said Detective Rose.

'Just after Christmas last year,' said Blezzard, 'Chance and I were playing poker in the Bella Union saloon here in Frisco. There was a new lady in town, a shapely widow named Violetta De Baskerville. We got ourselves places on her table. She was drinking Pousse Lamour cocktails and by the end of the night it was only the three of us. We got to talking about how much gold and silver was pouring out of those Comstock mines.

She was tipsy, and told us about a scheme she had once devised. She and a lawman friend of hers in Virginia City had planned to hire a couple of roughs to rob the stages. He would "capture and arrest" the desperados and split the takings with them, allowing them to "escape" on the way to custody. The traitorous lawman would then tell the authorities that the robbers got away without revealing the location of the stash.'

'Deputy Marshal Jack Williams,' I said to Affie under my breath. 'Violetta shot and killed him.'

Blezzard continued, 'Violetta told us her lawman pard had been killed in a shooting affray. She did not know anyone stupid enough to play the dangerous parts of Reb Road Agents. I told her we knew a couple of bit-part actors who would pretend to be brigands for a spell. I said me and Chauncy could play lawmen. You got any whiskey?' he asked Detective Rose.

'When you finish telling us.'

Blezzard took a deep breath. 'Violetta said she would fund us if we promised to exact revenge upon a brat in Virginia City. Violetta told us the kid was training to be a detective in order to join her pa's agency. Well, I have a friend in Chicago, owns a jewelry store near the Pinkerton Agency. I asked him to tell me everything he could about them. He sent me a letter full of useful information about Robert and Allan Pinkerton. Chauncy was good with accents so he decided to play the kid's pa.'

Jonas Blezzard shot me a glare. 'We had briefed Johnny and Jimmy to stop a stage with a little girl riding on top. That was how they would know the one with the silver.'

'How?' said Detective Rose. 'You could not telegraph a couple of Reb Road Agents hiding out in the high Sierras.'

'It was our plan from the beginning,' said Blezzard. 'Violetta thought if we could get her to admit she was a girl it would serve three purposes: it would hurt her friends and help mark out that stagecoach.'

'And the third purpose?'

Blezzard shrugged. 'It would be easy to shoot her dead.'

I thought, 'Dang! That Violetta is a clever one.'

'What happened to Chauncy?' said Detective Rose.

'He threw down on me,' said Jonas. 'I shot back in self-defense. It was justified.'

'That is a bald-faced lie!' I cried. 'You killed him in cold blood and with no warning. You tried to shoot me, too.'

Detective Rose turned to me. 'Where is Chauncy Pridhaume now?' he asked.

I said, 'You will find the body of my bogus pa in a shallow grave near a cave in a place called Grizzly Gulch a few miles west of Friday's Station. I had my account all written out,' I added, 'but it was in the pocket of my greatcoat and I lost that.'

Detective Rose smiled. 'We got your greatcoat,' he said, 'with all the incriminating documents and also a ledger book and a fine pair of buckskin gauntlets.'

At that moment the door opened and in came Violetta de Baskerville AKA Mrs. von Vingschplint AKA Mrs. Jonas Blezzard.

Her bosom was heaving and her violet eyes were flashing sparks. She looked mighty pretty. I heard all the men in the room exhale & even Ping & Affie were staring with their mouths open. Violetta was in the custody of another uniformed policeman. Jace was behind them.

It was now fairly crowded in that room.

All eyes were on Violetta. She looked around at us all & her gaze fell on me.

'I wish I had let you die up in the mountains last year,' she snarled.

I said, 'If you had not sought revenge you would now be living in peace and prosperity. I hope you have learned your lesson.'

'Why, you sanctimonious little blank!' she spat out. (Only she did not say 'blank'.)

'Ladies, ladies! That is enough,' said Detective Rose. 'I believe I see the way of it.' To the policemen he said, 'Take Mr. Blezzard and his wife and lock them up. In separate cells,' he added.

'Jacey, help me!' pleaded Violetta. Once again she swooned.

However, this time he made no move to catch her & she fell to the floor with a thud. One of the policemen helped her up and escorted her – now writhing and cursing – from the premises.

Detective Rose turned to me. 'Thanks to your

resourcefulness and bravery we have apprehended two possible murderers and nearly half a million in stolen gold and silver. Ever thought of setting up a branch of your detective agency here in San Francisco? I could use some operatives like you and your friends – that is, resourceful kids with a knack for disguise.'

'Ping, too?' I said.

'Of course,' said he. 'We have a big Celestial population and not enough good men to help us there.'

'Martha and Zoe, too?' I said. 'And Affable?'

'You bet. You are all good detectives.'

I nodded happily. It looked like I was going to remain a Private Eye after all.

A WEEK LATER, **I** FOUND MYSELF STANDING ON THE stage of Minnehaha's Medicine Show, listening to hearty applause.

It was Sunday, May 10th, and we were all at The Willows Amusement Park celebrating the capture of the criminals & the recovery of the money & our reward. Minnie had invited me to help her with the final part of her act. It was her last day in Frisco as she was bound for Sac City and parts beyond.

She was wearing her tight buckskin top and her puffy skirt with the stripes & zigzags on it. Her hair was wavy & glossy & black & fell down to her shoulders. She was not wearing war paint so you could see her freckles and pale skin.

I was wearing my fringed buckskin trowsers & beaded moccasins & beaded buckskin gloves & my red, blue and yellow zigzag jacket. I was also wearing the

wig of straight black hair. (I had bought it from Minnie.)
I was using my bogus pa's Smith & Wesson No. 2 with
its 6in barrel and rosewood grip. I like it because it fits
my hand real good and also because it takes the same
.32 rimfire cartridges as my 4-shooter Deringer. That
means I do not need to bother with cap & ball & powder.

Minnie and I had been shooting tin cans.

My ears were still ringing with the sound of gunfire
and my nose was full of the pungent smell of gun smoke.
We had hit every can!

I had also been using my fine new Henry Rifle which
takes fourteen .44 caliber cartridges and makes a bang
like a shout. It was engraved thus: *To P.K. Pinkerton,
with thanks from the Overland Stage Co.*

Mr. V.V. Bletchley had come all the way from Virginia
City to present it to me, along with a generous reward of
$2000. I had given $500 to Martha & Zoe & $500 to Ping
& $500 to Minnehaha. (That was when she had invited
me to be part of her show for just one afternoon.)

As the cloud of white gun smoke cleared on that fine
May afternoon, I could see the people looking up at us
and clapping.

I saw Ping & Affie & Martha & Zoe. Mr. Sam Clemens,
AKA Mark Twain, was there, too, with his friend The
Unreliable and also Mrs. John D. Winters who was smiling
and not looking down her nose. I saw my new colleague
Mr. Detective Rose & half a dozen of San Francisco's
finest. They were clapping as hard as anybody else.

Mr. Icy Blue was there, too, all in black. And Dizzy,

with his leg in plaster! He was making a good recovery. He had verified my side of the story & was now 'Yee-hawing' on account of he could not clap as he had to use both his hands for his crutches.

Best of all, Ping had got an indebted Virginia City client of his to ride Cheeya to Frisco in easy stages. So I was now reunited with my beloved pony.

I was about to jump down off the stage to join them when a man with oval spectacles ran up. He pointed to me. 'You! Stay up there!' he commanded. 'I am Mr. H.W. Corbyn. I am going to make photographic cards of you. I will sell them and make a fortune. It will only take a moment or two and I will give you half the proceeds,' he added.

So while Minnehaha was going round and collecting tips in her quiver, I remained on the stage.

Mr. H.W. Corbyn heaved his big black camera up onto the stage & drew the red velvet curtains so that the people in the audience would not disturb us. The sun was right overhead and it was shining for all it was worth. Mr. Corbyn made me stand with one foot up on Minnie's ammunition box, like when a hunter stands over the prey he has just killed.

While Mr. Corbyn was making adjustments, a dark figure stooped to enter through the tee-pee door at the back of the stage & then stood tall.

It was Poker Face Jace.

I could not move because Mr. Corbyn was making adjustments.

Jace stopped about two paces away from me. He had his hands behind his back.

'Go away,' I said. 'I am quit of you.'

'Hear me out,' said he.

I said nothing.

He said, 'Remember when you came to Steamboat Springs end of last month, and I said that in the whole world, only you and I knew the secret of your initials?'

I gave a curt nod.

He sighed. 'Well, after you left, I got to thinking. I remembered when I was with Violetta in Carson.' He paused & took a breath. 'She was interrogating me about you and we had been drinking and I might have mentioned something to her – about you not knowing what the P and the K stood for, that is.'

He still had his hands behind his back & suddenly his pale cheeks were pinkish. I had to look at him to make sure I was really seeing this. It was the first time I had ever seen Jace discombobulated. He even remained cool & collected under fire. But danged if he wasn't blushing or flushing or *something*.

'Keep your head still,' Mr. H.W. Corbyn told me. 'I am almost ready.'

'That was why I came here to Frisco,' said Jace. He spoke quickly & without his usual drawl, like he wanted to get it out fast. 'I wondered if Violetta might be scheming against you. I had just got into her hotel room and was about to search it when you showed up.'

'A likely story,' said I.

But part of me wanted him to convince me I was wrong.

'P.K.?' he said. His voice was kind of thick and he had to clear his throat and start again. 'You are kind of like a daughter to me. Or a son. Or – I don't know – maybe both of those combined. As you know, I lost my own . . . And I just wanted to say . . . I am sorry. I would like you to have this.'

From behind his back he brought out a straw hat of the kind they call 'sombrero'. Only it was not as big as most sombreros.

The photographer was fiddling with his camera again and had his back to us, so I reached out my hand & took it.

It was made of pale-gold straw and had a red hat-band and on that hat-band was a buckskin butterfly all embroidered with beads.

It was like the hat in my dream.

Had I told him about my dream? I could not recollect.

I looked at him and he looked at me.

I looked back down at the hat. I said, 'It is a bully hat.'

'Ain't it?' said Jace. 'I saw it on a Mexican gal near Sacramento on my way here and I thought it might suit you. She made me pay five dollars for it,' he added.

'Put it on!' cried Mr. H.W. Corbyn from his device.

I put it on.

'Yes!' Mr. H.W. Corbyn called out to me. 'But further back on your head, so it don't shade your face.'

'Let me,' said Jace. He stepped forward & set the small sombrero a bit further back on my head & then he folded the front brim up a mite.

303

'There,' said Jace in a low voice. 'That looks fine.' For a moment he lingered to brush a strand of wig hair away from my face.

Then he stepped back.

'Perfect!' cried Mr. Corbyn once more. 'That is the finishing touch we needed. Now put your left hand on top of the rifle barrel and put your right hand back so I can see your pistol and gun belt.'

Out of the corner of my eye I saw Jace moving away.

'Don't go,' I said.

He stopped moving away.

'Freeze!' cried Mr. Corbyn. Then he took away the cover of the lens & I stood as still as a jackass rabbit even though I could see Jace out of the corner of my eye. I could see him taking a cigar out of his coat pocket & he had some trouble lighting it as his hands were shaky.

In front of me, Mr. H.W. Corbyn replaced the cover on the lens and cried 'Got it! These are going to sell like glasses of iced lemonade in Hell!' he exclaimed. Then he added, 'Pardon my French.'

Mr. H.W. Corbyn took the photographic plate and hurried out the back exit, leaving us alone on the curtained stage.

I turned to Jace. 'We are all going to have a picnic down by the duck pond,' I said. 'The one by the emeu cage. Ping and Affie and Martha. Miz Zoe, too. Will you join us?'

'I would be honored,' he said. He puffed his cigar and blew smoke up. 'Can Stonewall come, too?'

'Sure.' I took a deep breath. 'Jace?'

'Yeah?'

'You know you said I was a bit like your son or your daughter or both?'

He nodded.

I took another deep breath. 'Would you maybe give me a bear hug like a pa gives his kid sometimes?'

Jace opened his mouth. Then he closed it. Then he tossed the cigar away & stepped forward & put his arms around me in a safe bear hug.

I usually do not like being touched but sometimes a bear hug is necessary.

This one felt good.

It felt safe.

I thought, 'I do not need to find out who my real pa is. No pa could be as good as Jace. He is true. And he likes me just as I am.'

My eyes filled up with tears & I felt a sob wanting to come up. Dang my changing body!

Just in time, my new hat fell off & we laughed & I bent down to pick it up & put it back on & when I looked at Jace, danged if his eyes weren't damp, too!

'Bit dusty today,' he remarked, taking out a pristine handkerchief and dabbing his eyes.

'Yeah,' I said. 'I noticed that, too.'

'Dang,' he said, putting the handkerchief back in his coat pocket. 'You look mighty fine in that get-up. How does it feel?'

'It feels good,' I said. 'It feels like me.'

Then I took out my pistol & cocked it & fired it into the blue San Francisco sky & shouted, 'Yee-haw!'

GLOSSARY

ALKALI – a harsh chemical found in both dust and water in parts of Nevada.

BLACKSNAKING – slang for using a whip (which looks like a black snake) on stagecoach horses or other animals that pull carts or carriages.

CALIBER – the diameter of balls and bullets measured in hundredths of an inch.

CARSON CITY – high desert town which became the capital of Nevada Territory in 1862.

CELESTIAL – slang for Chinese because the imperial court in China was known as the 'celestial court'.

CHOLLAR MINE – one of the many mines on the Comstock lode in Virginia City. People could trade in shares of the silver vein, measured in 'feet'.

CLEMENT T. RICE – Mark Twain jokingly called his good friend and rival reporter at the Daily Union Newspaper 'The Unreliable'.

CONFEDERATE – a supporter of the southern 'slave-owning' states that were fighting against the Union in the Civil War.

DERINGER – named after the inventor of a small pistol, it came to mean any small gun that could be hidden in someone's pocket or clothing.

FRISCO – slang term for San Francisco that was popular with Mark Twain and others in the 1860s.

GENOA – founded in 1851 as 'Mormon Station', Genoa (pronounced j'-NO-ah) claims to be the oldest town in Nevada.

GRIZZLY BEARS – a sub-species of brown bear native to North America. Their brown fur is often tipped with white, giving them a 'grizzled' look.

HENRY RIFLE – one of the earliest repeating rifles (i.e. you do not have to reload after each shot). It took fourteen .44 caliber metal cartridges.

LEVEE – an embankment built to stop a river overflowing; also a landing place on a river.

LUCIFER (Latin for 'light bringer') – an early type of wooden match tipped with a flammable substance and ignited by striking against any rough surface.

MAGENTA – a light purplish-red color named after the battle of Magenta (near Milan, Italy) in 1859.

MEDICINE BAG – a pouch carried by some Native Americans, often for magical purposes.

MUFF – a tube made of fur or velvet for women to warm their hands.

MUSTANG – a type of American wild horse, small but full of stamina.

PAPIER-MÂCHÉ (French for 'chewed paper') – a mixture of newspaper and glue made with flour and water that becomes hard when dry.

REB – Slang for 'rebel', a term applied to Confederate soldiers in the American Civil War.

ROAD AGENTS – highwaymen or robbers who lie in wait along the road to target carriages and stagecoaches.

SABBATH – day of religious observance and rest from work: Sunday for Christians, Friday evening & Saturday daytime for Jews.

SAM CLEMENS – a reporter for the Daily Territorial Enterprise from 1862–1864. He first began to sign his articles and books as 'Mark Twain' early in 1863.

SCATTERGUN – another name for a shotgun, a type of gun that fires 'shot' (usually lots of tiny lead pellets) rather than a single bullet or 'ball'.

SIOUX (pronounced 'Sue') – a Native American people who call themselves Lakota.

SLOUCH HAT – a soft felt hat with a wide flexible brim, usually in brown or black.

SMITH & WESSON NO. 2 – a six-shot revolver that took .32 caliber metal cartridges.

SOILED DOVE – a term used to describe a woman who worked in a saloon or brothel.

SOLFERINO – a reddish-purple color named after the battle of Solferino (near Mantua, Italy) in 1859.

SPITTOON – a metal, glass or ceramic container to catch tobacco-chewers' spit.

SPONDULICKS – slang for 'cash' or 'money'.

STEAMER – a common term for a steam-powered boat, usually with one or more paddle wheels at the side or stern.

STOVEPIPE HAT – a tall, cylindrical hat, famously worn by President Abraham Lincoln.

TELEGRAPH – a method of sending rapid messages (telegrams) over great distances by means of making and breaking electrical connections along a wire.

TERRITORY – a clearly defined area of land that does not yet have the full laws of a state.

THOMAS STARR KING – a celebrated Unitarian minister who supported the Union in the Civil War.

THOROUGHBRACE – a combination of belts, straps and springs that acts as a cradle for the body of a stagecoach so that passengers have a smooth ride even on a bumpy road.

TULE (pronounced TOO-lee) – a kind of bulrush that grows in Nevada and California.

UNION – northern states that opposed the withdrawal of the Confederate states from the United States of America.

VAQUERO – Spanish for cattle-driver; the earliest word for 'cowboy'.

VIZ. (abbreviation of Latin videlicet) – 'namely' or 'in other words'.

ZOUAVE – infantry unit in the French Algerian army whose colorful uniform was later adopted by several units during the American Civil War.